COMMANDO FORCE 133

They stood alone against the might of Germany:

MAD JACK CHURCHILL—Tough, dauntless officer of the British Commandos.

DR. JAMES RICKETT—He improvised and put together a hospital from shotdown bombers.

MADAME ZENA—Courageous leader of the Yugoslav partisans.

CHICAGO MARY—Pistol-toting commissar to General Tito.

SIR WALTER COWAN—Seventy-one-year-old British Admiral who wouldn't say die.

THE BANTAM WAR BOOK SERIES

This is a series of books about a world on fire.

These carefully chosen volumes cover the full dramatic sweep of World War II. Many are eyewitness accounts by the men who fought in this global conflict in which the future of the civilized world hung in balance. Fighter pilots, tank commanders and infantry commanders, among others, recount exploits of individual courage in the midst of the large-scale terrors of war. They present portraits of brave men and true stories of gallantry and cowardice in action, moving sagas of survival and tragedies of untimely death. Some of the stories are told from the enemy viewpoint to give the reader an immediate sense of the incredible life and death struggle of both sides of the battle.

Through these books we begin to discover what it was like to be there, a participant in an epic war for freedom.

Each of the books in the Bantam War Book series contains a dramatic color painting and illustrations specially commissioned for each title to give the reader a deeper understanding of the roles played by the men and machines of World War II.

COMMANDO
FORCE 133

BILL STRUTTON

BANTAM BOOKS · TORONTO · NEW YORK · LONDON

*This low-priced Bantam Book
has been completely reset in a type face
designed for easy reading, and was printed
from new plates. It contains the complete
text of the original hard-cover edition.*
NOT ONE WORD HAS BEEN OMITTED.

COMMANDO FORCE 133
*A Bantam Book / published by arrangement with
Hodder & Stoughton Limited*

PRINTING HISTORY
*Originally published as Island of Terrible Friends in
Great Britain 1961 by Hodder & Stoughton Limited*
Magnum edition published 1978
Bantam edition / January 1981

Drawings by Tom Beecham, M. Stephen Bach and Bob Correa.

Maps by Alan McKnight.

*All rights reserved.
Copyright © 1961 by Bill Strutton
Cover art copyright © 1980 by Bantam Books, Inc.
This book may not be reproduced in whole or in part, by
mimeograph or any other means, without permission.
For information address: Bantam Books, Inc.*

ISBN 0-553-13581-3

Published simultaneously in the United States and Canada

PRINTED IN THE UNITED STATES OF AMERICA

0 9 8 7 6 5 4 3 2 1

To
Jim Rickett
the most Terrible Friend of all

AUTHOR'S NOTES

This is a true story, though a few minor names have been changed. I owe a great debt to Dr. James Rickett, as well as to his wife, Dorothy for all their good-humoured help during its preparation; also to Margot Campbell, the novelist, whose idea it was. I am profoundly grateful to Mr. George Lloyd Roberts, F.R.C.S., now an eminent orthopaedic surgeon, for his own reminiscences and for his forbearance with the manuscript; to Dr. Francis Clynick, M.B., Ch.B., D.A., for whom the island of Vis marked a turbulent beginning in his rise to distinction as an anaesthetist.

My gratitude and admiration go to Madame Milo Zon, the indomitable "Zena" of this story. And though—as with her—the following have no connection with the views expressed in this book, I must also record my appreciation to Major-General T. B. L. Churchill, C.B., C.B.E., M.C., to Lieutenant-Colonel J. M. T. F. Churchill, D.S.O. M.C., to Captain M. C. Morgan-Giles, D.S.O., O.B.E., G.M., R.N., and to Alfred L. Blake, M.C., LL.B., formerly Brigade Major, 2nd Special Service Brigade and more recently Mayor of Portsmouth, for their kind and helpful interest.

ONE

When the Germans pulled out of Trani they were in too much of a hurry to blow up their imposing headquarters in the school buildings. All they could manage was to bust the lavatories.

British troops, entering, circled the stately white-pillared blocks of the Scuole Elementari and stopped. They came walking delicately through its large, silent classrooms, and finding no booby traps, voted it as splendid stuff for a general hospital. As to the lavatories, an R.E. officer observed that this Jerry general would have to answer for it after the war. Places of meditation were entitled to cultural immunity.

The elementary school made a good hospital. Elegant, spacious, modern, its blocks suggested the seat of some progressive colonial government. Only the Roman fasces, the axe-and-faggots designs which encrusted its cleanly columns reminded one that the Fascists, too, fancied themselves as builders. The pictures of Mussolini which had glared down on Trani's assembled tiny tots like an irate bullfrog had long been removed, and in the place where they had chanted their twice-times-tables, Major James Rickett of the Royal Army Medical Corps stood in a bright pool of light attended by a bevy of phantoms; he was engaged in a cystoscopy.

Rickett was tall, thin, bronzed by a summer-long in North Africa. Work had trained his shoulders high into something of a perpetual shrug. His speech was a product of the operating theatre too—soft yet abrupt, the words landing with almost feathery gentleness.

There were 400 beds in this hospital, and only Major Rickett and his O.C., Surgical Division, to handle the

1

theatre work. Though the war on this eastern sector of the
Italian front had ground to a halt, there was a steady flow
of cold surgery—hernias, pyelograms, appendicectomies,
other garrison work—mingling on his lists with the casualties down from the fighting.

There was a tap at the door of the theatre and one of
the nurses assisting Rickett left his side with a swish of
starched white to answer it. She returned, waited, met his
raised eyes over her face mask, and murmured: "Registrar
wants to see you. Soon as convenient."

Ten minutes later Rickett was through with the operation. He stripped off his cap, mask, gown and gloves
and crossed from the surgical block to the office. It was
raining steadily as he crossed. He lifted a long leg over the
puddles and thought, whiffing at a brief cigarette, *this
could be England*. It rains as much—in fact more, for
February. Ah, but when the sun shines, *then* it's Italy.

Major Jones, the registrar, was waiting for him. He
tossed over the slip of paper.

"This'll teach you to volunteer," he said. He stared up
at Rickett and watched.

"Why?"

"You're posted."

"Where?"

"Don't ask me. It's come direct from Allied Force
Headquarters." Jones was being rather intense about it,
and he was very interested in Rickett's face, which
mightn't have been giving him much change, for he added:
"Looks like something hot."

Anzio? Inside Rickett a voice was saying, *that'll teach
you all right. It's got you a ticket to Anzio, with a
parachute jump on the end of it, probably. What business
had you to put in for something like this, with your wife
and three children?*

With Anzio going the way everybody but the *commu-
niqué* said it was, that meant forward surgery in tents,
rain, mud, heavy shell fire. What made a man actually
ask?

He said, reading the posting order: "Forty pounds of
kit? I'd better start weighing out my underwear."

Colonel Black Jack Donnelly, who was Jim Rickett's
C.O., had earned his colourful nickname. Piracy was his
true vocation, and he admitted it. As soon as he heard

Rickett was leaving on an unknown but possibly adventurous assignment, Black Jack reached among his personal gear and produced a stack of Italian flour.

"I can let you have this," he said, "for a consideration." And he winked. The two men had first met back in Algeria where Black Jack had early impressed Rickett with his enterprise by getting the entire personnel of a N.A.A.F.I. store drunk—and then buying up its whole stock of whisky. Legend had subsequently adorned the incident with libellous sequels, one of which had it that Black Jack dined a few nights later with the very Guards Regiment for which the whisky had been destined. All its officers were steaming about not being able to get as much as a whiff of Scotch. Black Jack leaned across to their C.O., and said earnestly, *sotto voce:* "My dear chap—I can get you as much as you like!" He closed one eye. "At a price, mind ..."

So the stories went about Colonel Black Jack Donnelly. The more picaresque they were, the more he grinned —and added a detail or two of his own.

Now he fixed Jim Rickett with a fiercely speculative eye.

"The Brig told you the show you're being posted to?"

"He said it's called Force 133."

Black Jack grinned briefly, rubbing his chin. "I suppose you know where that lot operates ... ?"

Rickett shrugged.

"Across the Adriatic," Black Jack said. "Real hole-in-corner stuff."

"Never mind. I thought it was going to be Anzio."

Colonel Black Jack Donnelly was writing out a movement order. "You may come to wish it was," he murmured absently. "Now—a piece of advice."

"Yes, sir?"

"Wherever they send you, take a lot of cigarettes. They're worth all the currency in the world. You can work wonders with 'em. So roll up to the N.A.A.F.I. and get yourself a sackful."

"Yes, but how can one man get himself a sackful?"

Black Jack looked him up and down with astonished compassion. "Tell 'em you're a battalion, of course," he said.

Rickett took an ambulance down the straight flat thirty miles of coastal road, with the Adriatic glinting away to his left and throwing morning reflections into his eyes, to Bari.

He was now to be vouchsafed another peep into the mystery of his destination. The short, dynamic little brigadier who was Deputy Director of Medical Services, No. 2 District, headquartered at Bari, lifted another corner of the shroud for him by referring to a slip of paper before him.

"Vis—that's where you're to go. Vis." Brigadier Cameron barked it telegraphically.

"Where's that, sir?"

The Brigadier looked at him and referred again to the paper he held. "It's ah, an island. Yes, just off the Dalmatian coast. Let's see, where's a map—?"

When they found one, Brigadier Cameron spread it out on his desk and ran his finger over the Adriatic sea, questing up and over the cluster of islands which shoaled the coast of the Balkans. Rickett followed the searching finger till it stopped on one of the specks in a cluster of islands off the Jugoslav coast. He peered close at the name.

Vis.

It gave him a bit of a turn. It looked very far from anything British. They both stared for a while.

Rickett cleared his throat. "I thought the Germans had all that," he said.

"They have," the Brigadier said. "At least, all except this one island. Some Commandos are supposed to be hanging on to it with a bunch of Tito's partisans." He sat back, laced his fingers. "Your job's to start a hospital for 'em." The Brigadier's gaze wandered again to the map. He mused over it. He frowned and raised his brows and Rickett could read his thoughts like a book, because they were his own thoughts.

At length the Brigadier looked up. He rested his dark eyes on Rickett and said: "Looks as though they're going to *need* a hospital, doesn't it?"

When word got round that Major James Rickett was off to break his neck somewhere, one would have thought from the number of well-wishers that he was being launched on his honeymoon.

For a luxurious two days he made gloriously free with the Brigadier's own staff car and chauffeur. These took him in state to several bars, the Base Medical Stores, and finally to the lounge of the "Imperiale" where he ran to earth the man he was seeking.

He found his quarry, a medium-sized, fairish fellow with blue eyes, dressed in a sheepskin coat and beret, propping up the bar of the "Imperiale", with nothing to show whether he was a private or a general. Apart from his bohemian attire, there was little about him to suggest the swashbuckler, but this was Major Johnnie Forster, and his legend had preceded him.

"Vis, eh?" Forster said, and rubbed his chin. "Yes, I've been there. Hmmm . . . !" The blue eyes measured Rickett, then turned to catch the barman. Forster clicked his fingers. "Have a drink," he said. When the drinks came he eyed Rickett steadily over the rim of his beer and said casually: "I suppose by now you know where Vis is?"

"Yes. Where does this Force 133 come into it?"

"Force 133 is running the show on Vis. There's a Commando troop on the island, a handful of Yugoslav partisans, and bloody little else except a sardine factory. All the islands round it are full of Jerries."

"How many Commandos in a troop?"

Forster eyed him with a tolerant kindness of a Regular for a civilian in khaki. "Fifty," he said.

Rickett digested this, swallowing his beer. He said: "Then why aren't the Jerries swarming all over Vis, too?"

Forster chuckled for the first time and wagged his head, privately amused.

"Give 'em time," he said. "Just give 'em time." He reached out and gave Rickett a friendly consoling punch. "Come on. I'll steer you round."

The first thing Forster did was to direct the staff car a little farther down-coast to a tiny Adriatic fishing village lying below Bari. It was called Torreamare; it was the headquarters of Force 133, Rickett's new and unknown master, and it was here that the whole thing was to begin.

The car turned in at a quiet villa nestling among the

palms. Rickett got out with Forster and walked in, dusting his hands on the seat of his trousers and setting his cap straight.

They found their way to the Mess, opened the door, strode in, and there Rickett halted.

Several women stood looking round at him. It seemed that all of them were lovely. There must have been a half-dozen of them, scented, immaculately coiffured, distributed like spangles among the scruffy khaki figures.

They were dressed as though they had just stepped through from cocktails at the Dorchester for a brief, dutiful mingling with the boys engaged in trying to win the war. The Mess was loud with the accents of Mayfair and carried a high, feminine tinkle.

The stares measured Rickett idly. As he stared back, one of the visions took pity. She unhooked herself from her tête-à-tête with a tall moustached officer and stalked forward on delicate high heels, cigarette and drink in hand.

"Hullo, Johnnie," she said to Forster, and bent an inquiring look at his friend.

"This," said Forster, "is Major Rickett. He's going off to Vis."

The girl's brows rose quizzically at that. "You're joking," she said.

"Come and meet the others," Forster said, and propelled Rickett through them to the bar. There he turned and said: "Ladies and gentlemen—allow me to introduce Major Rickett. The new surgeon for Vis."

Some idiot behind Rickett guffawed and said ruefully: "Ooh-hooh!" and that started the ball rolling.

The hilarity finally nettled Rickett. He blinked and grinned back as amiably as he could. "All right," he said, and turned on the loudest laughter: "What's the joke?"

"Sooner you than me, old boy," said this one. "Vis has had its chips. The last partisan stronghold, y'know. The Jerries have cleared them off all the other islands, and now . . ."

"—now," drawled a captain, aquiline, bald, "they're all set to polish off Vis. And there's to be no back door. We think you ought to know." He drained his glass.

"How d'you mean, no back door?"

"No evacuation, no surrender," Forster volunteered.
"Their orders are to hold it to the last man."

"—and by the look of it," the captain said, "they'll get
to him pretty damn quick."

Force 133—"the Firm"—in its pleasant villa-base at
Torreamare, owed its unconventional personality to the
fact that it didn't really answer to ordinary army discipline.

Force 133 was under the direct orders and control of
the Foreign Office.

This association itself had been enough to promote a
certain feeling for social life, interleaved with the Firm's
preoccupation with promoting partisan warfare behind
the enemy lines. It had not been long before certain of its
officers were organising their lady friends out to Italy to
lend them a helping hand. Their instructions must have
read: "Just come as you are."

For as they were, they came, in the most splendid
mufti.

"Mind you," Rickett was told, "no hanky panky,
y'know. All these gals come from damn good families.
Background's very carefully looked into. It's not anybody
can get into this sort of show. And they're a fearful help
with this and that."

At close quarters the Firm was an even stranger
amalgam of types than Rickett had at first suspected.
Leaving aside the ladies who glamorised the H.Q. offices
with airy social gossip and a display of sheer-clad legs, the
officers of Force 133 were a mixture of playboys and
dedicated men.

The playboys, most of them, were at this base to stay.
They trickled in as refugees from the irksomeness of
ordinary army life, locomoted largely by elegant string-
pulling, drawn by a herd instinct as powerful as that
compelling game to a waterhole. Their delight at finding
each other would have been moving were it not so exclam-
atory.

They had converted the villa into a curious outpost of
the West End with their modish slang, their condescending
view of war and their terrifying insularity.

But among them moved the warriors, parachute-trained, sharpened by strange rigours in unimaginable campaigns, they came and went on their mission into North Italy, Jugoslavia, the wild mountains of Albania, and in their brief passage through the H.Q. at Torreamare they seemed to accept the existence of the chair-polishers and their chicken-and-wine menus with fatalism, even cordiality.

Christian names were *de rigueur* here. The Firm was carelessly named. It itched to be changed to the Club. For it was tribal; warrior or waster shared a principal qualification. They "talked the language".

The Firm was universally intrigued at the dust Rickett kicked up as he and Forster ploughed from store to store on an unrewarding pilgrimage for adequate gear. It amused them. Everybody knew that all you had to do was to fit out a surgeon with a little black bag, and all would be well.

Forster knew differently. He was a doctor himself, Indian Army, and he spent some brisk hours steering Rickett from store to store. They would need truckloads of lint alone. It disappeared so fast in action, particularly when one was cut off from future supplies. In fact, if Rickett was being posted indefinitely to found his own self-supporting unit on a remote island around which there was bound to be some bloody fighting, he was going to need a mountain of supplies.

It was soon plain he was going to get no such thing. The chit he flourished from Brigadier Cameron requesting all help for Major Rickett turned out in practice to be almost worthless.

The reason was—he could not say where he was going.

That alone was enough to make the quartermaster at Base Medical Stores lock up his boxes. Secret destinations were anathema.

"Sorry. We can only let you have stuff that can be written off."

Stores explained that there was nothing personal in this, but they had to know where the stuff was going so that they could account for it—just to show, as one of them put it, that it wasn't being flogged to the Eyeties.

The result was that even with a brigadier's backing, coupled with the formidable Forster's, their scrounging yielded only a battered portable operating table and a field surgical pannier containing little more than a limited supply of dressings and drugs and a few rudimentary surgical instruments.

Quiet though Forster seemed, the wildness which had earned him alternate promotions and demotions occasionally peeped through. Under his sheepskin jacket he wore his Indian pattern grey shirt, scorning rank badges. With senior officers like Brigadier Cameron, to whom they returned with their troubles, Forster began his interview with a marked show of deference and punctilio, saluting snappily, sir-ing with brisk regularity, and firing off all sorts of deferential observations—which gradually grew more pertinent, more personal. With these, Forster himself would undergo a change. He'd crack a joke, drop a "sir" and insinuate an old boy; sprawl in a chair, push his beret over one ear—and finally, to mark his conquest of rank, yawn, and under Rickett's hypnotised gaze, negligently stretch his feet, raising them till they were resting on the Brigadier's desk.

Brigadier Cameron eyed Forster's feet on his desk a little stonily and heard them out with a helpless air. He was as much a prisoner of the machine as anybody else. He said heavily: "Look here—all I've got is a request for a surgeon for this island. Nothing else, and I can't authorise it. Not even any personnel to assist you, if it comes to that—"

"But, sir, if I'm going to be self-contained, I'll have to tackle specialist operations, too. What with? They haven't given me much more than a knife and fork. How about anaesthetics? I'll need a qualified anaesthetist—"

The Brigadier shook his head. "They're short as it is." He pondered unhappily, trying hard. "Look here—I'll let you have a general duty officer. I shouldn't even be doing that."

"And a theatre orderly?" Rickett said doggedly.

The Brigadier sighed. "All right. A theatre orderly too."

"Thank you, sir. I know just the chaps I can use."

Forster swung his feet off the Brigadier's desk and did up his sheepskin jacket. "Let us pray that they're expendable, old boy," he said.

Rickett retreated up-coast to recruit his theatre orderly and to seek the help of that gifted strategist and *entrepreneur*, Black Jack Donnelly.

"I need gas and oxygen apparatus, beds, tenting, instruments ... I could fill at least two three-tonners with what I need. They won't even let me have *penicillin!* It's not expendable. I can't get a lighting generator to operate by, not even acetylene operating lamps. What happens in emergencies?"

Black Jack rubbed his chin. "I've got a Tilley lamp," he mused, and grinned slyly. "What'll you swap me for it?"

He was less pleased to hear that Rickett had also come to raid his staff. "A theatre orderly? I suppose you'll want my best, too. Well, you can't have Dawson, if that's what you're thinking!"

Rickett was rather smooth about it. He brought out a piece of paper. "I have a movement order here for a J. J. Dawson. Brigadier Cameron signed it."

Black Jack looked from the paper to Rickett. His glare, fierce, calculating, dissolved into a grin.

"You're a bloody thief, Rickett," he said with admiring surprise.

Rickett's smile shone, creasing his face. He unfolded his lanky limbs and got up, towering over Black Jack.

"I'm glad I pass," he said in his soft voice. "I've been learning from a master."

J. J. Dawson, Rickett's theatre orderly, allowed no enthusiasm to disturb him as he listened to Rickett's proposition. The lugubrious Dawson was not given to wearing his heart on his sleeve. He was pleased that Major Rickett had specially asked for him, but he would die before showing it. Dawson pondered the prospect of Vis without a glimmer illuminating his sad, horsey face. He sniffed and scratched himself.

"I suppose we'll be bloody corpses in a month," he said, with relish.

"How soon can you be ready, J.J.?"

Dawson eyed Rickett bleakly. For a moment his face threatened to crack into a wintry smile, but he controlled himself. " 'Bout an hour," he said. "I mean, counting the time to make a fresh will."

Captain Frank Clynick, R.A.M.C., Rickett's personal choice as an anaesthetist, was much sunnier about the whole thing. Luckily Frank was doing a malarial course at Bari, and he was easily found. He was fair, stocky, placid, a dreamer.

"We'll manage," he said, and grinned happily. "Mind you, I'll have to brush up on anaesthesia."

"I'm warning you," Rickett said. "There'll be no fancy equipment for it. I've just been right through Base Medical Stores on my knees for some."

"Never mind," Clynick said. "There's always the old rag and bottle." The idea of surgery with penknives under hurricane lamps seemed to find merit with him. The more they talked about the snags, the more the gentle Clynick beamed.

He had come to look positively seraphic by the time they had exhausted all avenues for stores and set off by truck to embark them for Vis. The pride of Rickett's collection was a carboy of methylated spirits for heating and sterilising. He had bought it on the black market in Bari for 200 cigarettes. He had several thousand more cigarettes in his pack, acquired by avowing himself to be leading a company.

Landing Craft Infantry (L)

Black Jack would have been proud of him.

Long before their truck reached the port of Monopoli where a landing craft waited to take them across the Adriatic to Vis, the rain started lashing down out of a black sky. The wind rose and whip-cracked the truck canopy. It was going to be rough. Dawson began to swear. Clynick was singing. Somehow they found the right L.C.I. in the stormy blackout of the quayside and the moment their truck ground to a stop, Dawson was out and pitching into the loading with macabre zest.

The L.C.I. crew was a bit disdainful about taking medical supplies aboard. Guns for Vis made a more direct appeal to their imaginations and they were ill-disposed to get moving with the rolls of lint and bandages which Rickett and company started heaving out. They enlisted a port officer to prove that the landing craft had no room left, and while Rickett argued that he was not going to be separated from the precious little pile of gear he had fought for by allowing it to be put aboard a schooner, to follow them across to the Jugoslav coast at its leisure, Dawson whistled up a couple of Italian dock workers, pointed to their supplies with a commanding finger, and with a curious combination of gibberish and mime, terrified them into carting it aboard.

By the time Rickett and several opposition officers had exhausted themselves in debate, it was all loaded on deck and snugly secured under canopies against the rain.

A wind laden with stinging drops tugged and whipped at their caps. Dawson cocked an ear in the all-but-total darkness to the sounds of weather which rolled ominously into the quay from seaward. "Tell you one thing," he said, as though a comforting thought occurred. "We'll all be sick as dogs . . . !"

He hawked, spat into the darkness where the sea slapped at the quay and jerked his head towards the heaving silhouette of the L.C.I.

TWO

If reputations can be made overnight, Dawson's renown as a prophet was established then and there. He, Major Rickett, and the fair-haired Captain Clynick had just sorted themselves out their resting places below when a raucous gang of Raiding Support Regiment troops came stumbling down over them, straight from their farewell revelries, and proceeded to pitch their gear about and fight for space, cursing and lurching as the L.C.I. got under way and rose to breast the sea which came surging out of the blackness to meet her.

Soon everybody was being sick, for they were battling into a full gale. Dawson, stricken by his own prophecy, lay prone, sheet-white and retching helplessly, his condition worsening till he was unconscious.

It was no time to think about food, but a tipsy youth in the Raiding Support Regiment did, with querulous irrelevance. He stood up, swaying, and demanded to know why they had come away with no rations; immediately a row blazed and spread throughout the deck as the re-criminations flew back and forth. A couple of violent rolls as big waves smacked the L.C.I. abeam put an end to it, and as the boat began to hit the real weather, the combatants began subsiding like reaped corn. A general groaning started. Even the durable Rickett loosened his tie, wiped a cold film from his face, bethought himself of getting up on deck for air. He had thought he was a good sailor, and it angered him to feel sick.

An officer came clattering down in glistening oilskins. He took off his cap and shook the drops from it. He looked round him at the stricken troops.

"Running for Bari. We can't get anywhere in this. Try again tomorrow."

He vanished up the companionway. Somebody raised a cheer.

The next night was little better, but Rickett was cheered by a very profitable raid ashore at Bari which yielded them two primuses—gifts of the British Red Cross. He and Clynick returned hugging these as though they were made of beaten gold. The bravoes of the Raiding Support Regiment had mostly been subdued by seasickness and hangovers into quietness—all except a large Glaswegian, vociferous and unintelligible, who from his own triumphal sortie into the low life of the town, had fought a rearguard back to the boat against a vengeful crowd of Italians and was now nursing a bloody hand. They bought him to Rickett. A couple of tendons in his wrist had been severed. He cursed thickly as Rickett put him off the ship and into an ambulance. It started off for the General Hospital as the L.C.I. warped away from the mole. From the back of the wagon their first casualty brandished a white-bandaged fist and screeched, to cover his dismay.

"I'll be seein' you, Jack! Ye'll be back in a week with yer goolies shot off! The whaul bloody lot of ya!"

The storm escorted the little craft relentlessly up the eastern coast of Italy, taking almost as heavy a toll among the soldiers on board as on the night before. The L.C.I. wallowed along in a tattered sunset which limned the distant monotony of the shore whenever the swell lifted them high enough to perceive it. It was bleak and without comfort, but they would hug it until nightfall. The boats nourishing Vis and its handful of defenders only ventured out to it across the Adriatic during the dark period. The waters of the Jugoslav coast were alive with enemy patrol boats, and even on moonless nights the clashes were frequent.

The darkness walled in about them, muttering with fretful winds, almost palpable in its density. The L.C.I. turned to run into its blackness.

It was about two o'clock when Rickett stirred at a hand on his shoulder. He wiped a hand over his face. He no longer felt sick. Frank Clynick was bending over him.

It had grown calm. The boat was throbbing steadily through a lagoon stillness.

"Come up and have a look," Clynick whispered.

He got to his feet and followed the stocky outline of Clynick up the companionway. They rose into total blackness on deck, groping like blind men towards the gunwale. There he stared about him. Stars shone in the water. Now he could see the shapes of sailors moving around him, the huddle of the deck cargo, the line of the gunwale—and a great shadow, blotting out a vast expanse of star-powdered sky, rearing above them, as suddenly and completely present as a revelation.

The boat thrummed slowly forward into its engulfing gloom. Now the faintest shapes were wheeling past them. Was that a bollard? A dockside hut? A soldier, standing quietly there, as immovable and unseeable as granite against the black arras of cliffs?

A match flared and lit a face—only a few yards away, a face without a body—then died.

Abruptly a voice shouted an alien command, almost in Rickett's ear, so that he turned. *"Stoi!"*

Almost immediately a machine gun opened up a little above them, with a morse of flame tongues, and the bullets screamed through the rigging. The dark hills took up the sound and threw it back. Out of the darkness a fruity English voice on the quay roared irritably: "Stop that, you silly bastard! Get the ruddy gangawy up!"

The L.C.I. touched. A gangway bumped heavily down on the gunwale. A figure rose out of the shore darkness on it and stood poised there, hands on hips. A torch flicked on and travelled over the canopied lumps of cargo.

"Right, get it off!"

A dozen beret-topped Commando silhouettes came swarming aboard in time to meet the Raiding Support Regiment which came surging up to the deck. Rickett shouldered his way through a confusion of disembarkers versus unloaders to the English port officer up on the gangplank. As he did so an irate shout above the din arrested him.

" 'Ere! What's all this? *Bandages!* 'Oo asked for bandages?"

"Cripes, look at this! A bedpan!"

"Well, chuck it off, then! Just get the guns!" the port officer roared.

Rickett reached him. "Those bedpans are mine." he said with dignity, and stepped aside to dodge the unloading chain.

"They're on top of our guns," the figure of the port officer said. "Get 'em off before my blokes heave 'em into the sea. What's this?"

The torch rested on the carboy of methylated spirits, and the voice grew interested. "Vino?"

"Medical supplies," Rickett said. "We're a surgical team."

The port officer paused and flashed the torch over him. A couple of the Commandos halted. One of them muttered: "Blimey, *R.A.M.C.!*"

"It'll be E.N.S.A. girls next."

Rickett ignored that, and aimed at the dark bulk of the port officer. "They said you'd be needing us," he said.

There was a brief pause while that registered.

"Evans! Brown! Help the major here with his gear!"

The port officer's name was Le Bosquet. He reached out a hand and introduced himself. "It's not the Jerries we have to worry about, so much as these Jugs. They're getting automatics from us now, first they've seen. Trigger-happy as kids, Slovenka!"

A dark outline standing at Le Bosquet's elbow moved forward. It was a woman. Her face shone faintly in the nimbus of the torch as her dark eyes inspected Rickett. She was aquiline and toughish to look at. with lank strands of hair flapping beneath a forage cap, but her eyes were deeply alive.

"Yes, sir?" Her accent was strong.

"Can you fix up Major Rickett with a place to sleep?"

"I will see." She turned and walked down the gang-way. Rickett looked after her until she was swallowed in the blackness. The port officer turned from watching them unloading. He was sardonic, "You can look. But that's about all."

"Are there many of those?"

"Women? About a third of the partisan army. About the only way you can tell them from the men is, they've got bigger bottoms."

"Rather rough place for them to be, isn't it?"

Le Bosquet laughed. "If you think of them as women, you're going to be in trouble," he said.

The surgical pannier had a pretty rough trip ashore but the Commandos doing the unloading were as gentle with Rickett's carboy of methylated spirits, under his pleading, as with a baby. He needed it to fire his precious Red Cross primuses. Gingerly they manoeuvred it across the gangway and stumbled safely on to the mole with it. There they stood teetering, breathing a little under its weight.

"Hey, sir! Where shall we put it?"

The port officer murmured: "There'll be a truck along for your stuff." Aloud he yelled: "Just put it down there!"

"Right!" The answer floated back cheerfully. Then Rickett heard the thump and the awful splintering of glass.

Out of the ensuing silence one of the Commandos growled: "You bloody twerp, Jonesy! *When I say ready!*"

Rickett came groping forth across the gangway and on to firm land. He stood looking down at the wrecked carboy, and he groaned.

But he was not able to mourn it long. Somebody said: "Listen!" They all heard the truck at the same time, growing louder. Rickett turned and saw it looming along the narrow mole towards them. It was coming suicidally fast in the dark. "Scarper! It's the Professor!"

The three Commandos turned and fled up the gangplank.

Twenty yards away the truck scattered the dark forms of several partisan soldiers who turned and hurled strange curses at it. It bore down upon Rickett standing there deserted on the mole until he, too, gathered his wits and leaped for the side. The big shadow of the truck hammered past him in a flurry of wind, completed the demolition of the carboy, and drew up with a screech at the dim gangway. A stocky figure climbed down followed by a woman partisan. The driver walked round the front, and peered underneath. "Bits of broken glass," the figure said happily. "Well, well!"

"A colleague of yours," the port officer said. "Captain Heron, Major Rickett." Heron, in the darkness, gave an impression of broad shoulders, a straggling moustache, an air of bland devilment, and he whiffed a strange liquor. He ran a Field Ambulance, and when they confessed to their identities, it was Rickett's which shook him.

"A surgical unit! I say! They don't mean to forget us after all!" Heron brought out a flask, had a nip, and passed it on. "By the way, who left that big bottle there for me to smash into?"

"That bottle," Rickett said bitterly, "was a carboy of meths. It cost me 200 cigarettes on the black market in Bari."

"You can't drink meths," Heron observed. "Though after the Jug rotgut, one wonders. Here." He thrust the flask towards him.

A guff of wild spirit from it did not entirely comfort Rickett. "It was all I had to boil my instruments with," he said.

Heron caressed his wide moustache and inspected him. "What General Hospital are you from? You sound like a worrier to me." He said it pleasantly.

It was Heron—the Professor—who conducted Rickett and his helpers, Captain Frank Clynick and J. J. Dawson, to the place where they were to spend their first night on Vis. The fact that he and Le Bosquet had been whiling away with some gentle tippling the long night spell of waiting for a possible supply boat to arrive did not seem to have impaired their efficiency a whit. They worked stoically and hard, cursing and joking in the blackout, with occasional recourse to the Professor's warming flask of *rakia*. Heron whistled up another truck and took aboard the mixed surgical equipment with high good humour and with no further losses. He drove off the leading truck with a dramatic lurch and a clanging of an enormous xylophone as they scraped the quayside bollards.

The truck bringing up the rear was driven by a cockney orderly who spoke almost entirely in rhyming slang. He and his ten comrades had been with Heron's ambulance right through the desert from Alamein. They had campaigned with the Long Range Desert Group and had seen lots of pretty lively action. Their job with battle casualties had been patch-up-and-shift-back, and for all they knew, that was where the matter ended, for they looked with suspicion upon anything as high-falutin' as a surgical team, which smacked somehow of base. It was clear that they wanted nothing to do with that.

Nevertheless, the cockney driver took pity on Dawson, aghast as they careered along the quayside after Heron's swerving truck.

"Don't worry, mate," he said. "The time to look out is when he's on the wagon."

Heron pulled up before a dark building and motioned Rickett out. They started to walk towards the door, when a figure leapt from its shadow with a levelled gun.

"Stoi!"

They had no time to reply before the sentry fired, and the roar and the surprise nearly floored Rickett where he stood.

"Engleski!" Heron yelled, and grabbed Rickett to halt him.

They both remained stock still while the partisan came forward, his rifle never wavering, until he was within a yard of Rickett and Heron. He glared at them both intently, then with an abrupt gesture of his gun motioned them to pass.

They started unloading the truck.

"Stand-to every night," Heron explained. "When they yell *stoi,* for heaven's sake stop. Every night's a panic now. They don't know which night Jerry's coming—only that it's any night now, and then—" He shrugged.

Under the light of Heron's torch the house turned out to be an empty butcher's shop. It still smelled of meat and fat.

"Dump your supplies in here till morning. I've got you a billet farther along the waterfront."

"Leave my surgical gear unguarded?" Rickett protested. "This place hasn't even got a lock on it!"

"Nobody'll touch it," Heron assured him. "These are not Eyeties. Besides, the island operates an excellent insurance against theft."

"It does?"

"Yes. If anybody lifts anything, he's shot."

Like the other buildings along the waterfront, their billet was in total darkness, partly shuttered, but breathing that indefinable awareness that told of watchers in the shadows. Sure enough, they had not walked three paces before they halted at a rapped challenge from the shadows. A partisan lounged forward, vetted them, and let them pass.

In the hall they stepped around a mounted anti-tank gun. Two partisan youngsters manned it, smoking, very awake, at the open door. A broad iron-balustraded stair reached up from the cavernous ground-floor room, with its wine barrels and its litter of sleeping soldiers, into a landing. Heron shepherded them into the first upstairs room, stumbled round a table to close the shutters, and switched on the light. After a whole night of groping in blackness it had the brilliant suddenness of a blow. Under its dazzle Heron's face, till now briefly sculpted by shadows and starlight and an occasional furtive match, was disappointingly absolute. He was fair, short, broad, with a sandy moustache. But there were sun wrinkles around his eyes and they were careless, amused, and a little sleepy.

He gestured and said: "Must be the housekeeper's day off."

The room was a shambles, its long table crammed with bully and other rations, some of them open and half-emptied among the litter of dirty plates. It was as though they had surprised an enemy, not an ally, at a midnight meal, and he had fled in the middle of it.

Dawson had already reconnoitred the food and had selected himself a tin. Rickett lowered himself into a chair, fished in his haversack for some treasure. He might as well show some goodwill, he thought, and brought a bottle of Black Jack's *Johnnie Walker* to light.

He plumped it on the table, and reached for some mugs.

"Have a drink."

Heron's sleepy eyes widened a little at the sight of that. He switched on his grin. "Christ, whisky! Now I know you're from base!"

The dawn woke Rickett, as it always did. He stretched, wiped his face, and swung his feet over the bed, groping with his toes for his boots. The light filled the whitewashed bedroom. In contrast to the mess room and the lower floor shambles it glowed spotlessly clean.

In one corner Captain Clynick lay with his cherubic face turned innocently to the ceiling. Dawson slumbered shapelessly under a blanket in another corner. Rickett shuffled to the window and looked out.

The peace of the place was as pristine as the first dawn on a new planet. There was the harbour, vaster than a lagoon, but entirely still, opalescent in the half-light. It was totally empty—void even of a fishing boat, a dinghy. The mole was uncannily silent. The boat which had brought them had vanished.

For a moment he felt deserted. With the sight of this meaning emptiness, with the light slowly beginning to gild the stonework of the houses fringing the quiet water, the reality of Vis and the uneasiness of it began slowly to invade him. But it was beautiful, and he felt for a cigarette to flavour his contemplation of it. The sunlight was spreading on the waterfront. He would go down and walk in it.

Me 109

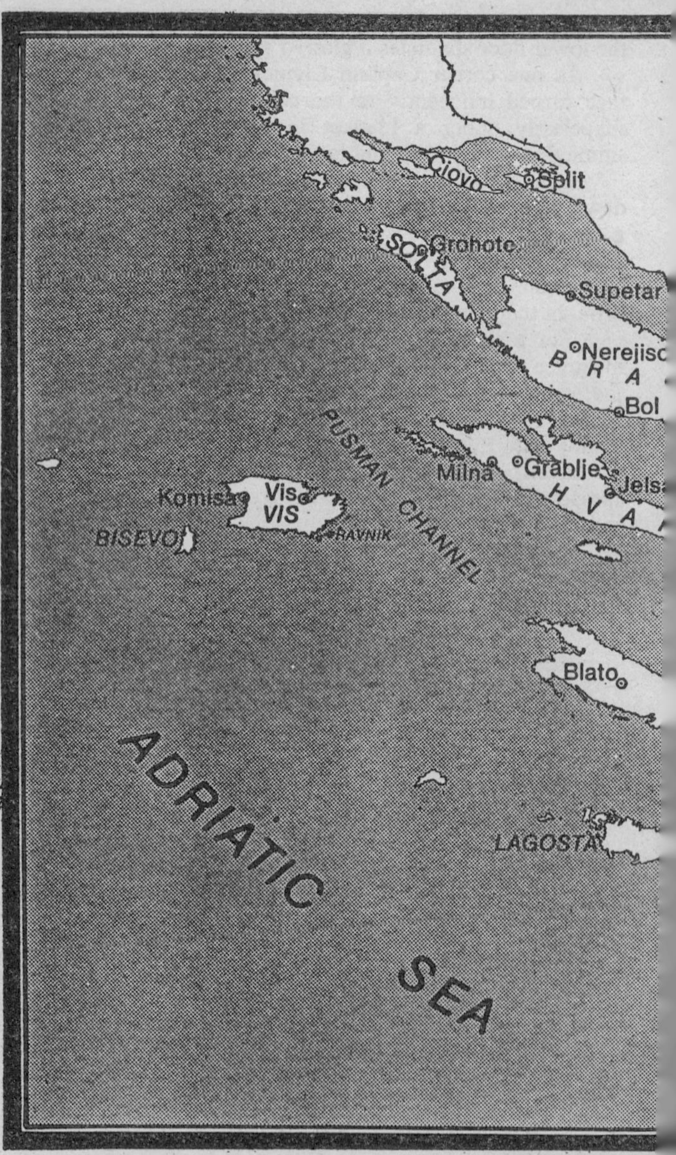
Ciovo
Split
Grohote
SOLTA
Supetar
Nerejisc
B R A
Bol
Milna
Grablje
Jelsa
H V A
PUSMAN CHANNEL
Komisa
Vis
VIS
BISEVO
RAVNIK
Blato
LAGOSTA
ADRIATIC SEA

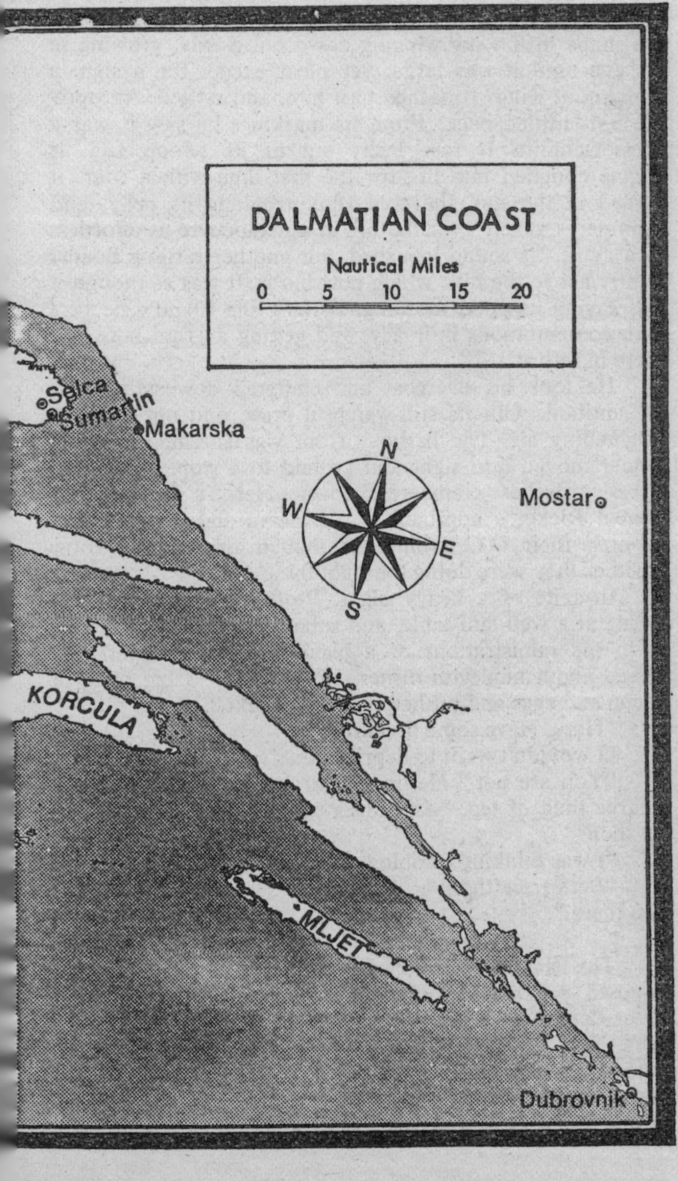

DALMATIAN COAST

Nautical Miles

0 5 10 15 20

Selca
Sumartin
Makarska

Mostar

N
W E
S

KORCULA

MLJET

Dubrovnik

Rickett was about to reach for his boots when he saw the shape in the sky winging down noiselessly, growing in his eye until it was large, yet silent except for a sigh, a whining of wind. It flashed past him, and rattled. Abruptly the hills rattled back. From its markings he saw it was a Messerschmitt. It rose lazily out of its swoop and its engine coughed into life for the first time with a roar. It turned in the sun, the gold rippling along its belly, and skimmed serenely over the hill in a manoeuvre as effortless as a gull's. Its sound vanished, but another rattling floated faintly above the hills which now hid it. It was as though it was saying its good morning, shaking the island's sleepers with contemptuous intimacy, and getting a grunt here and there in return.

He took his overcoat and clattered downstairs, past the antitank with its still-watchful crew, and out into the brightening air. The harbour front was stirring. A three-tonner moved into sight and ground to a stop. Some Red Cross orderlies clambered down—Heron's boys. They treated Rickett's approach with reserve and directed him towards their O.C.'s billet as though they didn't know whether they were doing the right thing.

In spite of a heavy night, Professor Heron was up, sitting at a well-laid table, and submitting somewhat bleakly to the ministrations of a black-clad housekeeper who fussed about him with dishes. He looked at a big plate of bacon and eggs and pushed it over to Rickett.

"Here. Have some breakfast."

"I wouldn't want to deprive you."

"You are not," Heron said dryly, and poured himself a large mug of tea. "Any ideas where you're going to set up shop?"

"I was thinking of doing a reccy—"

"Better see the man in charge," Heron said. "I'll take you there."

The island of Vis, like its neighbours, is one of several exposed peaks in a submerged mountain chain. It rises sheer out of an intense green sea to some three thousand feet. Two of its bays, Vis and Komisa—where Rickett landed the previous night—are almost landlocked by the steep mountainsides and form magnificent natural harbours. They lie at opposite ends of Vis, and though only five miles apart on the map, they are joined by a narrow, stony, tortuous mountain track which wanders over half the island before descending dizzily again to the sea.

In the centre of the island the rocky hills dominated by Mount Hum enclose a small central plateau, nourishing it with their rains and their siltings, which the natural chemistry of time and weather have transformed into rich red earth. On it grow vines whose grapes fill the wine vats in every house on the island.

It was the second time that the British had come to Vis. In 1810 the Royal Navy garrisoned the island to hold its ports open for trade which flowed into the heart of Europe, in defiance of Napoleon. Its ships also held a French fleet bottled up in Trieste—until, stung to action by an enraged Emperor, eleven French warships stocked with troops sallied out to capture Vis and destroy the small British squadron of four men-of-war.

Captain William Hoste, sighting the French, signalled his captains to "remember Nelson" and led them forth to rout the French in a furious and brilliantly skilful engagement.

The British built two forts on Vis, one beneath the topmost peak, and governed the island until it was ceded to Austria in the peace of 1815.

Now, once more to keep a foot wedged in this tiny back door to Europe, the British had landed troops on Vis—or rather, a troop: fifty Commandos.

It was an impertinently confident gesture, and a little belated, for the other islands in the Dalmatian cluster lying opposite Split on the Jugoslav coast had already fallen to a drastic German sweep of the coast. Nevertheless, the tiny band of men in green berets had joined up with the Titoist partisans manning Vis amid flowers and handshakes and embraces and sonorous speeches of welcome, and much firing of guns, to which the Jugoslavs—"the Jugs"—were dangerously addicted. It was a joyous *entente* between utter strangers, spiced with high peril, and for these reasons, romantic. It was to abate somewhat in the ensuing months in the face of political, tactical, racial and material realities.

More Commandos would be following—if they arrived in time. In the teeth of its threatened engulfment, Vis was pouring clandestine supplies across into the Jugoslav

E-Boat

hinterland, where saboteurs kept the railway lines constantly cut and rendered road communications so hazardous that now the sea lanes between the islands bore the heaviest enemy traffic of all.

While this small hump of craggy stone remained uncaptured, it kept at bay a fantastic number of the enemy. Its harbours were naked by day, but every inlet and creek, under the steep protective shoulder of the hills, swarmed with camouflaged small craft, both partisan and British, which emerged at night to hound the German shipping. British M.G.B.'s were boarding, bombarding, burning freighters, tackling the E-boats in running fights, even taking prizes in tow back to Vis.

Of the twenty-eight German divisions drawn and pinned down in the Balkans by partisan ebullience, the cream of these were now gathered around Split and these offshore islands. In their van was the crack 118th Jaeger Division. Korcula and Brac, close island neighbours to Vis, briefly snatched by partisans after the Italian collapse, had already been overwhelmed by big German forces a month before.

On New Year's Day, 1944, the Germans mounted *Operation Freischutz*—destined to mop up the remaining three islands defying them and to wipe the tiny garrison of Vis off the map. Away to the south-west, Lagosta fell. In a little over a fortnight the Germans had blasted the partisans off their last, and closest neighbour—the long narrow island strip of Hvar.

Rickett had landed on Vis with his bedpans and his primuses at a moment when, with an advance troop of Commandos and a couple of thousand ill-armed partisans, it now faced the Germans alone. His arrival put a clear emphasis on the *no retreat* order. There was no evacuation plan even for the wounded. He would operate on the battlefield.

His adviser on where to set up shop was Lieutenant-Colonel Jack Churchill, Commanding Officer of the British troops, lovingly known as Mad Jack. He was fair, quiet, and fierce, and whenever he stood opposite the Germans, they were in for a surprise. At times he piped his troops into battle; at others, led them, waving a claymore. On several occasions he had gone into action with a bow and arrow and there were several astonished but very dead Germans to bear mute witness to his archery.

"No use putting your hospital down in the harbours," he told Rickett. "They're the first places Jerry'll go for. Find a place up top somewhere. And, I say—none of this rot about marking the place out with Red Crosses, unless you want to be a priority target. Camouflage *everything*."

It was on the lofty central plateau of the island, just under the peak of Mount Hum, that Rickett at last found and commandeered a house. It was a square, dilapidated farmhouse and it stood aloof from a cluster of stone buildings called Podhumlje. The tiny hamlet sat at the southern end of the plain, halfway between sky and sea. Away on one side a track wound over the island's back. On the other the rock-strewn earth ran a few yards into space before crumbling vertically away into the sea. They reached Podhumlje from the port by a mean and tortured ascent which allowed them, in its hugging of the mountain walls, a few grudging inches between the truck wheels and a majestic eternity of far rocks and water. It would not be an ideal path up which to bring the wounded, but it was the only one.

Even in the sober early morning Captain Heron's slap-happy driving style was not suited to nervous passengers. He tackled the mountain track with the insouciance with which he had ploughed through the blackout the night before. Heron must have noticed his uneasiness when they slithered on the loose stones, for he said airily: "The time to worry is when you meet somebody coming the other way."

They reached the plateau, and got out at Podhumlje. Around them, in a tender morning sea streaked with ripple shivers, the enemy islands basked blandly in the morning sun. In this light they were so close that it seemed he would only have to fire a shotgun to startle any roosting birds among their dark, vegetable tumble, and then pick them off, one by one, as they rose. The sides of Korcula were as lucid of texture as the marks on a reptile, slumbering close and apparently unaware. How else did one reconcile this malign proximity with this quiet?

Closer still loomed Hvar, north of them. He could see the roads which veined it with white. He could pick out the bleached clusters of houses. Beyond it, across a soft expanse of watered silk, Brac reared a prehistoric spine, its crags clear-etched. Less than twenty miles off, the snow caps of the Dinaric Alps, the mainland itself, serrated the skyline. The morning sun iced them pink.

For the soldiers there might be profit in meditating how the wrath stored so close around would awake and fall upon them. For him, there was only a strange wonder, and his own task. He had to turn an old house that was little more than a bare stone shell into something like a hospital.

Their second journey to Podhumlje was to take possession of it. They undertook it recklessly at dusk, after a wearying day of negotiating to requisition it, and of begging stores from an amiably helpless quartermaster.

As if darkness were not hazard enough for taking the cliffside track, the road was choked with partisans winding their way up on foot to night action-stations. A fresh rumour had come blowing across the water that the German attack would come this night, and the expectation of it thrilled dangerously through the mass of partisans like some high-powered narcotic.

The army their truck crawled past was curiously exalted. The men and women, clad in their motley of Italian, American, British and captured German uniforms, topped with a sidecap and its Tito star, waved and grinned at them. They staggered under heavy machine guns, prodded at their donkeys bearing goatskins of wine, and gave themselves entirely to their harmonic battle chanting. The singing rang from the stone mountainsides. The truck, clinging desperately round the hairpins, the driver's face a pale, alert blob beside Rickett, ran suddenly into a great wave of their voices—Aeolian, gusty, tremendous, as if borne on a wind. It blew in their faces from a chasm ahead, washing them through, in spite of themselves, with a sudden heroic intoxication, a shudder, almost, of delirium. It breathed into their defiance a majestic beauty, and such was its contagion that in the splendid moment of coming upon this sudden glory of voices, it would almost not have mattered if they had gone over the cliff. It was as mighty as that, as terrible, as moving.

This was the way the partisans sang when they went into battle, but whether such sound as this gave those ragged soldiers the courage that was theirs, or whether their courage gave them this sound, Rickett did not know.

The house of Podhumlje had belonged to a priest who had fled on the day the partisans set foot on Vis. Whether he had pursued too guilty a relationship with the Nazis, or simply felt religion to lie too dangerously at variance with the partisan outlook, remained a mystery. The reality he left behind was a large shambling building whose lower floor was one square store-room, stone-paved, unlit by any windows, containing several great barrels of wine higher than a man, an untidy cluster of smaller racks of dusty bottles, and a wine press.

Dawson tapped a barrel and gave a rare grin when he found it full. So were all the other barrels. The fat gallon-sized bottles proved to hold *procek*, rich and fruity like Madeira, quite possibly sacramental. There was enough, if this were so, to provide religious comfort for several generations of peasantry to come.

To come into this place was to telescope time. One stepped straight through the double wooden doors into a Bible scene, with the goatskins hanging from the rafters, the crude wine-grower's implements rusting against the wall, the donkey nuzzling in at the door, the old woman gowned in homespun black who peered at them uncertainly from a crumbling window of the next house down a lane. A goat stumbled among the rocks, grazing and lifting its head to complain.

Once it became clear that Rickett, though senior and a surgeon, was unconcerned with rank or bossing it over

them, Heron and his somewhat ruffianly crew surrendered
the independence they would otherwise have fought to the
death to preserve.

A little guardedly, they elected to work close to him
at Podhumlje, and brought their own outfit up to move in
a couple of houses away. It involved them in evicting a
handful of partisans, which was not easy, and exhausted
most of their tact. The other houses swarmed with Jugs
and were patently impossible to occupy.

It was intensely gloomy inside the hospital. Rickett
chose the brightest upstairs room for the theatre, and set
up the portable operating table. Dawson, rummaging
about with the zeal of a pioneer, found an ancient dressing
table and detached its mirror. He strung this on wires over
one end of the operating table to help spread the light
coming in from the small window. At the other end of the
table they hung their precious Tilley lamp. With the
mirror, it might provide just enough light to see by, when
it came to operating at night. That is, if they ever got any
fuel for it . . .

Next door the primuses were set up for sterilising.

"All I need is some meths to light them," Rickett said.
"And for the lamp." He sighed and damned the men who
had dropped his carboy.

They invited Heron and his men in to christen the
place. Heron accepted rather touchingly. Though there
was all the wine in the world in the vats downstairs, he
brought over a bottle of *rakia* with which to toast the
hospital. Rickett accepted a mug of it from him, drank,
and gasped for air. It was explosively strong and it tasted
vile. He shook his head at Heron, who, jeering, tilted the
bottle invitingly to offer him some more.

Then an idea struck Rickett. He changed his mind
and reached out his mug.

"Say when," Heron said, and raised his eyebrows as
the mug filled and Rickett forebore to speak. He hesitated.

"Don't be stingy," Rickett said. "There's no ration on
this stuff, is there?"

Heron shrugged and filled it up.

Rickett took the mug to the primus, uncapped it, and
poured some of the *rakia* inside. Then he brimmed the
cup-like primer. "Stand back," he said, and struck a match

to the *rakia*. It burned with a wobbly, almost transparent blue flame.

In a few moments the primus was roaring. Occasionally it actually hiccoughed, but then it would roar into life again.

"Thanks," Rickett said.

Heron overcame his wonderment quickly, for he was a firm believer in the beneficent power of alcohol.

"I told you, didn't I?" he said. "People can worry too bloody much!"

THREE

As soon as Rickett could sit down with Heron to consider the medical situation on this island, they saw it as parlous.

Rickett's own job was to set up a hospital in the field for the Commandos, both present and yet to arrive.

It was plain after his first day that he could never leave it at that. There were already 2,000 partisans on this island. More were arriving every night. Also at night, by schooner, the wounded were streaming in to Vis from sorties across to the neighbouring islands and from operations on the mainland itself.

To cope with these there were two Jugoslav doctors, one of them an elderly general practitioner who directed the medical services for the whole of the partisan army in Dalmatia and who was thoroughly overworked simply sorting the sick and the wounded; the other was a man of doubtful pretensions who, while pluckily tackling all kinds of surgery, had little or no experience of it. His name was Petak and his *forte,* it was said, had been gynaecology.

"A gynie-man in this hole," Heron said. "How's that for a square peg?"

Heron saved the brightest item until last. There was another Englishman on Vis, doing surgery. He was another emissary of Force 133, sent to work among the partisans, and he was quartered down in the other port, Vis.

He was young but he sounded pretty good. His name was George Lloyd Roberts.

"I imagine Roberts is pretty busy down there," Heron said. "These Jug schooners are bringing in boatloads of casualties at night."

It occurred to Rickett that Roberts would be a damned sight busier when the attack started, with his theatre down in the port. He unfolded his lanky legs and put his cigarette out. He got up, buttoning his jacket, and turned to Dawson who was still scrubbing. He had scrubbed the sterilising room, the theatre, and now he was getting their bandage store clean.

Rickett said: "I'll be back by evening."

"We've got two stretchers, sir," Dawson said. "How are we going to find beds?"

Rickett hesitated. "I'll—send to Bari for some more," he said, as if that was all he would have to do.

"Let's hope we don't get our wounded before we get the stretchers, sir."

Heron struck up his favourite tune. "You worry too much," he intoned. "Just lay your wounded on the ground."

"By the way," Rickett said, halting at the door. "We're going to need all the shelter we can get up here. So—if you can grab another house from the partisans—"

"Or two—" Heron mocked.

Dawson stared at his O.C. and searched for something not to insubordinate to convey his manifest doubt. He said: "If you'll promise to pick the bullets out of me, sir—"

"I will," Rickett said. He liked Dawson's funereal style. He left with the truck to call on the young Captain Roberts. The road down to Vis port was a replica in its hazards of the ascent from Komisa. The harbour was a horseshoe, its curve lined with stone houses. An oval islet studded its bay, with a tiny church showing a spire like a pointed pencil.

George Lloyd Roberts had set up his partisan hospital in the stone schoolhouse at one end of the waterfront. He was dark, cheerful, assured, almost touchingly bovish· his accent had a careless elegance which was bizarre in these surroundings. He was also almost unreally good-looking—and, it soon proved, somewhat tougher than he either looked or sounded.

It seemed odd at first to come upon him here, sorting through a host of unwashed bodies amid a stench of decay and sickness and chloroform. The casualties swarmed in every room. They lined the schoolhouse outside in a seemingly endless queue. Inside, with earnest breeziness, Roberts waded through a ghastly procession of casualties, interviewing them with pantomime and pidgin while the others stoically waited their turn. Beneath the cultured phrases and the casual charm lay the lazy authority of one automatically schooled to give orders. He was Eton, only recently graduated in medicine, terrifyingly inexperienced, and so, by all the rules, incongruous.

Yet he was not. An orderly took Rickett through the squalid chamber which, he proudly pointed out, was the sterilising room, into young Lloyd Roberts's primitive operating theatre. As Rickett blundered in a brawny partisan orderly straightened, gave him the Communist salute, and said gravely: "Up your pipe, sair!"

At that a little woman assisting George lifted her head and glared with angry suspicion at the partisan. George looked up, too, and met Rickett's eye. He grinned. "Hullo." And bent to his work again.

The patient was about fifty, his head shaven against lice, and the bones of his face stood out in clear relief under a thin parchment skin. Rickett noted the hollowing in front of his ears. Automatically his professional mind registered a calculation: haemoglobin about thirty per cent. If he's lucky. A pretty girl, dark and luscious, was bent over the patient's head, caressing the air above his nose with a pad of gauze. This was his anaesthetist! The room stank of ether.

Roberts murmured: "Bit more, Suza." She was slow to understand, so he motioned, and she brought the ether-soaked pad close. Roberts had stripped off a filthy dressing to uncover the wound. An open fracture, tibia and fibula; must be months old, quite untreated. The white ends of dead bone showed through a gaping wound with purplish indurated edges. Gently, young Roberts tested for union. He raised his brows and returned Rickett's fascinated stare.

"What do you think of that?" he said, and smiled.

In spite of the sepsis, and the grotesque angle of the lower leg, there was quite moderate bony union. Roberts said briskly: "Right-ho, Zena! Transfusion, splints, eh? And then pop him on a schooner. There one going tonight?"

The older woman with him had a wild cloud of dark hair and a voice edged with vibrant power, heavily accented. "To Bari? Yes, I think—Johnnie! Lubo!" She clicked her fingers and the stretcher bearers jumped forward as though the click had stung them. Robert introduced her.

"This is Madame Zon—Zena."

"I'm Major Rickett. How do you do?"

She was in her forties, and her face immediately held him, for in spite of her smallness, it had a granite strength, a commandingly aquiline nose, eyes that were deep-set, dark, and full of a tragic power. The stare she had first turned on Rickett at his entrance had been terrifying. During the operation she had remained bowed and intent, but now, with a wild and arrogant lift of her head, it was her presence which commanded the room. And in her strength she was, against all the rules, beautiful.

She said in her harsh voice: "George teaches my partisans bad words." It was a simple statement of fact. George looked guilty. He entered a note in his exercise book on the patient. "That chap was on the run for eight months with that leg," he murmured evasively.

Even to a surgeon as seasoned to suffering as Rickett, the cases parading through this schoolhouse were a shock. The men still nursed their guns with a savage possessiveness. There were many women among them, brown, lined, swathed in heavy woollen shawls and black peasant tatters, so many with the cachectic look telling of illness from sepsis and starvation. They had brought their children.

These were the survivors of the partisan war which had rolled through their villages, of the German reprisals and massacres in Bosnia and Herzegovina. To the families, Vis was just another weary stage in a trek to a hopeless nowhere whose operative direction was simply away from war. Its evidence, interminable though their journey had been, still travelled with them. There was a boy who had been bayonetted through the mouth by the *Ustachi*, the Jugoslav quislings. Another with a foot padded with a dirty, bloodstained rag, which, when opened, revealed an instep denuded of skin, the white tendons standing out like bass strings, with maggots swarming among them. The maggots were a mercy, in a way. They had probably saved the foot from gangrene. It had had no attention since the

previous May, up in the Bosnian mountains, when the boy
who bore it was hit in a skirmish.

Rickett wondered how they had ever got him to Vis.
The journey and the suffering it had involved were unimaginable.

George was somewhat *blasé*. There was a hip wound
yesterday, he said, that was eighteen months old. He had
long given up wondering how they stood it.

"I've got my hands full trying to patch 'em up,
without thinking of anything else," George said. He
laughed, boisterously. It was his kind of apology for
having feelings about it. Thereafter Rickett tried to get
down to Vis harbour almost every day to lend some help
in the overcrowded hospital there. Though chaos raged
round him, young George Lloyd Roberts was gay about
the difficulties. The fact that he had been landed almost
straight from St. Thomas's into conditions which had not
been paralleled since the Crimean war set him back
amazingly little. His orderlies were clumsy and thick-
headed, but willing as horses, and devoted to him. Roberts
urged them on with the rich Balkan curses they taught
him. He knew about two other words of what he called
Jug.

Never far from his hands was a dog-eared school
exercise book in which he had stored, in his rounded
scribble, a lot of notes on hookworm, heat-stroke, fevers,
smallpox, antisepsis, diagnosis, hints he had snatched from
books and lectures en route for Vis. Most of them seemed
ill-designed to serve him here and so Roberts was using its
remaining blank pages to record the realities as they
confronted him, case by case: abdominal resections, amputations, eye operations, all the stark challenges of traumatic surgery. He had grappled with these alone, because
until now there had been nobody else to attempt it. He was
not shrinking from the grimmest surgery, nor the most
drastically specialised.

"Anyhow, it's do or die, what?" he said. That was all,
and it summed it up.

"What about the Jug doctors?" Rickett asked.

"There is Dr. Petak," Lloyd Roberts said. "Have you
met the *braf* Dr. Petak?" He said this all deliberately, with
a smile.

"No."

"I must see that you do," Lloyd Roberts said.

There was an etiquette in medicine which carried over into the Army. In another man's theatre, you waited till your advice was asked. Rickett's seniority did not entitle him to any exemption from this. In any case, the best kind of guidance in a tricky operation or a difficult case was to stand by and simply watch. In practice, a friendly presence was not inhibiting. It was an encouragement. An inexperienced surgeon was always more likely to lose his nerve and retreat from action rather than commit a positive folly. And if he did get in a tangle, there was always a way of steering him, by a display of interest, a casual remark, towards the right course.

But a couple of hours of looking on and Rickett had the younger man's measure. Under the classy stammer and the vestiges of boyhood, George was highly able, intent, extraordinarily resolute.

He was even his own pathologist. He had a blood donor service going, too. "Plasma? We don't get plasma, old boy. We get *nothing* from Italy. No, I use the local product. I go stalking the Jugs for it."

Most of his hospital helpers had to stop their work occasionally and give up some blood whenever George demanded it. They obliged cheerfully enough.

The hulking, grinning Johnnie, his stretcher-bearer, was his champion donor. For a couple of bottles of wine Johnnie would give up 400 c.c. at a time. He was strong, tender, and he lifted the sick in his arms as if they were babies. He never slept. After a long tour of duty and a donation of blood Johnnie would take his reward of wine out with him on a night's fishing and return at dawn, bleary, but with a full creel.

George had a specialist who siphoned off the blood into empty wine bottles. He was an aged, toothless peasant whose powers of suction, George Lloyd Roberts claimed, were remarkable. For this virtue he had appointed him his official Bloodsucker. George cross-grouped the blood and when he decided on a transfusion, he tested the patient's blood against his donor supply.

There was no refrigeration, of course, to preserve his bank.

He said: "I just fill my wine bottles with it and bung 'em into the ground under the cellar." George tapped a patient to put on his shirt again.

Then he added, thoughtfully: "Mind you, after a few days it goes a bit off."

That night Major Rickett ate in unthought-of magnificence. George took him to Zena's house, where he was billeted. There was a great social distinction attached to this, for Zena commanded—and commanded was the word—the finest house on the tiny harbour front.

She was the wife of the partisans' medical chief, Dr. Milo Zon, a gentle wisp of a man, as quiet as she was authoritative. Zena was also George's principal aide at the hospital. In her villa, she reigned as the island's acknowledged matriarch and social leader.

Few had ever been known to get the better of this electric little woman with the tempest of dark hair and the corncrake voice. She had had an expensive and worldly education in Vienna and Sarajevo. Before the war she had been a kind of medical theatregoer, helping her husband with his patients, attending operations his colleagues performed, finally, even, assisting them now and then—just as, now, she helped George Lloyd Roberts. In his hospital Zena was his Voice, and a very stormy one. She interpreted, directed the disposition of patients, the stretchers; as often as the pretty amateur anaesthetist, Suza, she helped administer choloroform or injected the pentothal.

Zena had a secret. She was short-sighted, and she was ashamed of it, as of a weakness. It gave her trouble, probing for a vein with the hypodermic.

But without her law-giving and power, George was all but lost. When she was away he had to diagnose by semaphore, sight, feel. Zena even disciplined George himself. He accepted her scoldings gracefully, like any son.

In the evening, Zena gave the lucky ones among them a home. Her house on the harbour was the meeting place for invited British officers and the partisan chiefs.

The terrace of the house, hung with a tumble of creeper, looked out on a postcard view of the slender islet in the bay, its arcaded campanile pointing above a thicket of cypresses—and beyond it, clear across a wide wash of sea, the enemy bastion, Hvar.

Inside the house the dining table was thick with flowers, for if Zena took a severe view of the war, her chief slave here, Cookie, took an obstinately feminine one. Cookie's linen shone. She was blonde and blushful, and her own battle was to preserve every civilian delicacy against the squalor of war. To her, it was as real a business as the partisan raiding programme on the surrounding islands. Cookie and her kitchen staff would scour the bare hills for miles in search of wild flowers for the dinner table.

This scandalised Zena, who would pass through the dining room like a tornado, confiscating the bouquets which made it a bower of sweetness, hurling them on to the fire. If anybody protested, she stabbed a finger at the view. "There are Germans across there! Are we getting ready for them, or for a carnival? It is indecent!"

As soon as she had swept through, more flowers appeared in her wake, magically, on the tables.

Cookie conjured wonders from the British and partisan rations, but she was flustery and easily upset. The one domain on which Zena marched at her peril was the kitchen. If she ever headed that way there was always a terrible scene which would end with a livid Cookie standing at the door screeching hysterical defiance and invective after her.

Rickett won Cookie's heart by the simple tactic of asking for a second slice of her Bosnian cake. Thereafter, she fussed about him endlessly and always whacked him out the biggest helping.

On this first night at Zena's they drank wine from the mountain plateau, and Scotch whisky—with a German label. It would have been interesting to trace the travels this bottle had had. Captured *en route* for America? Shipped back to Germany? Relabelled, despatched to the Fatherland's heroes garrisoning the Adriatic? Plundered by Jugoslav partisans who, in clumsy wooden schooners, emerged from the island hiding places at night like bats and waited athwart the German sea lanes?

Whatever the journey, the Scotch was now offered back, with a grin and a flourish, to a British guest of honour. There was a wonderful completeness in the compliment.

It occurred to Rickett, as he sipped it, that he was

enjoying life more than he had ever done before. Beyond
the harbour headland, pinpointed by the occasional spar-
kling of a light, the Germans were massing. The holocaust
impended, and in his own hut up on the hill he had a
primus, a portable operating table, some pentothal, and a
bare handful of instruments to meet the tide of casualties.

Yet overshadowing even those things was the spirit,
the gusto of this little woman who dominated their table
from her place at the head of it. He savoured the whisky,
halted, and grinned at her. The deep, hypnotic eyes met
his. The tragic shadows behind her stare thinned for a
moment. She smiled and said: "Is the British Army short
of doctors?"

"The *world* is short of doctors."

"What do they imagine you and this boy can do,
when the Germans come? There will be enough blood to
drown twenty doctors!"

Ricket mustered a jollity. "I've sent urgently for more
help," he said.

"You think it will come?"

He thought about this, and of the struggles he had
had, even to get basic surgical instruments.

"Sooner or later." He could not avoid an ironic
edge.

Zena sighed. "In time to bury us decently, I hope."

"Don't forget we've got your Dr. Petak, too," George
said dryly.

"I am not forgetting him," Zena said. She awoke out
of a dark reverie and patted George with fond reproof.

"He is our prize, this boy. He can bring any friends
he likes to my house. George is *partisan*."

Rickett nodded.

"Not like the first doctor who was here." Zena
slapped her forehead to remember. "What was his name,
George?"

"No names, no pack drill," George said.

"Huh! He thought he was a gentleman! He wore a
monocle all the time and put his boots up on the table. He
didn't even take them down when *I* walked in the room."

"What happened to him?" Rickett asked.

Zena waved an airy hand. "I had him thrown off the
island," she said happily.

That night on the way back up to their little cottage on the plateau, Rickett stopped the truck to watch a storm. It was away to the north and each time a lightning flash sheeted the horizon, it limned the steep bulk of Hvar, silhouetting it like a cardboard cutout in the sea. The rumble of the thunder reached him standing beside his truck on the frosty plateau, and he realised from its rhythm, crackling across the clear stillness, that these were guns. The M.T.B.'s were at it, wolfing at a convoy.

M.T.B.

His driver pulled on a cigarette cupped in his hand and said: "Up the Navy, sir."

"Yes," Rickett said, and climbed back. They drove on into the shadow of Mount Hum, and turned off the main track to bump towards the little stony huddle of Podhumlje.

Dawson had performed prodigies. He had been empire-building, very much at the risk of his neck. He had wrested possession of the ground floor of a neighbouring farmhouse for their hospital from a swarm of partisans.

Dawson had quickly sized up the island's mood. The partisans, he concluded, did not understand palaver. He chose his house, stalked into it, stared haughtily around at the stubbly ruffians who sprawled there smoking Balkan weed and polishing their rifles. He jerked a thumb towards the door, and barked: "Out!" When nobody moved, Dawson produced an old Routine Order and tried baffling them with that. He pointed to his Red Cross armband and began an impassioned tirade in broad Yorkshire. He spotted a couple of waverers, pulled them to their feet and started shoving them towards the door. One of them flung his hands off, glared and slid back the bolt of his short Italian rifle.

"All right," roared Dawson, "I'll get the bloody commissar!" The word *commissar* did the trick. They hesitated, looked at each other.

Dawson slapped his spurious authority. "Commissar! Commissar!" he bellowed. One or two got slowly up at that, gathering their things. In ten minutes Dawson was in full possession of the ground floor.

He clumped on upstairs. On the landing he came face to face with an aged crone, shrunken of feature like a skeleton, blackclad, quivering, speechless, and deaf. She stood there looking through and beyond Dawson out of deep eyes at a sad vision of her own.

He walked past her into the bedroom. There he halted, thunderstruck.

It was full of partisan girls. They lolled in the beds, fully dressed, resting after the stand-to. Their rifles lay against the walls but some still had grenades hanging from their blouses. A dark fat girl rolled over, removed her cap from over her face and goggled blearily at him. Dawson banished any idea of weakening into chivalry and struck a belligerent stance. Again he roared: "Out! That means everybody!"

The other girls stirred like so many beached seals to stare at Dawson incredulously. A couple of them tittered. Dawson crimsoned and, uncertainly now, roared again. It had absolutely no effect. They only looked at each other and made jokes about him, and giggled. That stumped him.

"Well, you got the ground floor, anyway. Well done," Rickett said.

"Don't worry, sir, I'm working on another tack," Dawson said. A strange expression spread over his face.

"You just leave it to me," he said, and turned back for the embattled house.

As Rickett was settling into bed he heard shrieks from the house down the stone-walled lane, a roaring, and more shrieks. Frank Clynick halted in the act of turning down the Tilley lamp and they looked at each other. After a while Dawson came charging up the stairs, stopped, then entered, breathing rather hard.

"It's all right now, sir," he said. "Got rid of 'em all." Though he tried to maintain his usual poker face, he could not repress a leer.

"What did you do—expose yourself?" Rickett asked.

Dawson paused on the way out. "You'll never know, sir."

And they never did.

Major Rickett was up with a cold but rosy dawn to inspect their new house. He found the old crone sitting in the chilly gloom on the upstairs hall, bereft, uncomprehending, and alone. Her senility had defeated Dawson. There was nothing one could do about her—except show care. Rickett raised her to her feet and led her gently into the bedroom. He indicated one of the pallets vacated by the partisan girls. The old lady seemed to understand. She nodded and subsided slowly on it, turning the almost-

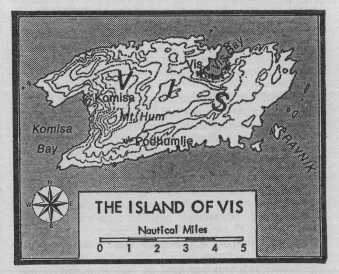

THE ISLAND OF VIS

Nautical Miles

0   1   2   3   4   5

sightless hollows of her eyes wearily from him to the wall. He stood and looked down on that fragile withering of flesh on bone which was all that remained of a human

being, and knew that she was simply waiting for the time
which was coming to die. The one remaining thing one
could do for her was—to do nothing; to forbear from
evacuating her with all the other lost civilians; simply to
let her sleep her days away in the quietest corner of the
house, with no more bewilderment.

He walked out and along the stone-walled road back
to his hospital.

There was a noise growing in the sky. Soon it filled
the whole world with anger and with it came the rattling
that blew chips off the stone walls and spurted up rusty
driblets of earth. Rickett dropped flat, but by that time it
was past, and he watched the Messerschmitt lift again into
the sky on a faint oily wake. It wheeled, in a sun that had
not yet touched the plateau, wavered, irresolute in the
clear sky, then decided for home, and steadied for the
blue-black hump of Hvar.

Dawson, white with shaving lather, had a virgin
swathe down one cheek, and a revolver in his hand which
he had emptied into the sky. He was still staring at the
speck with the wounded astonishment of a man who
doesn't know how it got away from him.

Almost every morning at first light the Messerschmitts came circling round in hopes of catching a
straggler among the M.T.B.'s, homing from a night's
piracy among the islands. Any late boat with still some
way to make towards the steep protective inlets of Vis
where they sheltered by day had a hot last mile or so.

Short of actually landing on Vis, the enemy planes
had the run of the island, a privilege which they indulged
contemptuously. It usually happened just as Rickett and
the others were at their washing. They soon learned to
wash with their revolvers handy, and improved their morale by loosing off at least three rounds from the time the
fighter swooped out of the sky until it was past and
climbing again. Rickett, with nostalgic memories of pheas-
ant shooting in Hampshire to sustain him, was never quite
without hope that one day he might score a hit, even with
a revolver.

Even Dawson had a kind of gloomy optimism. He
wished he'd brought a camera.

"It'd be just my luck to knock a Messerschmitt
down—and nobody to snap me with a foot on it . . ."

A dispatch rider bumped his motor cycle down their lane from the road. He was torn and dirty from slithering off his machine to get his head down. The Messerschmitt had caught him out in the open.

"Naval Commander's compliments, sir, and are you open for business? There's a Jug doctor down at Komisa, sir, looking after three of our lads. Shell burst on an M.T.B."

"Send them up. Captain Heron's ambulance is down there."

"Sorry, sir. The Jug doctor won't let them go. Says they're his."

Rickett swung a leg over the Don R.'s pillion. "Take me down there. Who's this Jug doctor?"

The Rider kicked his bike into life. "Pee-tack, sir. Some name like that."

They wobbled off for Komisa.

McWilliams, the officer who had taken the wounded sailors to the little port hospital, met Rickett on the quay down at Komisa. He was anxious that Rickett should not upset the Jugoslavs in a tug-of-war for patients.

"He's been very good to us," McWilliams said. "Mustn't hurt his feelings."

Not for nothing did McWilliams care about goodwill. He had a troop of fighting men to care for, and with only a newcomer from base, Rickett, setting up some kind of casualty station in the hills, he was anxious to keep his entrée to the only orthodox-seeming hospital on the island.

It was a tall ugly building which might have sprung from an English town in the era of Florence Nightingale. Several quite lofty rooms served as wards and these were jammed with partisan wounded and sick. A weak naked bulb on a squeaky porcelain adjustable pulley lit the operating theatre, which was also crammed with the paraphernalia of an office, laboratory and dispensary. A horsehair couch stood in the middle of the room. It turned out that this was the operating table. While Rickett stood and stared round at the mess, Dr. Petak walked in.

He was tall and skinny, with flowing grey hair, a long white coat which nearly trailed the ground, and a pair of steel pince-nez lying askew on his thin nose. He wore rubber gloves, and smoked. He whipped off a glove, proffered a hand, bowed, and said in terrible French: "I am charmed."

Rickett began to explain himself and Petak stopped him with an elegant gesture. "You would like to see the patients, perhaps? Please—this way."

The sailors had been wounded by their own shell. It had been fired at too low an elevation, had hit the M.T.B.'s railing, and exploded on deck. They lay in neighbouring beds and Rickett saw at once that Petak had been at work on them. One of them grinned wanly at Rickett while, under the guise of an affable interest in Petak's skill, he examined his surgery. The first man's arm was encased in plaster.

"Broken arm?"

Petak shook his head. It was a jagged shell-splinter wound, he explained. He had excised it, sewed it up, and popped it straight into plaster. He had not waited for any sign of infection before doing a delayed suture, and to immobilise the wound he had plastered it up immediately, without any kind of padding, nor any allowance for swelling.

The second patient, a leg wound, had had the same treatment—cleaning, immediate stitching, tight plastering on to bare skin.

They turned to the third man. He was fair-haired, still a boy. "Name's Godby, sir," he whispered.

He was in a bad way. The wound had penetrated his abdomen. Mercifully Petak had not operated on him—yet. But on Petak's showing with the others, God help a case like Godby's.

He had to get him away.

Rickett turned to find Petak's eyes on him, shining and hungry for approval. Rickett groped for some French.

"I see they're in excellent hands, doctor."

Petak beamed.

"However, they are British servicemen," Rickett said, "and, therefore, ah, my responsibility . . ."

Petak considered this, moving his head profoundly from side to side. All he said was, contemplating Godby: "This is a very difficult case . . ." He said nothing about the danger of moving a stomach case. With an objection as valid as that alone, he could have silenced Rickett.

"Personally, I should be very happy to leave him in such capable hands. But—I have orders ... my senior officers at headquarters ... I shall, ah, have to take them with me."

Petak clicked his heels, bowed, smiled. "I understand your position. In that case, of course, doctor."

Rickett expelled his breath quietly. "I'll bring our ambulance around," he said.

They parted with florid displays of courtesy and goodwill. At the door, when Heron's orderlies had loaded the three patients into the ambulance, Petak held Rickett's hand. His eyes glinted fervently behind the tilted pince-nez.

"I have a piano down in the cellar. If you are interested in music—?"

"I should be delighted."

"I am very fond of playing. I sometimes wonder if I should not have become a pianist."

Rickett nudged him slyly. "Well, it is perhaps harder to kill a good tune—eh, doctor?"

"Ha ha, quite so! *Au revoir, cher confrère!*"

The ambulance took the stony ascent to Podhumlje more delicately than ever. It was cold but the driver perspired in his effort to dodge the bumps. Every time they jolted Rickett consoled himself with a vision of what it would have meant to have left Godby behind.

But, whatever the reason, moving a stomach case was still a blasphemy. In the campaign in Italy, during an Allied advance, they would pitch a couple of tents on the battlefield and leave a sergeant, four or five orderlies, a sister—all to look after three or four abdominal wounds, rather than move them too soon.

At all events they were taking this man to a wretched stone hovel on a hilltop without a single amenity for this task—except his own experience. Thus inauspiciously they were to christen their so-called field hospital on Vis.

The sight of their first casualties had Dawson moving very briskly. The Tilley lamp was little use for shedding any illumination downwards, but wangling the dressing table mirror on Dawson's patent wires helped to shed a weak glow on to the table. Dawson was already well organised. He had a drum of sterile dressings in readiness and a quantity of mackintosh sheeting for boiling up. All his gear had been sorted and he had his hands on what they wanted the moment they unloaded the ambulance. He started the two primus stoves, boiling instruments and sheets.

They sat down first and had a mug of wine with some bully and biscuits. Godby's pulse had increased. He was getting the anxious look, *Hippocratic Facies*. They had no watch, but it was about three hours after dark. Rickett got up and said: "All right."

They brought Godby in and put him on the table.

Having come from general duties, Frank was new to the business of getting a needle into a vein and Rickett had to master an urge to relieve him of the hypodermic and take over. It was just that this was their first case, and a bad one, a voice inside him argued. He kept quiet and Clynick got on with it. Kicking off with an abdominal operation here was not the best starter, but the first test which confronted them was mercilessly absolute. With it they declared the whole pattern of how they would work together, primitive as this was to be. The first requisite to be enunciated was trust. They were both relieved when the messing about was over and Frank had contrived the injection. A faintly awkward smile announced it.

Because blankets were short they had kept Godby in his battle dress and trousers. They simply started the operation by pulling his trousers well down and his shirt and vest well up. His torso, glistening white and vulnerable in the harsh light-and-shade, gave Rickett a moment's awful pause. There was something so personal, squalid, almost guilty, in what they were now presuming upon a human body, so far from the calm rituals, the array of resources of a proper hospital.

Rickett swabbed the abdomen with spirit. He laid out a surround of boiled mackintosh, took his scalpel. Made the first incision.

Then the familiarity of it took charge. He was treading a well-known path of surgical routine. Dawson helped, swabbing, handing ligatures, cutting after Rickett tied off the bleeding points. The paramedian incision went smoothly. But as soon as he opened the peritoneum, he found free dark blood.

The big difficulty was to localise the source of it and trace how much danger there was, under this light. Soon he knew Godby was in luck. He was a slight boy, not overmuscled, no superfluous fat, and so Rickett, manipulating the spleen easily up into the open wound, found almost at once the cause—a ragged wounding of its anterior edge. He decided to remove the spleen.

The Tilley lamp was coughing on its *rakia* diet and now was the time that it gave him anxiety. The difficult part was tying the splenic artery. One clamped, cut the pedicle above it, tied a ligature very firmly down out of sight behind its mushroom-shaped top. As he removed the Spencer-Wells clamp, he dreaded a gush of blood which would tell that the artery had slipped from the clamp and the ligature was not tight enough.

For a brief moment a thought laid a cold hand up him. *If the lamp goes now, he's a goner.*

It kept coughing, but it stayed alight. He loosened the clamp gingerly, hoping against a spurting of blood.

It was all right. He took the clamp out.

He straightened. The spleen with its jagged piece of shell plopped into a bucket. He felt justified in assuming this was all the damage. In any case, it was not possible to make a further exhaustive search in these conditions. He sighed, and set about closing the abdomen.

Within half an hour the three of them were grinning rather proudly at each other over another mug of wine.

That night, Gill, one of Heron's orderlies, assumed the watch on Godby. Heron's crew had come to the rescue with blankets as pillows and supports for putting the sick man in Fowler's position, half-sitting up so that any infected blood would drain to the pelvis, where it could be dealt with. They put his stretcher on a trestle in the other upstairs room, now a ward.

The plasma was changed to a saline drip and the orderly took his pulse every fifteen minutes. As he started coming round from the pentothal, Rickett ordered a morphine shot.

The Tilley was darkening, its mantle blackened. It had served them well.

Next morning Godby's pulse was down in spite of the upset of the operation. His eyes were open. He recognised Rickett with a faint nod.

Rickett worked on the other two wounded men, Slack and Ross. He undid Petak's damage, removed the stitches, cleaned out the wounds. There was no penicillin for them, as there would have been in Italy. He powdered them with sulpha. Ross had lost sensation in his hand. It might be paralysed. But when Rickett took off the plaster and reopened the wound he saw that Petak had managed another prodigy of clumsiness. In tying off a blood vessel, he had also ligatured the funnybone nerve.

FOUR

They were still desperately short of almost everything—
above all, the manual labour needed to service an operating theatre. They all spent the next few days busily
scouring the island. There was little they could borrow
from young George Lloyd Roberts down in Vis harbour
but advice—and his influence.

George had the Jugoslavs in his pocket, for the
roughest of them sensed his mettle, and what he was
doing for them. Major Rickett's correct approach for
partisan help was to ask the *Obdornik*, chairman of the
local civil committee. He tried this, but retreated before
the language problem.

It was George Lloyd Roberts who introduced Rickett
to Chicago Mary.

Chicago Mary was a tough, grey-haired woman in her
middle fifties who carried a gun strapped round her ample
waist and spoke broad Bowery out of the corner of a
trapdoor mouth. She had lived in Chicago for sixteen
years. Now she was a commissar, and, as such, a power in
the island, somewhat feared. The active Communist ele-
ment comprised only a tenth of the partisan force, but
under Tito's autocracy it was solidly in control. However
fiercely individualistic the ordinary soldier was, his leaders
wielded absolute power with holy and incorruptible zeal.

Chicago Mary did not look the girl for any hanky-
panky, but for all her battered toughness, she responded to
ribbing and flattery. Rickett made it clear that his ideal of
a woman about the house was someone moulded in the
image of Chicago Mary herself, well-built, mature, wise,
and a good cook. Chicago Mary grunted a little sceptically
at him, but hunted around the port and dug out the first of

51

Rickett's new band of retainers—a shrivelled old dear in widow's weeds called Marie who did not want to leave her beloved island and who agreed to come and cook. Next Chicago Mary assigned to his unit two scared lost teenage girls who had been found huddled together in a farm outbuilding in Podhumlje, fending for themselves. They were called Anka and Filica, and they were jumpy as rabbits, but willing. They acted as housemaids, table orderlies, and they washed and mended.

As the casualties started drifting in, Dawson put them to scouring and scrubbing the theatre clean of the post-operational mess. Dawson spoke a little Italian, which they understood, and for this they came docilely under his wing.

The girls did their best to accustom themselves to British ways, but this was not always easy. As word of old Marie's cooking began to spread, visitors began to drop into their mess on one pretext or another. Anka had a promising bosom, and a bald-headed Commando captain who began to frequent the hospital around meal times was quick to show his appreciation as she leaned over to serve him. He would give a throaty growl and suddenly bite at her. Anka would leap hasilty back with a squeal, and flee.

"Pity they don't speak English," he said to Rickett. "I could teach 'em a thing or two."

Marie's husband Miki moved in, with his donkey. He elected to be their woodcutter. His total vocabulary was a nod and a grunt and he wore a battered peaked cap—even to bed. A unit of Royal Engineers moved in near by on the plain. Rickett asked them over to build a hot water boiler above the rainwater tank outside his theatre. They served this by cutting the stunted pines which struggled for life on the slopes around them. But the blackout was strict, and the sentries were so trigger-fingered that at night they had to have a man standing by ready to douse the boiler fire the minute an air raid alert sounded.

Hardly a night passed now without fresh alarms of the imminent German attack. The schooners and M.T.B.'s came back nightly with stories of landing craft concentrating over at Hvar and Brac. They lived in hourly expectation of the shower of green Very lights which was to announce to the whole island that the balloon had gone up.

A partisan order even forbade people to undress for bed. Rickett and was helpers ignored it. Their usefulness lay in being well rested and properly ready for the wounded. For what *they* were required to do, they would have warning.

Rickett was naively proud of his home-built supply of hot water for the theatre, but he still had no beds and no shelter for the wounded. It was winter and they could not lie on the ground in the open. He had signalled back to Italy for 200 stretchers, and had received a bewildering answer. The answer came in the form of a query. It said: STRETCHERS NOT REPEAT NOT AVAILABLE TO WHAT USE WOULD THEY BE PUT. Rickett had balled the signal in his fist and flung it speechless on to their log fire. He and Clynick and the others began to tear down the matchboarding partitioning which divided their upstairs rooms in the house now serving as their living quarters, and Dawson was instructed to have these converted into beds.

In his quest for hospital shelter, Chicago Mary directed Rickett to Commander Cerni, Jugoslav Commander of the island.

The Jugoslav Command was quartered in a sprinkling of cottages farther up the mountain. Commander Cerni, slight, lean, dark and dynamic, received Rickett civilly enough, but was unmoved by the flatteries which had worked so well on the amiable Dr. Petak.

"I heard that a British officer had arrived to start a hospital. What can I do for you?"

"I am told you have six British E.P.I.P. tents in store. We need cover badly."

"For what purpose, Major?"

"For hospital wards—to shelter casualties."

Cerni flicked his sleeve, read a document, put it in a tray.

"I am sorry, but they are ours."

"With respect, Commander, you are not putting them to any use."

"They were sent by the Allies for the partisan army. You are here to attend to British troops."

Rickett said: "I don't propose to make distinctions. I am equally ready to serve the partisans.

"Thank you. However, I am sorry. These tents are for the partisan army."

Rickett stormed back to Podhumlje. He ate his evening meal in silence. Nobody could get a word out of him—not even Heron, the Professor, now an intimate of their mess. Heron got up, patted his stomach, and said blithely: "Coming, Clynick?"

"Yes," Frank said. "Come on, Dawson."

Rickett looked up. "Where are you all going?"

"The *Prodigal*'s in tonight. Might be some stuff on board." It was Heron's habit to drink with the port officer and wait for the armed trawler supplying the island to come in.

"Yes—for the Jugs," Rickett said bitterly.

"Might be able to lay our hands on something, sir," Dawson said, and his innocence made Rickett prick his ears. "You never know."

Rickett considered this. "You might," he said. "After all there's a blackout . . ."

When they had rumbled off towards Komisa in Heron's truck, Rickett went up into their tiny ward to take a look at the stomach case, Godby. It was the third day after the operation and Godby was taking some broth from one of the housemaids, Anka. His pulse remained reassuringly steady. As Anka finished, he thanked her with a faint nod and his eyes followed her briefly to the door.

Rickett got up, pleased. "You're doing very well," he said.

It was true. He was their first battle, and it was only the third day, but things looked well.

Early in the morning he awoke at the noisy return of the dock raiding party, glowing with *rakia* and triumph.

"Look what we got!" Heron said, and hiccoughed. They had three crates of British army boots, all destined for Tito's men. Dawson, Heron and Clynick had snatched these by dodging the sentries among the boxes coming off the armed trawler, *Prodigal*, as she disgorged her cargo from Italy. They were as exultant as if they had fought a successful action: well they might have been. Looters were shot out of hand. And from the day they had arrived, the Jugoslav partisans had made one thing uncompromisingly plain. *They* ran this island, and everybody, the British included, obeyed *their* law.

But Rickett was agape with delight at this haul. He

was beginning to get an idea of what kind of rules one played on Vis. He tapped the Professor. "Where do you keep this firewater of yours?"

Heron hefted out a bottle. Rickett snatched it and poured some into a mug. He raised it and grinned. "I think I know the kind of diplomacy that operates here," he said.

They stayed up the rest of the night, celebrating. Later in the morning, having dipped his head in a bucket and togged himself out in a newly-pressed battle dress, Rickett paid a call on the island's commander, Cerni. After an exchange of polite preliminaries he ventured to inquire how the partisans were off for boots. Cerni grunted. Footwear was their worst problem, he said.

"I have a crate of boots I think I can let you have," Rickett volunteered, Cerni's face lit up at that. Rickett added: "But I would, ah, like to mention that we're still awfully short of tents."

Cerni pondered this. "I see," he said. And then: "I will send men down with the tents. Perhaps at the same time they can collect the boots?"

Next day a fatigue party pitched their six tents on the sloping stony platform of ground between the houses and the cliff edge. There seemed always to be some kind of wind up here, even on lucid, startlingly blue days like this. Far below, the sea was almost still against the jagged inlets, and ranged in hues from a pellucid turquois to rich, clear emerald. From this height they looked deep into the heart of the ocean, for the sun pierced its dazzling transparency like a searchlight through tinted crystal. A little over a rifle shot away a domed mountaintop reared out of the water—the island of Bisevo. Now it was credited with a grim usage. The partisans, one or two of the Commandos were already saying, carried out their executions on it. But its sinister purpose, indeed the whole savagery underlying guerilla warfare had as yet wafted no more than the faintest whiffs to them in their isolation here among the stones at one end of the plateau vineyards.

Rickett had prudently kept two crates of boots in reserve. They were the raw material of diplomacy on Vis, he decided, to be used in future deals with the Jugs. The idea of more raids on Komisa quayside during unloading nights in search of loot with which to trade appealed to the buccaneering strain in Dawson and the Professor. For there was little else to do but drink and wait for the Germans.

While they were feathering their nest up at Pod-humlje, Colonel Jack Churchill was hastily strengthening the fortification of the island with the partisans. North of Vis harbour he made the historic little grey fort, Fort George, a strong point. Its weathered grey stone still bore the royal arms of England engraved on the walls from its occapation nearly a century and a half before.

Major Rickett, working to transform their hovel into a semblance of a hospital, observed that even Nelson's leeches would have been better equipped for war surgery than he was.

Colonel Jack had installed a Commando Heavy Weapons Troop not far from the hospital to hold the central plain. Another troop, with the wild boys of the Raiding Support Regiment, was ferried across to hold the tiny outlying island of Ravnik. Churchill was not the man to wait to be attacked. His little force went straight over to the offensive. They had hardly swallowed the anchovies and the wine with which the Jugoslavs welcomed them to the island before Colonel Jack launched their first night raid by L.C.I. across the water to Hvar. His three troops, with thirty newly-arrived American Rangers, surrounded a German strongpoint in the port of Milna and snatched four prisoners. Interrogating these yielded valuable—if awesome—intelligence concerning the German disposi-tions and strength on the surrounding islands. Digesting this, the Commandos decided to try and hold the Germans in check by a bold programme of sorties and raids to batter and bluff the enemy into the belief that the British *must* be on Vis in force to be attacking frequently and with such spirit. Another Commando troop sallied across again a few days later in a leaky schooner loaned by the partisans and tackled the Germans garrisoning the village of Grablje.

Shouting at the top of their lungs and hurling gre-nades, they launched their attack with such ferocity that the Germans in the outpost threw up their hands after only a brief but violent siege. The Commandos returned with the body of their leader, Captain Bare. He was killed in the first few moments of action. They left behind three men, one a Commando presumed dying with a hole in his chest the size of a fist. The other two were missing. All three turned up two days later to meet a partisan ferry boat which slid quietly in under darkness to take off a Commando major who had stayed to observe a British naval bombardment. The "dying" man, Private Tuck, had crawled three miles in that time to the meeting-place, nourished by his emergency ration and by drinking melted snow.

By the time they carried Tuck ashore at Vis and into the tiny partisan hospital there run by George Lloyd Roberts, he was in bad shape. George operated. It was his first British casualty and under his nursing, Tuck rallied astonishingly. They put him on a boat for Bari where he eventually made a full recovery.

It was into this atmosphere, tense but exuberantly aggressive, that Rickett had arrived with an orderly and an assistant from base—all three of them brimming with zeal at getting a real job to do, and with dismay at being given nothing with which to do it. Between forays for equipment —raiding the quays at night, imploring a British "Q" to do something for them, carpentering their own beds out of wood and sacking—Rickett descended often to Vis harbour to help George cope with the inflow of sick and wounded partisans arriving on the night schooners.

These first days were the honeymoon days of the *entente* with Tito, when crisis united them and there was no time to allow differences of outlook to corrupt it. They were feverishly fortifying and constantly plotting their attacks. At night British destroyers from Italy cruised about the island sending up flares. Both ports rattled spasmodically with small arms fire. At Komisa the sentries, on the assumption that anything moving in the darkness was hostile, shot at the British motor gun-boats as they moved out to create their nightly havoc among the German convoys.

Nor was the enemy shipping getting much rest by day. The *Luftwaffe* might lord it over Vis, but the R.A.F. was out almost daily from Italy to bomb German boats in the Pusman Channel between Vis and the Jugoslav mainland. Partisan intelligence, flashed from island to island and brought in at night by the schooners, was putting the tally of sinkings as high as fifty vessels.

The morale of the Jugoslav guerillas was equally as buoyant as the Commandos'. Every night in the ports a bronchial loudspeaker relayed the B.B.C. news in Serbo-Croat, and the partisan grapevine bore it on as swift as the wind to the neighbouring islands. On these, in spite of the Germans swarming in the garrisons, those guerillas posted to watch enemy movement and carry out sabotage would boldly celebrate an Allied victory by lighting bonfires. From their hospital at Podhumlje, Jim Rickett and his helpers could see these fires twinkling on Solta and Hvar, and the sight of them gripped the heart with the same exhilarant power as the singing to which the partisans marched.

And still, in spite of the nightly alarms and the increased enemy air curiosity, the expected storm did not break. For his own hospital, Rickett was easily able to handle the intake of wounded from the night raids and the routine sick, between spells of helping George.

His own staff was now as oddly adapted to the task as his gear, much of which was now home-made. Someone had located a battered sterilising drum in one of the houses in Vis and though he doubted if an egg would cook in its steam, they went solemnly through the motions of using it; hygiene, after all, was largely an attitude of mind. It would do till they had something better.

The two teenage girls, Anka and Filica, though still petrified by the British protectors, slaved from morning till night among the sick, at the table, in the theatre. Like all their Jugoslav helpers, they received no pay, but their devotion to the work was as fierce as anything Rickett had encountered.

Old Marie's ways with bully beef and M. &. V.—on a prehistoric stove donated, surprisingly, by Chicago Mary —was not as good as the cuisine down at Zena's, but it was better than any army cook's. They had adopted a young goat which Rickett had found tethered and starving in a deserted yard; this now wandered around on the ground floor and no amount of booting ever dissuaded it from taking an occasional excursion into the hospital rooms upstairs. To carpenter their gear, for which Rickett drew weird designs, they also had a sad, taciturn old Jug called Lovro, donated by the partisans to fill their labour short-age. Lovro was one of those mixed partisan gifts. His wife

was still on German-occupied Hvar, and Lovro was morose company. Further, an aura of suspicion came with
him. The other partisans cast side-long looks at him, and
wisps of speculation that he was a spy floated in his
shambling wake. But nobody could be sure; if there had
been a shred of proof, the partisan way with Lovro would
have been short indeed. Instead they off-loaded him on to
the British. Rickett was unconcerned. As long as Lovro
worked, he reasoned, he was welcome to transmit as much
top secret information about urine specimens and hernias
as he could lay his hands on.

And then Private Dodd arrived among them. Dodd
was light-haired, strong, wickedly good-looking, and he
had the eager, friendly, exploring air of the born army
scrounger. It was not enough to call Dodd a Fixit. He was
the Eyes and Ears of any unit—the kind of man who,
while the rest of a force is still getting ashore, vanishes
ahead into the mysterious darkness of an alien place and is
subsequently rediscovered in entire and familiar possession
of it, his legs tucked under the best table in the town, his
haversack already reposing in some ample lady's boudoir,
his laundry deposited with another, and himself dishing
out the really vital data about the place and its inhabitants
as if he has been there all his life.

An aura of special privilege accompanied Private
Dodd. He won it by the sheer diligence with which he
burrowed into every corner of a new place, but he wore
his distinction modestly enough. Even in a fiercely disciplined body like the Commandos he managed to elect his
own duties—and chose to become everybody's handyman.
It gave him, a private, entire freedom of movement, the
entrée everywhere. The hospital attracted Dodd. Perhaps
its helplessness was a challenge. It was also farther than
any other unit from his own.

Rickett, plagued by the lack of decent lighting by
which to operate, finally wrested a derelict German generator from the partisan command with the gift of another
crate of boots. It was Private Dodd who stepped forward,
all shiny expectancy, and offered to help install it up at
Podhumlje. The O.C. of Dodd's Commando Troopdown at
Komisa let him go with a resigned sigh, and they brought
the generator up in a truck. Private Dodd made an eager
tour of the whole hospital—poked his cheerful head into

the wards, counted the beds, explored the theatre, brewed himself some tea in the kitchen, discussed the stove with Marie, tasted her M. & V., slapped the gloomy Lovro on the back and won a pallid smile—all before he re-emerged to install the generator beneath an outside stairway. To help him he borrowed an electrician from a newly-arrived R.A.F. advance party. They scrounged some wire from the signallers and spent days wiring up the operating room and trying to coax the generator into life.

When a Don R came roaring up with a signal from Italy for Major Rickett, Private Dodd all but lifted the bike from under the rider's seat and was off, scooting down to the Heavy Weapons Troop in search of petrol. At the corner of the lane turning on to the main track he slithered and fell in a shower of stones. Got up, dusted himself cheerily, vaulted back on, and was away again down the plateau.

Dodd returned with petrol, but crestfallen. "No light bulbs, sir," he said.

And so it proved. There was not an electric light bulb to be had on the island. No trading deal could tempt the Jugoslav commander this time. He simply hadn't any.

Private Dodd said: "The *Prodigal's* in tonight. She'll have electric light."

"How do you know?"

"She uses a searchlight to unload with."

"How are we going to get them to part up with bulbs?"

"Give them the good old partisan treatment. Trade them something they want."

"Like what, Dodd? Boots? Some lint? A hernia truss?"

At this sarcasm Dodd merely smiled and over the rim of his wine mug kept his eye on Rickett's goat which was emptying the refuse bin outside the kitchen door.

"They could do with some fresh meat, I should say," he said.

That night when the squat bulk of the *Prodigal* warped into the mole at Komisa, a deputation consisting of Captain Clynick, Corporal Dawson and Private Dodd came aboard, the latter with the kid slung round his neck. They came off again bulging with 110-volt bulbs. The generator produced double this voltage, but the R.A.F.

electrician and Dodd wired them in pairs. They fashioned switches made by poking nails in metal slots.

At last, with coaxing, the ancient Siemens coughed shakily into life, and with it the cluster of overhead lights set in a reflector cut from biscuit tins glowed into a wobbly brightness. Major Rickett yelped with sudden joy, thumped Dodd and the electrician on the back, exulting that he could at last *see*. He issued orders for a christening party.

They poured a libation over the engine and named her Jenny. A woman's name, as Dodd advocated, because she made such a bloody awful fuss and because she had to be flattered into performing. They tapped one of the priest's big vats and drank toasts all round to the advancement of science. Everybody began to think of lighting the reception tents and the wards as well. These, added now to Heron's Field Ambulance accommodation, with the barns and sheds they had cleared around them, could now cater for nearly 100 casualties.

Some sort of order could now be perceived out of all the chaos, and they were winning it only by larceny, horse-trading, and make-do. They owed no thanks to any quartermaster.

A little later in the revelry someone suggested a short silence in memory of the goat, but this was cut short by a roar from the generator outside. The theatre lights glowed hectically bright, now to a demented racket from the engine—and then blew. A stumbling inquest revealed the generator's throttle was broken, and that henceforth it would have to be governed by assigning someone to hold a hand lever whenever they needed light.

As to more electric light blubs, everybody at this time of night took a rosy view. All they needed for this, the Professor said, was more goats.

Still the invaders were massing. High up, the *Luft-waffe* was almost on constant watch now. The R.A.F. reported glider concentrations over at Mostar on the mainland.

Rickett's visits to help George Lloyd Roberts were a good excuse to enjoy Zena's hospitality down in Vis harbour. Her villa with its gleaming furniture and its conversation, tempestuous as this sometimes was, was the last remnant of civilised living that this place had to offer.

Zena's motherly devotion to George was manifest, but it was not blind. She was apprehensive of his inexperience, and wise as she was in the ways of the world, was professionally incapable of hiding it in the way that Major Rickett or the gentle Dr. Zon could.

When she saw George preparing for a risky operation, one involving a stomach case or a thoracic wound, involving an approach with which her instinct disagreed, Zena voiced her fears to Jim Rickett.

He met her with a stare, silence; a change of subject. Rickett had had a gentler induction into medicine. He had not been thrown neck and crop into a savage jumble of general practice, major surgery, and the most delicate reaches of specialisation as George had. He could only admire the way he never flinched from a thing.

George depended utterly on Zena and they bickered like mother and son. George played naughty pranks on her. He prompted her to English swear words and choked in his soup when she innocently used them—especially if there were visitors.

In these first days General Templer arrived on a visit to inspect the defence. George's partisan hospital in the schoolhouse of Vis harbour was a scheduled stop on his tour. With great seriousness George had schooled his orderlies to form a guard of honour. They would salute and give the usual obscene salutation with one mighty voice.

Zena discovered the plan. She already had her suspicions about George's strange phrases, and she tackled Johnnie, the most villainous of his orderlies. Johnnie shrugged. He didn't know what the words meant, and he didn't care. When she told him they were bad words, Johnnie leered. He rather liked the idea of being rude to a general, under orders.

But his face changed when Zena threatened with a rasp in her voice to share the joke with the commissars.

General Templer duly came through. As he did so, the guard of honour came to attention. George eyed them with furtive expectancy and when they hesitated, semaphored urgently at them behind the general's back.

Silence.

The inspection over, George returned in thwarted fury to hold an inquest into what had gone wrong with the reception.

Zena entered in the middle of it. She listened calmly. Then she said in a voice dark with power: "I know what means up-you-pipe!"

George sat down suddenly. The inquest was over.

She was a tiny woman to radiate such power, such uncompromising truth. George needed her autocratic zeal to discipline his staff and to organise him, for he was totally untidy. She also took turns with Suza, the soft, doe-eyed theatre assistant, to administer anaesthetics. Both had difficulty with pentothal injections.

The other thing these two shared was that they both loved George.

But Suza was *in* love with him.

Rickett noted it very soon. New arrival that he was, he sensed that this was dangerous. This partisan creed towards love was quite uncompromising. There was no room for it.

It was, quite simply, outlawed.

A third of the partisan fighters were women, and the rule was designed for their survival as a disciplined force. Sexual relations were punishable by death. So, it was said, was pregnancy. The British troops had got hold of a rumour that several women had been shot in recent weeks on Vis.

This attitude, coupled with the rigorous partisan way of life, had largely succeeded in producing a merging of the sexes—with some strange results. Many of the partisan women had lost their alluring, outwardly feminine ways. They had become hard of face and scarcely distinguishable in their stride from the males with whom they fought, shared the same tents, even the same blankets.

After a few days in this atmosphere Rickett understood the mysterious joke with which he had been greeted on arriving: "You can look, but don't touch."

It came as a refreshing surprise, working among them, to find a *partisanka* reverting to weakness and indulging in a truly feminine fit of hysterics. Those who remained unable to adapt themselves to the harsh life were gradually weeded out and drafted to Italy or to hospital work—or they took semi-civilian jobs, like Cookie, who ruled the kitchen at Zena's villa.

Another thing that Rickett noted in this examination of the manly *partisankas* was that many of them had amenorrhoea. Their menstrual periods had stopped.

One of the self-appointed guardians of the island's morals was the local chemist in Vis harbour, a high partisan woman official with the rank of major at the time of Rickett's arrival in early February, 1944. She was called Jela—a jut-jawed, stout, middle-aged woman with flaxen curls and even, white teeth, who toted a gun and carried about with her a sense of grandeur.

George's hospital was a natural hunting ground for Jela. For one thing, she was a hypochondriac. George prescribed gymnastic lessons for her varicose veins. Zena also had to administer massage, which Jela liked. But her great passion was for injections. Scarcely a day passed without her summoning Zena to her quarters above the pharmacy for an injection, either for a new pain, an attack of rheumatism, or simply to maintain her intake of Vitamin D. Jela had no addiction to drugs, but she had an unmistakable addiction to the needle itself.

And the watch of this Comrade Grundy on everybody's behaviour was unrelenting.

Zena disliked her. There was not only the business of pandering to Jela's fascination for the hypodermic, but her busybodying had already caused tragedy—the kind of picturesque operatic Balkan drama that an Angle-Saxon found difficult to credit, let alone comprehend. Rickett got the story out of Zena.

"There was a young commissar I knew—oh, he was a fine young man!—who had kissed a girl. Maybe they did more than kiss—who are we to know? But Jela got to hear of it and she summoned the young commissar to report to her."

"He was very frightened. He knew what it meant. He was so terrified that he shot himself."

"I was very angry. Whatever the rules were, Jela had no right to meddle in our love life. I told Cerni about it. He flew into a terrible rage. 'That bloody Jela!' was all he could say. He kept screaming: 'That bloody Jela!'"

Yet Jela did not have to answer for it. To Rickett the story, if he was to believe it, was a revelation of the freelance power a party member wielded among the partisans, and of the fear they inspired as a consequence, even among the tough and individualistic Jugs.

Whether George returned Suza's affections was not clear. He gave no sign of it. And even though Jim Rickett as yet still only half-believed these tales of the partisan party line of love, he felt powerfully relieved at that.

FIVE

The British decision to put troops on Vis and help hold it at all costs was the first real token of an Allied change of mind—a grimly practical one. Ideology was overboard. After a disillusioning flirtation with Mihailovitch and his *Chetniks,* who were marking up a grim record of murdering fellow Jugoslavs and even, on occasion, fighting *for* the Germans, the Allies transferred their patronage to Tito and his fighters. However distasteful it may have been to fight cheek-by-jowl with the Communist partisans, it had to be admitted that they were the ones who were killing Germans.

It was Tito's ragged guerillas who were largely keeping this fantastic German strength immobilised in the Balkans.

As if this was not compliment enough to their hardy skill, German frustration declared itself with a fury exceeding that in any other occupied country. They burned, looted, tortured, murdered on a scale which made their behaviour in the guerilla strongholds of western Europe seem like a pallid recital of isolated misdemeanours. In Jugoslavia their brutality had become senselessly indiscriminate, with village after village wiped out, every house left burning, the entire roll of inhabitants slaughtered to the last child. In the towns the people were being herded into the squares before machine guns and mown down in their thousands—the unoffending, the peaceful, the aged, the children, all to deter the growing partisan activity.

In consequence, more survivors vanished to join Tito every day, the more peaceable among them consumed with a terrible hatred—and a desperate concept of the nature of war. The vast remainder of the civilians were brutalised into a conviction of what the word "enemy" truly meant. Instead of being terrorised into submission, they sought sullenly, surreptitiously, believing in no other hope and with little left to lose, to subscribe what aid they could to the partisans. It was as if the Germans had taken the whole country by the scruff of the neck and shaken it into showing the maximum amount of fight.

To most the name Tito signified simply patriotism and leadership. Of those who finally reached him by the hazardous paths into the Bosnain mountains or by those furtive nightly schooner trips which wound and dodged between the German-held islands, few knew or cared much about Communism. The party had won their respect —and their military allegiance—by its deeds. A few were perhaps converted by the indoctrination which ensued, assuming creed and uniform together. But the majority who wore the red star in their rough forage caps were united under Tito—Serbs, Croats, Montenegrins—with one ideal only, which was to fight the Germans. *A grande dame* like the diminutive Zena owed her influence on the island of Vis simply to her effectiveness and to the power of her formidable personality. Watching Zena as she presided over a splendid table in the best house overlooking Vis harbour, and talked of the days when her father, a big industrialist, lived in Vienna; of her finishing school and the preparation there, at once tribal and frivolous, of a young girl for the fashionable marriage market, Rickett could only enjoy the incongruity of her, so suicidally opinionative, trying so bravely to curb her tongue and march arm in arm with a swarm of commissars. He tried to draw her with his teasing. He suspected Zena scorned them. She would fix him with her stormy eyes. Zena never defended; she only attacked.

"You think maybe I ought to be with the *Chetniks,* those you dropped arms to, to murder my own countrymen with, eh? Or with the *Ustachi,* who are worse than the Germans themselves? You forget—I am Jugoslav, *partisan!*"

She brandished a finger and rolled the word *partisan* out like an oath. It was an oath which for them all had a deep religious ring. It shielded her from the necessity to argue too far or reason too deeply, since its worth was self-evident.

In some ways the blunt, humorous English surgeon and the wiry Madame Zon were alike. Both liked to create an argument, to see a rumpus blossom out of nothing, to sit back and enjoy with innocence the fireworks, caring really little for the issue they had raised. They perceived this instantly in each other and Jim Rickett's visits to Vis harbour were marked by the salvoes they fired happily and at random across the dinner table.

Until she joined the partisans Zena had been writing anti-fascist propaganda in Sarajevo. To join her husband and the partisans, she ran the gauntlet of the Germans and *Ustachi* who searched the trains in which she journeyed to Dubrovnik. From there she crossed in a small boat to Vis. Whatever her politics, Zena was very positively for Tito. He was the magnet, the legend, the hope. He was the only living soul, as far as Jim Rickett could judge, for whom she had any real respect.

To the ordinary partisans, to most of the helpers round George Lloyd Roberts in his hospital, Tito was a god. He was this to the hulking Johnnie, or to Lubo, whose ideals were otherwise simply fleshly; both wanted their wine as often as possible and a woman more often, if possible. They seemed to do satisfyingly well on both counts in spite of the watchfulness of Jela, the blonde commissar who was in love with a hypodermic, or of a new and dangerous nuisance who now haunted the hospital—a morose zombie of a girl who suffered from scabies and a surfeit of party zeal. They called her Propaganda. She cast doubting eyes on everybody and stalked her way enwrapped in a great gloom.

The mild and mannerly Dr. Zon, Zena's husband, was an innocent elder, faced now with a nightmarish administrative task. Medically, the Jugoslavs possessed little more than knives and forks and hard liquor—the foul *rakia* which, admittedly, had powerful anaesthetic properties if one drank enough. Their available medical talent was little better.

But if the Balkan peninsula was part of the soft underbelly of Europe, Vis was its umbilicus. The sea around it was busier after dark than Piccadilly in the blackout. In addition to the schooners plying illicitly to the mainland, destroyers were patrolling to intercept any sea-borne offensive, German convoys were criss-crossing on their hazardous ways up-coast and southward to Greece, British light craft were preying on them, Commandos were probing across to raid the encircling enemy in L.C.I's and, on the southerly quarter, more schooners were evacuating the refugees and the badly wounded to Bari in Italy, and returning low-laden with supplies and reinforcements.

The race was now on to equip and garrison Vis sufficiently to withstand the weight of the German attack when it fell. A breathing space of even a fortnight while the supplies tumbled out on to its dark quays from the small boats would give it a fighting chance.

It was an undertaking whose significance rang no great bell with those genies in Italy who sat on stores. Rickett's own appeals for surgical gear fell into a bureaucratic abyss.

His personal pirates, Dawson, Heron and Clynick, lurking in the shadows of the docks, managed to appropriate some medical stores destined, as usual, for the partisans. The hijacking was additionally justified when Jim Rickett discovered what they had grabbed—plasma. "Good," he said shortly. "The Jugs would think it was something for crabs."

A heavier-than-usual convoy on the night of the 20th February brought No. 43 (Royal Marine) Commando ashore at Komisa, bringing the British on the island up to around 1,000 fighting men. Their bearing, smart and disciplined, could not fail to impress. They were superbly fit and self-respecting, and the partisans, in spite of their own fierce pride, copied them. They began marching and drilling to the shout of their N.C.O.'s, giving the step— "Jedan da! Jedan da!" They watched the Commandos at their unarmed combat practice, and tried that, too. The results were mildly disastrous.

One of the Commando's showiest tricks was to turn the tables, unarmed, on a man tackling him from behind with a revolver. He would make a pretence at surrender— and then suddenly dodge, whirl round, wrest the gun out of his opponent's hand and fell him.

It was the kind of trick that appealed to the bloodthirsty Jugoslavs and some began practising it themselves. They disdained to take the precaution of unloading their revolvers first. The result was that before those tackled from behind with a loaded revolver could perfect the technique of evasion and countering, their clumsiness earned them a pretty forfeit. Their opponents fired. The first results were as gruesome a hole through the guts as Captain Rickett had yet seen carried into his hospital, followed almost immediately by a further case with a perforated kidney.

He operated on both, using injections of pentothal to anaesthetise the wounded men. When they recovered consciousness they began groaning and whimpering a little and appealing to Rickett for help. Dr. Zon was passing by on the road to Vis and called in. Rickett asked him: "What on earth are they grizzling about?"

Dr. Zon spread his hands. "They're asking aren't you going to do anything about their wounds—or are you just going to leave them here to die?"

"Great scott, I've only just finished sewing them up!"

Zon smiled. He turned to the partisans and explained they had already been operated on while they slept under a new type of anaesthetic. There was some difficulty in persuading them of this but, once convinced, they beamed their delight and with their morale restored, began to take an obvious turn for the better.

Not that this served as a lesson to their comrades. The armed combat went on, and the casualties continued to come in to George Lloyd Roberts and to Jim Rickett, whoever was nearer to the scene.

The carelessness of the swarthy Jugoslavs with weapons was astonishing when one considered the desperate lengths to which most of them had had to go to arm themselves in the first place. Most had acquired their guns by the tough, classic partisan method—getting close enough to a German sentry to tackle him from behind, choking or knifing him without raising the alarm, and not only grabbing his rifle and ammunition pouches, but often divesting him of his trousers and boots as well, and then dodging for the hills. It was an almost ritualistic initiation for new recruits.

Inured though the Commandos were to bitter campaigning, their sudden introduction to an ally as fierce and pitiless in his attitude to war as the Jugs came as a shock. Each tended to consider himself the better fighting man and to show it in his attitude to the other. Later, in the warmth of action together, Commando and partisan were to discover a grudging admiration for reach other's fighting qualities and courage.

Other differences, small but cumulative, began to declare themselves. The atmosphere on the island was electric with expectation of the coming German attack. All troops moved into their positions at night and stood-to until after dawn. There were hourly alerts, and the steep hills overlooking the sea resounded to the abrupt crackling of guns.

While Rickett and his helpers were still hard at it constructing a ramshackle semblance of a field hospital up at Podhumlje under the shadow of Mount Hum, three Commando soldiers strolling the hills behind Vis stopped at the sound of shouting and a wailing among a small gathering of partisans, men and women, on a slope. As the British soldiers stared, they saw that the group stood in a half-circle round two women, one of whom screeched and sobbed hysterically. The other, moaning, gestured an appeal to the group. She was holding a spade. A partisan thrust her back, motioned with his rifle, and weeping, menaced by guns, the two women started shovelling again.

As the Commandos approached, a partisan wheeled, spotted them, waved them warningly back. They halted, perplexed.

"What's going on?"

"Dunno, mate. Some kind of punishment, I s'pose . . ."

They were about to turn away when a fresh outburst of crying and protest riveted their attention. The two women cowered by the shallow trenches like cats at bay, spitting and wailing. Their screeching reached a crescendo as their guards, assembling into some sort of order, raised their guns. A ragged volley mingling with the crackles of a tommy gun rang out and the screams ended abruptly on a high note. The sound of the gunfire echoed in giant metallic slappings round the hills, and the two women crumpled and fell. One half-slid into the grave. A partisan moved forward, bent low to inspect the bodies, and toed them into the trenches.

"Why, the murderin'—!"

"Blimey—an execution!"

The Commando soldiers ran forward, agape in protest, and as they came up several partisans turned and motioned threateningly away. Two women partisans shouted at them and a hubbub arose as one of the Commandos, using his hands, began asking what it was all about. Volubly and with unceremonious mime, several of the executioners indicated it was none of their business. A couple nearest the Commandos began shoving them roughly out of the way, using rifle butts. One of the soldiers stepped back clear, unclipped his webbing holster. At that a number of guns came up, levelled on the little group.

"Come on, Geordie, you want to get us shot too?"

"Murdering bastards . . . ! Killing women . . . ! What for . . . ?"

But under the menace of the execution squad, they had to fall back, glaring, pursued by incomprehensible threats, hurling back abuse to satisfy their futile outrage.

That night the Commando camps seethed with the story. One or two partisans had vouchsafed explanations which only heightened the Commandos' disgust. The two women had been condemned by a tribunal of woman partisans to be shot after having been convicted, one said, of pregnancy. No—another declared—it was for promiscuity after warnings. A third version was that the girls had transmitted venereal disease. And a fourth, even, that they had been German officers' whores.

All the British knew was that they had been ruthlessly shot for breaking the partisan chastity law. They were not alone in their shocked indignation. George Lloyd Roberts heard of it and came into his hospital, raging. "They shot those girls! Of all the lunacy . . . !"

It was some time before Zena could get a coherent account out of him. One of the girls they had been treating for stomach trouble. There had been no query of pregnancy or disease. Then old Dr. Zon returned to their villa on the seafront. He looked at Zena and said: "Have you heard?"

Zena nodded. "Did they do right, Milo? Do you agree?"

Old Milo Zon was pale, and he trembled. All he could say was: "No. It was a *terrible* thing." In these days, the world was making many assaults on his innocence.

Of course, Private Dodd had the news as early as anybody and came to Rickett's hospital with it, aghast. His bouncy smile was absent. It might well have been. He had established acquaintance with several *partisankas* scattered at strategic points over the island, wherever it was his habit to call. When Dodd poured the story in Dawson's ear, Dawson merely paused in the act of loading instruments into the steriliser and listened with scarcely a flicker of expression. At the end of it he laid the last instrument in the steriliser and scratched himself thoughtfully.

"Not what you'd call conservative treatment," he observed, "for the clap. Eh, Doddsie?"

The pattern of the projected invasion became clearer —parachutists, glider troops and infantry in landing craft. More units of the *Luftwaffe* were moving in around Vis. The ports on the islands of Hvar, Brac and Solta on the northern quarter of Vis were filling with troops. The signs merely served to prompt further displays of truculence from Colonel Jack Churchill who kept thrusting parties of Commandos across to spy out the military activity and to harass the garrisons with hit-and-run attacks. Led by partisan guides outposted in hiding on the enemy islands, they ambushed isolated German detachments and stormed houses billeting officers of the German Command. These actions—particularly the ambushes—which bands of partisans from Vis were also paralleling in their own bloodthirsty way—began to show their effect in a greatly heightened German nervousness. In spite of their numerical strength the enemy began withdrawing their smaller outposts and huddling together in numbers, mostly in the towns and ports. Single Commando scouts, crossing to reconnoitre, pushed their aggressive daring ever further. No. 2 Commando's Lieutenant Barton, who slipped across on one of these nights to spy out the enemy positions on Brac, the most heavily-manned of the islands, typified the audacity with which the Commandos probed and thrust right into the heart of the German encampments.

After three days' snooping and noting, dressed as a peasant and with two partisans to show him the way, Barton loaded his Sten gun on a mule under a burden of firewood and walked past a number of German sentries right into the village of Nerejisce, garrisoned with 200

German Paratrooper

Germans. One of the partisans stood guard outside while he knocked on the Commandant's billet, was admitted, thrust past a screeching woman to a bedroom upstairs, and there, in the faint light of a candle, fired a burst at the German Commandant who, half-risen and gaping wordlessly, leaned over and fell. Barton calmly helped himself to the dead commandant's automatic, his compass, an excellent pair of binoculars and a rifle. With these to substantiate that he had been busy on important work, he beat it with his two Jugoslav comrades through a thicket of sentries, now full alarmed, who shot and joined the chase.

Barton got clean away, pursued by whistling bullets and relays of yelping dogs.

One of Rickett's new cronies on the island, a young desperado from Jack Churchill's No. 2 Commando called "Pissy" Parsons, was prominent in these ring-the-bell-and-shoot raids. Partisan scouts flashed word from Hvar that the Germans were preparing for an outing—a cinema show had arrived. Parsons boated across the waters in darkness—"on spec, really, you know"—in hopes of finding their Commandant at home. He stole into the town and rapped on the door of the German Headquarters. It was easier than he had hoped. The German O.C. was alone, and opened the door himself. Pissy shot him in the stomach, pushed him inside and came in with him, shut the door, stepped over him, and ransacked the deserted headquarters. He came back to Vis loaded down with office files and intelligence material.

"Pretty good gen that time, old boy," he said, and put his mug under the big wine vat in Rickett's cellar. "What's this—sacramental wine, you say? Oh well, for what we are about to receive . . ." He drank and smacked his lips.

Co-operation with the individual partisans on these short hand-to-hand raids was splendid and always full of excitement, for in valour alone the Jugs matched the Commandos at every turn. They were, if anything, more impetuous, and almost entirely careless of life. Where they differed—and it mattered little in the early guerilla brushes with the enemy—was that the Jugs had a simple, earthy concept of warfare which embraced not even the most rudimentary military tactics. They had only their cunning and their courage. They were impatient with any detailed

plan—a source of much headache to the Commando
officers in the larger engagements which were to ensue.

Sten Gun

But if the Commandos imagined they were fighting a
tough war, the Jugs were fighting a far more desperate
one, right by their side. The British had rules, a whole
complex of them which, though often broken, enabled
them to slaughter and be slaughtered with a semblance of
decorum. And under similar pretences of observance the
Germans, also fond of formality, accepted them as a
soldierly enemy. As guerillas, the Jugs had no such status.
If caught, they were mostly butchered. They received no
mercy and gave none. Not a single rule by which men
sought to rationalise the business of killing applied between Jugoslav and German. The issues of Fascism versus
Communism or democracy apart, it had come down to a
bitterly personal war, its hatreds fanned by countless
outrages, between races who had come to despise each
other. And if some idealists among the Commandos chose
to show disdain at examples of Jugoslav savagery and to
resent being allied to a rabble of supposed barbarians, they
were simply venting another discord in the disharmony
that occasionally seethed between the two camps on Vis.

The realisation of this came to Rickett early. From
among the terrible wreckage washing nightly across to Vis,
Johnnie and Lubo carried in a characteristic example of
what the war now seemed to be about; a boy of twelve—
thin, staring, his eyes returning now and then from a
remoteness to examine those now tending him. The Ger-

mans grabbed the boy in a village and demanded the whereabouts of the partisans. The boy shook his head. The Germans hung him down a well, by his genitals. His was the martyrdom, not even of a young hero defying them, but of an innocent. He could not have talked because he did not know. His whole crotch was a gangrenous mess and he was near to death. Their surgery saved him—for such future as was his as a cripple.

It was a children's war, all right. Rickett descended to Vis in a truck to give George Lloyd Roberts a hand. It was the morning after another amphibious partisan raid on a German island strongpoint, and this time it was the German intelligence system which had worked well. They were ready and waiting, and the partisan casualties were heavy. Among them was a fourteen-year-old boy. He wore the three stars of a full captain in Tito's army. He was thin as a whip, not fully grown, but old in the ways of war. He had earned his captaincy in a characteristic partisan way— by election. His troops had voted him on merit to lead them. He was hit in the upper leg. This was his twelfth wound in campaigns which had ranged from the mountains of Slovenia to the Dalmatian islands. But it was not the leg wound which bothered him. It was his ear. Rickett found a mastoid, the result of an old head wound from a mortar fragment, and he ordered the boy to be evacuated to Bari on the next schooner going.

Rickett patted him farewell, grinned, but the youngster glared back suspiciously and started firing questions at Zena. Zena answered him soothingly in his own language and when it dawned on him that he was being evacuated, the boy flew into an awful rage. He stormed wildly at Zena and Jim Rickett, the tears flooding into his eyes. His bandaging finished, Johnnie and Lubo took him out, cursing and kicking and screaming insults.

Zena sighed and wagged her head sadly, fondly. "Very bad language," she said. "Very bad."

"Yes, but why? In Italy he'll be operated on under proper conditions. He'll be back all the quicker."

Zena looked at him out of her deep dark eyes and shook her head. "It is the disgrace," she said in her most doom-laden tones.

That halted Rickett in what he was doing. He considered this, and shrugged, and smiled.

SIX

Every morning after the lone Messerschmitts had finished sharking up and down the island and vanished low across the water to home, it was the Allies' turn to give an air display.

A great concerted droning not long after braakfast usually announced it, and soon the bombing fleet from Italy was high overhead, its rumble shredding in the wind and its unseen escorts lacing it about with vapour trails. Glinting here and there up in the infinite blue, it passed like a huge shoal of transparent fish migrating directly northward to the feeding grounds at Wiener Neustadt, thirty miles south of Vienna.

There was plenty for them up there. It was a big railway junction for the Balkans, an industrial centre with locomotive and small arms factories, and its aircraft works were turning out 400 fighter planes a month—more than a third of Germany's total war product. It was the home of the Messerschmitts themselves. The Allied Air Forces had been subjecting this industrial fortress to a ceaseless battering for the past six months, first with long-range Fortresses from North Africa, and now from dromes in Italy.

The opposition these fleets met as they neared the target was bitter and intense. Early in the afternoon they would return, crossing high over Vis again. Not far from Rickett's hospital the R.A.F. had installed a small radar unit whose leader, a Flight-Lieutenant called Scottie, had the job of directing bombers strayed from the pack and of giving advice to those returning, their fuel tanks holed, or crippled by flak and anxious for a place to set down.

Less than a week after Rickett had installed himself he was returning from a foraging trip to Komisa, where, tired of meaningless promises of stores from an amiable but ineffective supplies officer, he had at length given way to anger. Thumping the table, Rickett had threatened to quit Vis and go back personally to Italy to stir up enough gear for his job.

Now, still seething, he allowed himself to be driven back to Podhumlje by the cockney driver he shared with Heron. As they wound under the shadow of Mount Hum and came in sight of Podhumlje's bleached stones, the driver nudged him and said: "Take a butcher's, sir." And pointed. Rickett looked up. A bomber loomed in the sky, wings tilted and streaming oily smoke. It was coming down and heading for the island in a slow arc.

"Liberator," the driver said. "They'll be cookin' inside." They had stopped the truck and could now see flames licking under the wing from one of the port engines. It passed over them with a great whine, showing a blackened belly and the U.S. markings through drifts of smoke. As Rickett craned his neck upward, a parachute blossomed and hung in the sky, almost motionless. The plane took a steeper dive, a higher whine. Another parachute puffed suddenly in its wake, a tinier speck almost at eye level from their point on the island's platform. Then the bomber plunged, and they saw it hit the sea in a distant white flurry. The choppy waves, dancing under the northerly wind, erased the circle of foam almost as quickly as it spread.

The first parachutist, his chute dimpling and swaying in the buffets of wind, came down somewhere behind the hills at the other end of the plateau where the road wound down towards Vis. The other disappeared out of sight beyond the mountain into the sea. A little over an hour later a rider was dismounting at the hospital with news of a casualty—a navigator with a busted ankle. From Komisa the air-sea rescue launch roared out in pursuit of the other airmen, but by the time they had spotted the parachute lifting soggily on the waves and had reached the pilot, he was dead. He had strangled in his own harness.

Thereafter aircraft crashes and parachute drops all round the island were frequent. Those able to make it would take two runs over the island, under Scottie's radio directions, baling out half the crew on each run. Mostly the planes missed the island and crashed into the sea.

There was always a lot of air-sea rescue work, not only racing to salvage airmen who might still be trapped in their aircraft, but to rescue parachutists coming down far out in the water. Sometimes these crashes brought a strange tug-of-war for possession of the survivors—a struggle as between rival monsters lurking in their island lairs and emerging only to quarrel over a prey. For from Hvar and Brac to the north or from Korcula to the south-west, depending on the position of a crash and their chances of reaching it first, the Germans would emerge from port and race the British to snatch the victims out of the water and make them prisoner. If one side saw the other was undisputedly first, it sheered off; which was wise, for to be lured into pursuing a craft close to its stronghold in broad daylight was madness. Occasionally, as it was, a Messerschmitt chose to intervene and came streaking across the water to shoot up the launch and harry it back to port.

The bombers which hit the island usually caught fire. But another Liberator crashed into Mount Hum, and this time it was a land race between the island's rival scavengers for loot. A couple of Rickett's men, hurriedly mobilised and bundled into the truck, won the race, and held all others off. Having dismembered the Liberator with axes, hammers and stones, they returned in triumph with a pile of twisted heavy-gauge wire stripped from a gun turret, some ten-amp switches and enough parachute silk to make nighties for a company of F.A.N.Y.'s.

At the hospital, gleefully, they unloaded it all and, ripping out the flimsy Italian signalling wire, set about a proper wiring job, installing luminous switches and sockets where once nails had done duty. Scottie's radar magicians ran out extension lighting to the reception tents in front of the house and to the tented wards to seaward.

Heron's orderly held up a huge swatch of parachute silk destined for his lady-love in Blighty. "Cor, no kewpons, neither. She's gonna love me for this. Enough panties 'ere to last her till sixty!"

In the first-aid kits they had rifled there were also drugs they had never been able to prise out of base, like benzedrine, which Rickett promptly appropriated for their modest store. He was stunned by their haul. He accepted an extra-large mug of wine, lowered it fast, and banged it on the table. He shone with triumph.

"Hold the Jerries off this place long enough," he said, "and we'll build a hospital out of what drops from the sky."

"We'll get it quicker that way than from Italy, sir."

"Up the Air Force."

"Here's to man's, ah, ingenuity in, ah, adversity."

"*Sdravo.*" They gave the partisan salute, and drank to the confusion of all stores wallahs.

"I wonder," mused Scottie, "if any of these Yankee bombers carry pianos. We could do with one of those down here."

"Another glass of vino?" This to Rickett.

"Just a spot," Rickett said. "Just a spot."

The first among the adventurers to be attracted to Vis in its strangely embattled situation among the enemy islands was an aged British admiral. His name—Admiral Sir Walter H. Cowan, Bt., K.C.B., D.S.O., M.V.O.; aged seventy-one, diminutive and ferocious.

The Admiral had been officially retired these many years, but had managed, by attaching himself to one fighting unit after another, to fight in almost every theatre of war where trouble was flying thick.

Now the Commandos had adopted the Admiral as their mascot. Wearing their green beret, he could be seen almost any morning slowly making his way past Rickett's hospital on a donkey. The Admiral was out on his daily constitutional, which took him up to the top of Mount Hum. Thanks to his Spartan and aggressive life, Sir Walter was in superb fighting trim. He accompanied the Commandos on all their inter-island raids. In addition, he wangled trips out on motor gun-boats when they went marauding.

The Senior Naval Officer on Vis, Lieutenant-Commander Morgan Giles, brought Admiral Sir Walter Cowan with him on a jeep visit to the hospital. Major Rickett was busy operating on a mixed list of Commando and partisan wounded, assisted by Clynick and Dawson, Rickett sent word to Heron to invite the Admiral into their modest mess, to lay on a "bit of a show", but Sir Walter reminded hunched in the jeep, resolutely withstanding all efforts to entice him from it. He didn't want to cause any bother.

The reverence in which he was held by British soldiers and sailors was in marked contrast to the official treatment meted out to Admiral Cowan's Jugoslav counterpart, Admiral Ivo Preradovic, one of the former chiefs of the Royal Jugoslav Navy. A dapper and affable little figure, anxious to serve against the Germans in any way he could, Preradovic had been stripped by the partisan command of any kind of importance matching his value and experience, and reduced to a liaison job with the British. He endured the humiliations cheerfully enough, even to having to line up personally with his mess tin for his meals, among the motley of partisan fighters queueing at the cookhouse.

If Admiral Sir Walter Cowan did not for his part wish to cause any bother, he contrived to in spite of himself. On those dark schooner expeditions, for instance, which put forth to explore the German emplacements, their paths would often cross those of the E-boats or a heavily armed Siebel ferry. Prudence dictated that the slow-moving partisan schooner stop, shut off her engines and wait in silent hope of remaining undetected until the enemy's dark shape slid past. On these occasions, the Admiral's voice would rise, loud in protest in the stillness, demanding to know why they didn't press on and "ram the ——s!"

There were two legends current to account for his almost excessive pugnacity. One—an unkind one—had it that his wife gave him a rough time of it at home, and it was his pious ambition to get himself decently killed before the war was out. The other was that he was still smarting from a deadly humiliation received at the hands of the enemy when, having attached himself for a while to an Indian Cavalry Regiment, he stood in the path of an enemy tank at Tobruk and tried to hold it up with his revolver. Having exhausted his ammunition on it fruitlessly, he ended by flinging the gun at it. Whereupon the enemy popped open the lid, pounced on him, and took him prisoner.

They subsequently sent him back, speechless with humiliated rage when he learned of the announcement which accompanied his release. "We do not keep seventy-year-old admirals," the Axis broadcaster told the world.

It seemed now that he was intent on making them rue those words.

Sir Walter's spry condition could be an embarrassment to the toughest young Commandos—as an attack on the southerly island of Mljet proved. There, not a whit out of breath, the Admiral stood and made a splendid target on top of a two-thousand-foot mountain he had scaled, while he waited for the others still scrambling up its slope in his wake, nearly fainting with exhaustion.

He was the first of the true swashbucklers, but certainly not the last. For Vis and its situation was soon drawing them from all over the Mediterranean like flies. Even hardier spirits from base camps were wangling L.C.I. trips across to Komisa or stowing away in schooners to get a binocular view from Vis at the German preparations on Hvar, ten miles across the bland-smiling sea.

Some came on visits of "inspection", and among these was an orthopaedic surgeon, Watson, whom Rickett took a certain delight in squiring around the sheds and tents and hovels where they had fitted up lighting from bomber scrap, beds from torn-down match-boarding between the rooms of their farmhouse quarters, an operating theatre reflector cut out from biscuit tins, their ten-gallon water boiler, their home-made equipment, Dawson's own conveyor-belt contraption for making plaster bandages, and the broad brick-built external stretcher stairway Rickett had cajoled the engineers into constructing straight up into his first-floor theatre entrance from ground level outside. Below these stairs the generator roared and racketed in a lashed-up shelter, and the lighting alternately glowed and faltered to its caprices.

But Rickett had an especial delight in taking Watson on a professional visit to Petak—"the *braf* Dr. Petak", as kindly old Zon would describe him. Petak received them briskly and with delight, clad only in pants, a long white coat open to reveal his lean, hairy body, and the inevitable rubber gloves which he wore even for social occasions.

Rickett watched Watson's eyes pop as they toured the wards and saw what the *braf* Dr. Petak was up to. They were full to brimming, as usual, with refugees and partisan wounded. There was the usual stench of sepsis and antiseptic mixed with the odour of verminous bodies. Petak, pattering in broken French, gestured proudly to a row of partisans whose wounds had been immobilised in plaster of Paris and said: "You see? *Toujours le gypse . . . toujours . . .*"

Watson saw for himself. He looked up from examining a patient, straight at Rickett. He couldn't say anything for a while. Then he managed, dryly, to murmur: "I see they've heard of Trueta." After a pause, bending again: "But that's about all."

Until the advent of penicillin the prescribed treatment for a badly jagged wound was to dress it, pad it well with wool, immobilise the wound in plaster, and leave it until it swelled and stank—but gradually healed. Trueta, a surgeon in the Spanish Civil War, had been the first to use this technique. The padding was to allow for the swelling. The British even practised splitting the plaster while still wet to allow for swelling and occasional examination of the wound.

Without padding to allow for this swelling, the patient was soon in agony, and the wound turned gangrenous. None of this was new to Rickett. On his social calls on Dr. Petak Rickett had become inured to the horrors of his treatments. With hand wounds, for instance, the essential thing was to get movement going as soon as possible. Petak went against all modern teaching by immobilising hand injuries completely in plaster—with the result, at best, of crippling them, and at worst, of creating a gangrenous mess which demanded amputation.

After a few cursory examinations and questions, put with the usual polite interest in stumbling French, Watson had had enough. He and Rickett allowed themselves to be led downstairs to a vaulted cellar where Petak was anxious to dispense some of his hospitality. The cellar was furnished with two rickety chairs, a wine barrel, and an old upright piano. That was all. Petak jerked his head, beaming, at the barrel, for them to help themselves, and himself sat down abruptly, spread his long white coat out behind him like a concert pianist fluffing his tails—and proceeded to hit hell out of the piano.

Watson, dazedly, drank two tumblers of wine with scarcely a pause for breath, then sank into a chair with his chin on his chest and appeared to listen to the cascades of Chopin from under Petak's flying fingers. The fury of his attack dislodged Petak's wobbling pince-nez entirely and he broke off dramatically to grope for these. He shot his guests a smile of bright apology and with his frizzy grey hair flying, returned to the assault.

He really was a very fine pianist.

On the way back in the truck, Watson was silent for a long while. At length he awoke from his daze sufficiently to remark, delicately: "Charming fellow, that Petak."

"Indeed. Quite delightful."

They drove in silence again.

"My God!" Watson said.

Rickett had to grin. "There's one thing he's got that we haven't."

"What's that?"

"A piano," Major Rickett said.

While the small partisan and Commando parties struck out at the Germans the urgent build-up on Vis went on nightly. So did those eerie choral stand-to's against the invader as the partisans wound uphill to their night positions, singing their wild harmonies and prodding their wine-laden donkeys, like the cast of a mammoth opera. The stars glittered on a cold sea, quiet except for the most bizarre effect of all—the flare fishermen.

It was as though the fishermen alone were exempt from the rules. Throughout the whole invasion alert, as the Germans had swept one island clear after another till they now stood all around Vis, the flare fishermen had gone placidly on ignoring blackout restrictions, mined stretches, volleys from the lookouts and the constant threat of being caught up in an amphibious landing. Their bobbing lights, like candles floating on the sea, provided the most unreal, the most truly operatic note of all.

It was at dawn that the reality ebbed back with the quiet throb of the small warships making their ways round to their camouflaged lairs, and with the shape of the schooners looming through the paling gloom, loaded with refugees and with the returning raiders.

By the second week in March the savagery of these ambush-sorties was beginning to daunt some of the Germans into throwing up fortifications, concentrating in garrisons, and patrolling only in big parties. Their engineer teams now carried out the minelaying of beaches under heavy escort. They were easy to stalk. Wherever they went, partisan scouting parties shadowed them, silent and immensely curious, plotting exactly where the mines were laid. When the German parties withdrew again to the safety of their emplacements, the partisans wriggled forward, dug the mines up with their hands, smoothed the ground over again, and bore the mines back with them to Vis.

Carcane Carbine

At the time of the Italian collapse, when Tito's men had enjoyed a brief control of the Dalmatian islands, big stocks of Italian ammunition of all calibres had fallen into partisan hands. To complement this miscellaneous stockpile of war booty on Vis the Allies were pouring over the guns with which to fire their ammunition—captured Italian artillery pieces, mortars, and small arms. In addition, much Allied war material was arriving—grenades, stens, uniforms, blankets, medical supplies of all kinds, none of it for Rickett or for his Commandos. Big stocks of food were piling up on the quays. Specialist-instructors in technical equipment were arriving. The Jugs had little knowledge of weaponry beyond rifles. So elementary was their mode of warfare that in the first combined engagements which they fought by the side of Commando comrades, partisan troops were astonished at the sight of artillery firing over hills at an unseen enemy beyond. They imagined it was all done over open sights; the principle of indirect laying mystified them entirely.

Though the Jugs adored weapons of every sort, they showed no more care with the mines they had confiscated from the Germans than they did with their rifles, from which the accident rate was enormous. As the steep-plunging volcanic formations of Vis were entirely without beaches, the partisans began burying their mines all over the island, without either maps to record where they were, or warning signs for the unwary.

The result was that it became suicidal to step a foot off any of the goat tracks which laced the hills. On an otherwise-still afternoon with the island's contours bathed in sun and a momentary peace, it became a commonplace to hear a sudden explosive WHOOF, followed usually by another, the roar spreading among the hills like a wave.

At the hospital at Podhumlje, Dawson would pause. Without looking up from his work, Rickett would say: "Wait for it to ring."

He was referring to their field telephone. The signallers had laid it for them and they were inordinately proud of it.

Sure enough, within half an hour the phone would be ringing. Soon the casualty would be borne in—either already dead or with the calf and thigh muscles shredded like the sinews of an old fowl that had been over-boiled, and involving amputation of both limbs. As often as not the casualties were Commandos, and on two occasions the dead were officers.

It was on such a day that they brought in the body of Captain Wilson. Two nights before Wilson had stood warming his back before the log fire which roared in their primitive mess at Podhumlje and watched Rickett dispensing hospitality to a haphazard accumulation of Jugoslavs and British who had dropped in for an evening glass of wine. To give them a meeting-ground, the hospital mess had lately been keeping open house.

The Commandos who brought their dead leader in were helpless with a vague anger at the waste of a respected life.

"Them bloody Jugs, sir. They don't mean no 'arm, but, well, look what it's done!"

All Rickett could remember was a few snatches of the conversation he had had with Wilson a couple of nights before. The mess had milled with every sort of guest, for Rickett's open-house rule banished any distinction of rank. Johnnie, the hefty orderly from George's hospital in Vis harbour, stood with a glass of *rakia* and a wide happy beam. That morning he had come all the way up to Podhumlje with a netful of fish for Rickett; they had grilled these over an open fire. Now Johnnie, a true primitive, was reaching out to clout everybody within his distance on the back and roaring at them happily: *"Dobro! Eh? Dobro!"* Obviously he approved of this kind of a mess.

Wilson, the Commando captain, had surveyed it all. "This mess of yours has become quite the place for a party."

"D'you think it's too, er, mixed?" Rickett said slyly.

Wilson shook his head. "Not for me," he said.

"Fearful hooligans, of course, these Jugs," Rickett said. "But then—so am I, rather."

They had drunk in silence amid the *mêlée*. Wilson had set down his glass. "I think you've got the right idea," he said.

"About what?"

Wilson had gestured. "—all this. I think we ought to do a lot more drinking with, um, hooligans . . ."

SEVEN

On March 5th Brigadier Tom Churchill arrived on Vis with the headquarters of the 2nd Special Service Brigade to take over the command of the island from his brother, Colonel Jack, at their hill post of Borovic, not far from Mount Hum.

Brigadier Tom was younger, quieter, more scholarly than his dashing brother, of whom he was immensely proud. A great bond of affection united these two. Colonel Jack went happily back to lead his No. 2 Commando and moved into a flat in Komisa which became noted for the potency of its celebrations whenever his troops chalked up a new strike against the Germans.

Tom Churchill had come from the gruelling fighting at Anzio and the Garigliano with its high toll of casualties among the men of his Brigade. There was to be no relief from the strife of hurried battle or from anxiety for his men, stuck out here on a precarious piece of Balkan rock. Added to this he faced the formidable task of co-ordinating plans for battle operations with the partisans on an increasingly ambitious scale.

The Commandos planned their first really big-scale raid on the Germans for March 17th, twelve days later. They were not to know at the time how apt was their choice of this date. It was precisely the day which had been set by the German High Command for the invasion of Vis—an attack with a heavy amphibious force from the south-east via Korcula, with the Komisa area marked to bear the brunt of the assault. But the vigour of the Commando strikes and the intense activity of British light warships were already giving the *Wehrmacht* pause to reconsider the military situation and to argue tactics with German naval chiefs.*

And so instead of taking up a defensive stance to beat off an invasion, the Commandos launched an attack on the island of Solta, a satellite island separated from the heavily-held fortress of Brac only by a narrow, mine-infested channel. They had probed and reconnoitred it from all angles—not without a couple of head-on clashes with the Germans. German nervousness at the belligerence of these reconnaissances manifested itself in a concentration of their garrison, and according to the latest Commando probes the enemy troops had now entrenched themselves behind heavy defences in the small town of Grohote.

This raid on Solta was to be a combined operation, opening with a dawn attack by aircraft of the Allied Mediterranean Air Force on the town. As an experiment in co-ordinating with Italy-based air support, and with their headquarters in Bari, as well as with the island's own slender naval resources, it promised to be tricky, to put it mildly. But at least on this occasion they were to be spared the additional headache of partisan participation with all its attendant liaison troubles. Churchill's Commandos took only partisan guides.

As usual they chose night for the assault, for surprise was of course essential, and their little flotilla under M.G.B. escort was vulnerable from the air. On the plain near Podhumlje that night the Heavy Weapons Troop left their tents near the hospital silent and empty as they embarked down in the port in L.C.I.'s with troops of No. 2 Commando.

They vanished into the moonless dark between the harbour headlands, towing their boatloads of light artillery. Admiral Sir Walter Cowan, of course, was aboard. They could not have kept him out of it. With them also were some Rangers from a small party of the U.S. Operations Group which had planted a flag on Vis, and an R.A.F. Officer with a V.H.F. set for talking to their bombers.

When the small assault force reached Solta, their

---

*The *Wehrmacht* requested a postponement of the attack on Vis—already postponed since the third week in February—until the 4th April, 1944.

landing craft came inshore unchallenged and the Commandos began climbing after their guides over steep rocks and high terraces banked with stones. It involved alternate mountaineering and slithering down steep slopes, a heavy task for the support weapons, as they made their way over the island to take up their perches among the orchards and vineyards which dominated the town of Grohote on three sides. Then they waited. The trickiest part of the operation was to be the daylight fighting. First, there would be the curtain-raiser of bombs at dawn, before they stormed Grohote's defences. If the Germans on Brac, right next door, got wind of the operation and started pouring rescue reinforcements across the channel in daylight, they could be up to their ears in trouble.

In their pre-dawn creeping through the slopes commanding the town the Commandos came upon an alert

Kittyhawk Dive Bomber

defence. Well before first light it spotted them and the alarm went up. Within moments the Germans were blazing away at the leading troops, wriggling close to the town's defences. At that, the Heavy Weapons Troop opened shop and replied with mortars and Vickers—but the main body of the Commando besiegers waited for the dawn.

At six o'clock the formations of Kittyhawk dive bombers came droning into the fight, peeling off in the paling sky to fall on Grohote. From the village, columns of dust mushroomed and eddied amid the thunder of bombs as house after house was hit. It was a brief but concentrated sample of hell, and in the short, uncanny silence which followed the delivery of the last bomb, while the defenders still had their heads down or scrambled dazedly among the rubble, the leading Commandos were in the dust-hung streets, dodging from house to house, grenading and Sten-gunning. In the first bout they collared the German commander and brought him before Jack Churchill who stared grimly and thrust a loud-hailer into his hand.

"Tell 'em to come out with their hands up," he barked.

Haggard and dust-flecked, the unhappy officer stared round at his captors searchingly. In his dazed way he seemed to gather some reassurance from the message Churchill began dictating. They were British and they didn't shoot prisoners.

The German commander accepted the loudhailer and relayed the invitation. In trickles, sullenly, the enemy emerged from the battered houses and the piles of stone with their hands high.

On the north side of the town a strong point resisted and then, with a perfidy that occasionally characterised the Germans in defeat, hoisted a white flag. At that a Commando soldier, Cox, ran forward to take their surrender. Immediately he emerged into open ground the Germans opened up with a machine gun and Cox crumpled, riddled through the guts.

That strong point did not get another chance. The Commando pounded it into silence and polished it off with grenades, leaving the German dead littered round their guns and draped grotesquely in the firing slits.

Within an hour the whole village was in the hands of

the Commandos. Their tally was 107 German prisoners for the loss of two dead and less than a score wounded.

They left the village empty, a ghost garrison, but it was an uneasy and vigilant wait throughout that day on the rocky slopes for the expected vengeance from Brac—so close that its high peaks crowned with nacreous cloud frowned down on them.

No vengeance came.

Dusk fell about them at last and the Navy was back. They returned loaded, and in triumph, their first Combined Operation a complete success. The small island of Solta was left empty of Germans. The air liaison from Italy had worked brilliantly well; the dive bombing had been perfectly timed, devastatingly accurate. This kind of support was a shock to the Germans, and it repaid some the lordly arrogance of the *Luftwaffe* over Vis.

The beating up of Solta and its haul of prisoners provided Rickett with his first spell of battle casualties. They came winding up from Komisa in the darkness and unloaded the wounded, a phantom cavalcade of bearers lit only by the flames which the hospital helpers got going under the boiler outside of the operating room. This boiler proved their first weakness. A droning in the sky and the wailing of sirens announced the *Luftwaffe*, prowling in search of the returning boats, and they had to douse the fire each time the planes came nosing in towards the island until they had sheered off again. It made sterilising difficult, but the resourceful Dawson managed to keep Rickett supplied with clean instruments, sterile towels and well-boiled mackintoshes over a rush operating programme which lasted slightly longer than twenty-four hours.

There were fourteen major operations among the Commando wounded, and among the first they brought in was the lad Cox whom the Germans had chopped down from behind a surrender flag. Cox was still alive. His intestines were lying in his vest in a mess of blood and faeces. They had been riddled with the burst. Rickett cleaned and excised and repaired the awful damage as best he could, removed seven feet of intestine, closed the abdomen—and knew, for all that, that the boy was doomed. They kept Cox comfortable with morphine. He held on four days, and then died.

Several German prisoners came in too, among them

some dying or already dead. The Germans were left until Rickett had finished operating on the Commando casualties.

The dead and those for whom there were no beds were laid down on the floor wherever space could be found in the tiny passageways of the houses. Next morning Rickett, touring between operations, twice tripped over dead Germans lying across the corridors. This roused him to a rare display of petulance and he stormed off to round up his orderlies. He halted a couple and glared. Said he severely: "Pass the word round. I am damned if I am going to have German corpses cluttering the place for me to trip over."

And he moved on to repair the other weakness their first spate had revealed—the absence of mortuary space.

Down in Vis George Lloyd Roberts was busy on the first partisan casualties from a combined Commando and partisan attack on Hvar. For this the partisans assembled an armada of the most unseaworthy-looking craft in the world, ranging from concrete-reinforced schooners to fishing boats from the caves. The ports and hills echoed to tramping and the wild beauty of the partisan battle songs as they poured down from their encampments into the waiting craft. This sea-going rabble of ships set a ragged, wallowing course in the gathering dusk across the strait to the rearing crags of Hvar. Ahead of them the Allied Mediterranean Air Force, summoned by radio, had opened proceedings with a bombing attack on their objective across the other side of the island, the port of Jelsa.

It was here that the Allied commanders had one of their first tastes of partisan impetuosity in a combined attack. The invaders climbed and force-marched across the island till they were overlooking Jelsa port. Below them German shipping was burning fiercely, but the port was otherwise silent—and empty. The Germans had fled the bombs and lay in refuge in the surrounding hills. The partisans were all for storming the port and taking possession. The Commando leader had the greatest difficulty in restraining them from this and coaxing them to play their allotted role—to wait, and cover the Commandos while they stole in and explored the town.

It was fortunate that the Commando tactics—in this case, at least—prevailed, for at dawn the Germans rose from hiding and assembled to spring the trap and swoop down on Jelsa. Instead, the ambushers became the ambushed. As they emerged, they were met by partisan fire from all round them, and in the ensuing battle piled the slopes with their dead. That night the Jugoslav schooners returned with a fraction of the casualties they would otherwise have suffered, but nevertheless, there was enough work to strain the resources of Lloyd Roberts and his little hospital down at Vis.

The Germans immediately marked their displeasure with a particularly heavy raid on Komisa port. The bombers came in low among the shipping which, for once, lay fairly thickly in the usually-deserted harbour. At the same time as the warning sounded, the port was an inferno of

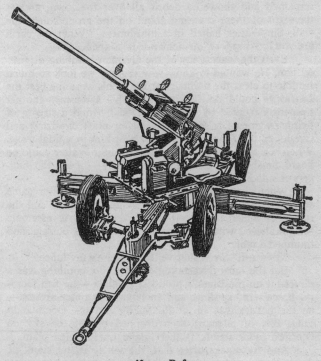

40 mm Bofers

bursting bombs. Several of the boats were hit or swamped
by near misses and a bomb nearly put an end to the
brothers Churchill. It burst in the water three yards from
the narrow mole on which Brigadier Tom and Colonel
Jack stood supervising the disembarkation of the last-
comers.

As usual, Admiral Sir Walter Cowan was in the thick
of it, enjoying himself hugely. The anti-aircraft defences of
the port, totalling several Bofors, were pathetically inadequate; their fire was ragged and ineffectual, and most of
their bursts went wide of the wheeling planes. The old
Admiral, striding up and down, divided his blistering
language between exhorting the gunners to better effort
and flaying them for rotten shooting.

Several sailors crouched flat on the mole as the bombs
screamed and showered debris all over the town, and at
the sight of them crawling about on the ground near the
wall, Sir Walter halted in astonishment. "What on earth
are you looking for?" he demanded. "Sixpences?"

Even the inaccuracy of the German bombing disgusted him. He wanted to know why the hell we took so much
trouble to clear the harbour by day if this were the best the
Luftwaffe could do. To punctuate his sarcasms, another
near-miss erupted by the harbour wall. Amid a stream of
flying fragments it sent some smaller craft capsizing and
enveloped the Admiral and those near him in a tidal wave.
When the spray had subsided, Admiral Sir Walter could be
heard finishing his sentence witheringly—"if all the bug-
gers can do is wet you . . .?"

When the raiders headed for home Sir Walter came
striding back to the naval mess, amid the plaster and the
rubble of which the orderlies were beginning to assemble
their scattered wits. He stared around him in outrage and
thumped a table.

"Steward!" Sir Walter yelled. "Where's my lunch?"

But the most devastating effect of the bombing was a
direct hit on the island's proudest building—the fish factory. It scattered sardines and anchovies for miles around—
on the houses way up at Podhumlje, on the Commando
H.Q. Bits of pilchard even dropped out of the sky on
Scottie's radar shack, farther inland on the high plain.

And for weeks after that, the whole island stank of
dead fish.

From Vis the Commandos would ship their prisoners back to Italy in darkness. The partisans had no such arrangement and by this time the fate of Germans who fell into partisan hands was pretty general knowledge. Those not immediately executed were put to work—and when the fatigues they performed seemed no longer to justify their rations, they were shipped across to the nearby rocky islet of Bisevo. Thereafter they were never heard of again. Theirs was the same fate as the Germans themselves reserved for captured guerillas in any occupied country. And in the bitter traditions inherited from their mainland campaigns, the Jugs neither wanted prisoners, nor could they afford them. Moreover, they had abundant labour of their own.

It was a talking point in the mess at Podhumlje, where Rickett's reputation as a host was spreading. It was here that the Commandos and the commissars, who tended to remain socially aloof from each other elsewhere, drifted in, and met, and drank, and taught each other tunes, and argued.

His spate of surgery from the bombing or the raiding over, Rickett liked nothing better than to join the drinking and get a really good argument going. When he had accomplished this, he would sit back and watch the fire-works, and occasionally grin. It was unorthodox therapy, he would own, if anybody taxed him with this failing, but it helped people get things off their liver. Between Jugs and Commandos, it occasionally cleared the air.

The Jugs liked Rickett. He had an instinct, shaped from years of general practice, for identifying himself with people. He kept this faculty well camouflaged under a blank stare, a sudden creasing of his rubbery features in a grin, an air of confidential, frowning earnestness which he reserved whenever he decided to pull anybody's leg—hard. He had a strange weakness for buffoons, ruffians, eccentrics, and like George Lloyd Roberts with his squad of Jug orderlies well-drilled in profanity, Rickett itched with strangely boyish rebellions against protocol. His method with the Jugoslavs was hearty: slap them on the back, adopt a bullying tone, give them a bit of buffoonery. Shock tactics. Under this treatment their rough peasant diffidence vanished. They invariably responded with happy broadening grins. Challenge them. Give them the old Joe Blunt.

Wag a finger. "I know all about you fellows. Never take a prisoner, eh? What? Of course you don't! Prison camps, over on Bisevo? Don't make m laugh! You take them over there to shoo 'em!"

And then, fearful that his Commando guests, too, might grow smug at this, Rickett would jerk a thumb at them: "Don't you believe that *they* take prisoners either. Not always, anyway. Eh?"

"Well," hedged a Commando officer, "not *always*. It depends."

"On what?"

"On circumstances."

"On military necessity, you mean?"

"We-ell . . ."

"Suppose you had orders to kill a German Commander, and you had to sneak in alone into a town swarming with Jerries to do it, and you opened the door and poked a revolver at him, and he threw up his arms and surrendered to you? And you knew you hadn't an earthly of getting out with him on your hands as your prisoner?"

"I'd say sorry first, and *then* I'd shoot him."

"Exactly. What if you were campaigning in small parties and had no prison camps to send them to and no food to feed them with and you had to take them everywhere you went, as the Jugs would have to do, what then?"

By this time a glorious argument would be boiling up. Rickett would happily retreat into a back seat and watch it rage.

There was a time when it was thought that the Jugs might have no further use for the grim islet of Bisevo. At one stage in this strange and merciless war a proposal had actually been made for an exchange of prisoners. The partisans, who had a temporary mixed bag of wretches under guard—Poles, Austrians, Germans, quisling Greeks and even some hated *Chetniks*—considered these proposals which were brought to them by intermediaries. And in what must rank as one of the most abortive truces in the history of the war, they agreed to an exchange.

Accordingly the partisans gathered their prisoners into a schooner and sailed across for an appointed island rendezvous near the enemy stronghold of Hvar, under a flag of truce.

The result was a triumph of treachery and murder to enter in the bloody annals of the war in Jugoslavia. Zena told Rickett the story. The Germans appeared at the rendezvous, she said, inspected the batch of prisoners brought to the exchange, and went down the ranks sorting them out.

"The Polish and the Austrians they didn't want." Zena said. "They picked out only German officers. They took those and refused to hand over their own prisoners. These they took back with them and hanged them all on Hvar."

Zena wagged her head bitterly at the recollection. She did not even blame the Germans all that much, but themselves.

"We should have known better," she growled, broke a cigarette in half and lit it. She smiled at another recollection. "One of the Austrian prisoners we had complained: 'The Germans treat us like Slavs!' He said it was such— what do you say?—*outrage*, as if he meant 'like lice!' All this he said to me, a Slav, when I spoke with him! I ask you, what kind of people do *you* think they are that we are fighting?"

So deep was the hatred, even of a cultured woman like Zena, that George Lloyd Roberts, who burned with young ideals of chivalry, had doubts about leaving the occasional German prisoners who were brought in to her mercies. Zena's own brother and sister, both partisans, had been taken prisoner by German soldiers—and shot. Zena had walked through streets in Sarajevo where her friends, strung up by the enemy, hung dead from the lamp posts.

George already had one German prisoner in his ward when another was brought in from a partisan raid with a bullet in his leg. George decided to operate. Zena injected the pentothal and as soon as the patient was under, George went ahead excising the wound.

After a while he straightened and sighed. "I'll have to go and make another plaster," he said to Zena.

"Yes, George," Zena said.

George Lloyd Roberts hesitated still in going. He looked at the gun Zena wore in her holster. The invasion still overhung the island and Zena had orders to wear it.

He said weakly: "Will you give me your gun?"

She rounded, glaring. "You stupid boy! Do you think I would harm a wounded man, a *prisoner?*"

And George retreated before the storm of abusive reproach she hurled after him. She was bitterly hurt that he did not understand her—and yet in the atmosphere of hatred which reddened this whole war, perhaps he *did* . . .

Zena stayed on duty, watching. Slowly her fury ebbed away, and she could even smile to herself, fondly, at the memory of George's confusion as he backed before her out of their theatre. She returned to the German patient. He still hadn't recovered consciousness from the pentothal.

Zena moved from bed to bed, looking at the other sick men who stirred or moaned in the squalid ward, lit by a weak, naked light bulb. The tour took her some time, with the checking of plasma drips, making the men comfortable, fetching and giving water, but when she returned to the man George had operated on, she grew anxious. The German had not stirred. Zena shook his shoulder gently. But there was no response.

She thought, *I have given him an overdose of pentohal. And George will think—*

Zena called a girl orderly, Sofia, to watch, while she walked to George Lloyd Robert's dispensary. George was rubbing plaster into bandages and glanced at her a little warily to see if Zena was still angry. He wiped his hands in a towel. "Mm?" he said, and smiled on her his nicest smile.

"George, the German is not awake yet," Zena said.

"Nothing unusual," George murmured, and tossed the towel down. "Sofia will keep you posted."

They ate at Zena's house, and when the meal was over and no message had come from the hospital, Zena, always so sure of herself, was sure no longer, and in a voice that was astonishingly humble, she broke a silence. "I am frightened, George," she said.

"Don't worry old darling," George said. "They sleep for twenty-four hours sometimes, just on one dose. Specially if he's had a morphine shot as well."

It took the German twenty hours, in fact, to awaken. By this time Zena had taken up a bedside vigil and as the man's eyes opened, her grim distaste softened and she

actually smiled on him. Then Zena turned and flew into
George, radiant with relief. He grinned. Zena clasped her
hands, and, astonished at herself, shouted: "I am so
happy!"

"Then have a drink," George said.

"You know I never drink! Don't try to make me! But
I will smoke a whole cigarette!"

When Zena returned later to the ward the patient was
sitting up, in high spirits, and talking loudly to the other
German prisoner. She heard his voice long before she
came into the little shed-like ward and she stopped at the
sound of it. He was boasting of his battle exploits.

He was a *Luftwaffe* bomber officer.

"... ah yes, Split ... indeed I know it ... *hör mal*,
I ought to! Our squadron strafed the hell out of it. In those
days one never saw any flak ... You could fly up and down
as you pleased. You could see 'em running this way and
that in that square, you know, next to the big hotel. Most
of the time you never saw what you hit ... we were so
low we had the machine guns going ... you could even
see the bodies out on the road and along the esplanade
there ..."

A great madness gripped Zena at the sound of this
voice; at the loud, careless satisfaction of it, the proleptic
relish with which this man she had helped to operate on
was describing the aerial massacre of a Jugoslav town,
Split, just across the water on the mainland.

She started to walk in, and Sofia, the orderly came
rustling out to greet her. That stopped Zena. She took a
grip on herself. She said, with great care: "Ask him how
he feels."

Sofia looked at her askance.

"Go on, girl! You know I never speak German to
these people!" Zena walked slowly in behind Sofia and
came up with them as the girl bent and made the German
comfortable. Zena kept her own eyes on her work, refusing to meet the glance the pilot flicked up at her. He would
have seen murder in her eyes.

She took his pulse in silence. As she did so, the
German leaned slightly away towards his companion and
murmured: "A real witch, this one. Do you know, when
she took up that hypodermic for my anaesthetic, I could
have sworn she was going to kill me!" He smirked she

didn't catch the other's low reply but they laughed. She released the German's wrist and said calmly to Sofia, in her own language. "Tell him if he needs anything, ask for it."

By now her rage was so great that she walked unsteadily out of the shed. A Jugoslav commander lounged in the hospital reception room. Zena walked up to him and jerked a hand towards the ward she had left. She said, stonily, "There is a *Luftwaffe* bomber officer inside."

The Commander looked straight at her and removed the cigarette from his lips.

"How do you know?"

"I heard him say he bombed Split."

"You're sure?"

"Very sure."

The Commander straightened and stepped on his cigarette. He motioned to two partisan officers. "Perhaps we should ask him to tell us the story," he said, and took Zena's arm. "You will come, comrade, and translate."

Zena stood her ground. "I cannot."

"Why not?"

"I do not speak German," Zena said. Would they accept the other reason? *I hate him too much even to talk his language to him.*

The Commander halted. "Then how did you understand what he said?"

"I just did," Zena said flatly.

The others gave her a strange look and walked in to the ward. George Lloyd Roberts came in and, not understanding what they had been talking about, but knowing that something was up and wary for his charges, went after them. He came upon the group of partisan officers standing round the bed of a somewhat changed *Luftwaffe* pilot and said: "What do you want with my patient?"

"He is our prisoner. We have been interrogating him. We wish him to come with us now."

"He cannot be moved from hospital."

The German had a ghastly look now, as his gaze shifted from one to the other.

"There are doubtless many partisan sick who need your attention more, doctor."

"They have it. I cannot allow this man to be moved."

The partisans hesitated. The Commander said: "Very

well." He motioned to the other two to leave with him. At the door he looked back.

"We shall wait till he is well," he said. He gave the German a long look and went out.

Zena told Jim Rickett all this. He was an amiable confessor, uncritical. His silence was one of understanding and it enwrapped her in a strange warmth.

"Did they come and get him?" he asked.

"Oh yes—eventually."

"Did they shoot him?"

"I don't know," Zena said. She was sullen. She could not help it, the murder still in her heart, the memory of a dead brother and sister and the sight of dead children, and so she had to come out with it: "I hope so," she said.

Rickett was smiling on her, with gentle interest, and wagging his head, but whether in admiration or reproof it would be hard to say. All he said was, mildly: "I shouldn't like to have had your war."

"Stop here," Zena growled, "and you will get it."

EIGHT

It was Zena who provided them with a piano. She tracked it down, from a remark dropped by a patient, to a house on the waterfront now crammed from ground floor to attic with partisans. Zena marched in, swept off the caps and mess tins which encumbered the top of the forgotten piano, and commandeered it. And on a typical impulse, she shipped it up to Major Rickett, "for social purposes."

That was very like her.

When it arrived by truck, it was trundled in amid cheering by a great squad of Rickett's neighbouring Commandos and engineers. For the unveiling ceremony they plucked Scottie from his radar shack down the road, steered him, stuttering with delight, for the keyboard. Scottie was a very useful bar-room performer. He could play anything by ear, not well, but with gusto and certainty. The piano was frightfully out of tune, but one didn't have to play *Colonel Bogey* on a Bechstein.

That was the real beginning of their parties. With it their mess became more than a social centre; an institution. The gayest spirit, always in the thick of the revelries, was Professor Heron. He had an enormous thirst for conviviality, and he started quenching this as soon as the sun was over the yard arm. As evening wore on his bald pate grew pinker, his round face merrier, and the buffoonery of which he was often the ringleader grew wilder. Heron was the terror of that timid twosome, Anka and Filica, who fled squealing with delight at his mere approach, for he ragged them unmercifully. *Rakia* seemed to be the ideal fuel for him too. On its stimulus his energy and mischief knew no bounds. The astonishing thing about Heron, though, was his resilience. Whether he owed it to fitness, to his careless attitude to any problem, or to a sheer *joie de vivre,* he would spring from his bed as if each new day were a gift from heaven and, irrespective of what had happened the night before, would come bustling happily to work. Some of these parties went on till dawn. Heron was always the last on his feet, and first up next day. He had discovered his own balance between war and wassailing, and it had never floored him for work yet.

For Rickett, a surgeon, it was different. First aid and ambulance work were one thing, but for him, tomorrow might bring a brain operation, the removal of shell splinters around a man's heart, the supremely delicate trial of eye surgery without the special instruments or the experience, for which he only had a few hurried notes on technique and a pep-talk from a Bari specialist before he embarked.

It might bring a sudden welter of the ghastliest casualties right out of the blue—from a Commando sortie, a partisan raid, the bombing of the ports, the awaited German offensive. Come what may, his was a one-man band—utterly too small, heaven knows, for any deluge of casualties such as they secretly expected, dreaded. His was also the *only* band.

And so, as the revelry mounted, Rickett would eye the fun, regretfully put down his glass, and roll in under a blanket.

That didn't work too well, with a party still proceeding in the same room. So after a week or so Rickett carried a one-man bivouac tent a hundred yards down the road and pitched it there, putting in a home-made wooden bed.

Dawson, ever solicitous for his welfare, protested at this. Rickett listened. He said: "A doctor doesn't prescribe pills for a patient and then take them out of his mouth."

"What do you mean, sir?"

"I mean, Dawson, that these parties are prescribed. The place needs them."

Dawson shrugged and went off muttering, but got the point, and soon prepared his own tent. Professor Heron emphasised it with a characteristic performance the very next night. The *Luftwaffe* came over, and no sooner had the alert sounded than the bombers were roaring in low over the hospital, which they had discovered in spite of its net camouflaging. Soon they were carpeting the place with incendiaries.

In the midst of the noise and the shouts Captain Heron dived out and ran pelting for the girls' quarters. There he found Anka and Filica cowering and blubbering. He grabbed them and dragged them upstairs to Rickett's mess, together with Marie the cook, and forced them to join the party. "Dance!" he instructed them. He grabbed several hulking partisans and with a lot of grinning and clownish miming, got them in a circle with the British orderlies and the girls. Heron put his arms round the necks of the nearest and raising his voice in execrable imitation of a partisan song, led them off in a clumsy ring-a-rosy.

Soon they had all caught the spirit of it and were dancing madly, the British yelling their heads off in pidgin Serbo-Croat which convulsed the partisans. They had to pause and hold themselves while they reeled about, guffawing and wiping their eyes. Even Anka and Filica forgot their fear in shrieks of laughter and squeals as Dodd and Dawson grabbed them, whirled them off their feet in a mad clog dance.

At the end of the party the girls and Marie were struggling to teach Rickett and the orderlies the steps of the *kolo*, but Heron, assuming a pansy's grace with hand on hip and curveting sweetly, turned the whole thing into a burlesque and the lesson collapsed in hysteria.

They hardly heard the all-clear go.

That sort of thing, naïve and collegiate, nevertheless went down very well with the Jugoslavs, for at least its language was unmistakable.

Garbled legends about this island, drifting back across the Adriatic, were attracting more visitors from Italy. There came a medical brigadier whom Jim took down to Zena's house in Vis harbour, where they wined and dined him royally. Cookie put more flowers for him on the table, despite Zena's strictures. Her wondrously exotic dishes were no more than their daily fare, though they lived on the edge of a volcano. It would have staggered a British housewife. It floored the Brigadier.

Rickett's mess up at Podhumlje refused to stand on any kind of ceremony. Brigadiers and other V.I.P.s found themselves sitting down to Marie's cooking in company with Dawson, Heron's slangy drivers, medical orderlies, and any partisans or odd-job troops Rickett had on constant loan.

The old Brigadier liked this. He lingered there, taking a discreet back seat at the parties but, despite the tension and the strangeness, unwilling to leave. He sighed as he finally bade Rickett goodbye and muttered glumly, "Suppose I'd better be getting back to Italy, Rickett. Been like a breath of fresh air, up here, away from all the——."

Rickett shook his hand and watched the Brig go off in the jeep down to Komisa and the boat which would take him back to base. He returned to work.

One of the first cases that the orderlies bore in was a Commando with a suspected fracture of the ankle. The terrain on the mountain was awful and ankle injuries from troops stumbling about in the darkness—sometimes no steadier from whiling away the waiting with wine—were common. Rickett probed and tested the ankle and appeared nonplussed.,

"I think," he said aloud, "I ought to have a consultation for this."

Frank Clynick and Dawson gaped at him.

"Get on the blower, Dawson, and get a message off to the Brigadier aboard the *Prodigal*. 'REQUEST URGENT CONSULTATION ON ORTHOPAEDIC CASUALTY.' "

On receiving this, Morgan Giles sent an M.L. racing out after the trawler, which was already under way and clearing Komisa harbour. They put the Brigadier off in the launch and he returned joyfully to Podhumlje in a jeep. It gave him three, perhaps four days' surcease from the routines of base administration before the trawler's return, for transport was still at a premium.

The Brig was immensely touched at being consulted in this way, and a profane Commando private who had tripped on his face in the blackout was bewildered to find himself the centre of a grave consultation, presided over by no less than a brigadier, on the damage he had done to his ankle.

In a similar way a wild man joined them from the sky. He was Gerke, an Australian Spitfire pilot. On an impetuous foray too far into enemy territory, Gerke had run out of fuel, and he crash-landed his Spitfire on Vis. It was now becoming the habit to bring all strays up to

Podhumlje for a spot of hospitality, and Gerke, sponsored by Scottie, immediately joined the nightly revelries with Heron, whose zest for parties he shared.

Gerke was lean, dark, a humorist. He liked this place with its desperate raffishness, its noisy defiance in the face of what tomorrow might bring. The Australian pilot haunted the place for several days, exploring the island by day and carousing by night, before he returned with some reluctance to Italy. By now, after many arguments with the partisan leaders over the clearing of precious vines from the platcau, the Air Force was working hard on an emergency landing strip. It was to be used first for patching and refuelling light planes, fighters, and as a base for observer craft; later, as it grew bigger, Dakotas and crippled bombers were to make use of it too.

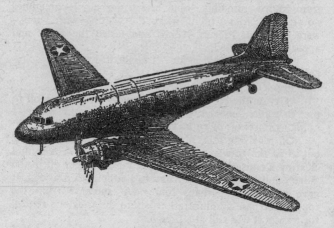

Dakota C-47

A few days after Gerke flew off, another Spitfire emergency-landed on the rough strip, in search, too, of petrol. Rickett returned to the mess from a session of the incidental surgery that took place between actions—and found Gerke lolling in a seat there as if he owned the place, with a mug of wine in his hand.

"What-ho, sport," Gerke drawled. "Pull up a chair."

This time he had buckled the landing gear of his Spitfire, which meant an enforced stay of several more days. This time, also, he had his pyjamas and a toothbrush with him.

Finally, back in Italy, Gerke helped himself to some leave and announced to his astonished superiors that he was off to Vis for a holiday. "If that's your idea of a holiday," one of them inquired sarcastically, "why don't you try boating up the Rhine?" To which Gerke retorted that if they could show him a pub on the Rhine where you got free vino for as long as you liked to stay, and without a lot of fat Fritzes singing the *Horst Wessel,* he'd be there like a trout up a stream.

After a pretty hefty session with him, Rickett left Gerke and the Professor in their familiar attitude—leaning around Scottie, waving their mugs of wine and instructing him in the cadences of a ribald Australian folksong called *The Man from Gundagai.*

Next afternoon Rickett's field telephone rang. It was Scottie on the blower. He was stuttering somewhat more than usual.

"M-my G-god, Jimmo, I say, poor old G-gerke's got an awful h-hangover. W-worst I've ever seen. He's been spewing all d-d-day . . . !"

"You know," Rickett remonstrated mildly. "You fellows do rather tear the pants out of it. All right, I'll come on over."

He hiked down to Gerke's hut. Gerke's hangover certainly hadn't improved his condition, but it took Rickett no more than a brief examination of his abdomen to diagnose his trouble. He straightened, jerked a thumb at the field telephone and barked at Scottie: "Ambulance— quick as you like."

The way Scottie's jaw dropped was comic.

"W-what's up, Jimmo?"

"He's got a bloody awful appendix."

Rickett operated urgently as soon as Dawson had Gerke shaved and loaded on to their operating table. In a few minutes he was fishing out an organ that was grusomely gangrenous. There was early peritonitis. The gay Gerke had run it a bit close.

But apart from a revolting appendix he was in splendid fettle. The vino had made no inroads on Gerke's condition. It was his condition which pulled him through quickly, and in ten days he was back in Italy.

There Gerke escaped from his convalescent depot and within three weeks of having been opened up for a "hangover", he was flying sorties again.

They knew, because occasionally he would be on the air to Scottie as he swooped past Vis, dictating rudely affectionate messages to one and all.

The next crisis which young George Lloyd Roberts had to deal with came, not from a spate of partisan casualties—and these were keeping him very busy now—but from within his own hospital. The lovely Suza, his anaesthetist, was sighing after him, a fact which no longer escaped the zealous eye of Jela the Apothecary. Whether it was from the mothering that George was getting from Zena or from George's own breezy-seeming indifference was hard to tell, but Suza acquired a strange jealousy fixation, flattering in itself, laughable otherwise, for she started to inveigh bitterly against Zena.

That splendid soul did not even notice any of this in her brisk rounds of the hospital, which she ruled in such masterly fashion for George. One of the first inklings George Lloyd Roberts had that the matter had assumed sizable proportions was a cryptic message he received from Colonel Penman, R.A.M.C., who had visited the island and was now attempting to help him and Rickett from Italy by battling for stores.

Penman's signal simply read: GEORGE FOR HEAVENS SAKE BE CAREFUL.

Elucidation was not long in following. He was confronted in his own hospital by Jela who accused him of carrying on a nonprofessional relationship with a *partisanka* assisting him at his operations. It turned out that her informant was the morose, mysterious girl snooper they all called Propaganda. She had, it appeared, been rummaging in a room adjoining the operating theatre in search of some balm with which to soothe her scabies when she happened to peer into the theatre and saw, she alleged, the *Engleski* doctor in close, non-professional conference with Suza.

This aroused a whole welter of emotions in George—indignation for one thing that they had accused him of one of the defections he had *not* been guilty of, anger that his own privacy could be invaded and trampled on, irritation that he should even have to answer it at all—which he did, by denying it and telling them to mind their own damn business.

That didn't go down at all well. The row spread and was taken up the hill to the partisan command on Mount Hum. It was only after high-level intervention on the Allied side and some rarely diplomatic thinking among the Jugoslav commanders that they decided on a course of moderation.

Suza was banished to the mountain of Bosnia, where Jugoslav guerillas were eluding the German columns groping into the high snows to capture the leader, Tito. She embarked tearfully in the darkness of Vis quayside on a schooner loaded with emissaries and arms for the mainland.

And George, incensed by it all to the point of incoherence, was informed that, mindful of his splendid services to the partisans, they were prepared to forgive him and overlook the matter on this occasion.

In reply George could only glare blackly and answer with blistering sarcasm: "Well, thank you *very* much."

NINE

Slowly a change began to show in the attitude of the partisans towards Rickett's British hospital. Zena's influence had a lot to do with it. Rickett's own rough wine-and-song diplomacy was working, too.

The fact that he made no apparent distinction between partisan or refugee wounded and the Commandos thawed them. Rickett was stricken by their plight. He still counted any badly wounded Jug he could politely save from the clutches of the amiable Petak as a man snatched from a dangerous ordeal.

In return, the ordinary partisans began to conspire with him to acquire equipment and the means of improving the hospital. It became almost a community aspiration. They brought wood for bedding, logs for the boiler, *rakia*, anchovies from the factory stocks, and Johnnie came frequently with delicacies from his fishing net.

Tragedy helped to weld them. The senseless minelaying continued; at isolated spots on their plateau the ground would erupt with sickening frequency, and the casualties would flow in to Rickett. When old Dr. Zon came by on his welfare visits, Rickett's partisan wounded glowed with praise for their treatment.

None of these accidents seemed to affect their careless worship of lethal weapons, even when it jeopardised the children.

On two successive days the partisans brought in a total of five child refugees, all horribly wounded from grenade accidents and a mine explosion. Two of the children, deathly white, whimpering pitifully and resenting any movement or examination with screams, had bad multiple wounds including perforated abdomens. One had a severely lacerated liver. Another, a little girl, had a fearful wound in her left thigh and most of her left hand had been blown off.

When they emerged from their operations, Rickett and his helpers spoiled them atrociously. Even the solemn Dawson clowned for them. The hospital was a gay enough place at any time, but as the badly-wounded children slowly mended, and the lustre and mischief returned to their dark eyes, their laughter made every day sound like Christmas. The place began to wear a permanent smile.

And these days, Rickett found, more of the wounded and the sick Jugoslavs arriving in the ports were diverted to Podhumlje. He hoped circumstances would never force him into making distinctions, for his prior duty, however he disguised it, lay with the Commandos.

Meantime he even had to undertake midwifery, in urgent cases, among the great flow of refugees passing through Vis on their way south to camps in Italy. Only those able to fight or to serve the fighters were detached from this stream and allowed to remain.

It was late March now, a few days after the combined Allied raid on Hvar, and Rickett still had a ward full of casualties from the ensuing bombing of Vis. From Hvar and the mainland the German *Luftwaffe* continued to treat them to a minute daily inspection, raking with machine-guns everything that moved. So assured were they in their domination of the skies here, that they even began to use the island as a practice bombing range.

The culminating outrage was that they didn't always even use live bombs, particularly if the instructing bomber was putting novice pilots through their paces. This kind of treatment aroused a positive frenzy in the swarm of men now garrisoning Vis, who augmented their pitiful ack-ack by loosing off with every gun they possessed—even pistols. Going into his operating room one morning Major Rickett was surprised by an ancient Italian Savoia bomber which came nosing round the mountain—so low that from the partisans further up the hill came an angry fusillade of fire that spattered the hospital wall and kicked up so much dust in the pathway around Rickett that he had to do a quick hotcha dance inside to safety.

Savoia-Marchetti S.M. 79

The very next day the eager Private Dodd was rumbling up to Podhumlje in a borrowed truck on his round of social visits when a growing roar behind him made him brake, look out, leap from the truck, and flatten himself desperately out on open ground. Too late he realised he was on the very patch of outcrop where a few days previously he had seen them carting off a wounded mine casualty. Private Dodd had only a split second's horrible distaste for the patch he was lying on when a great feathery whistle made him bury his head. There was a thump which shook the ground only a few yards away. He waited, but there was no explosion, only the roar of the bomber as it climbed, rejoining its parent bomber which circled offshore, watching.

Dodd raised himself, looked around, got gingerly to his feet. He came skipping like a cat on hot bricks out of the field and vaulted into the truck, and as he did so, another bomber came roaring in out of the sun. Dodd wrestled to get the truck in gear and bolted, just as a fresh missile came whistling about his ears. This time he heard the roar of an explosion. He looked hurriedly about and saw a great cloud of white dust hanging in the air.

Private Dodd came belting into the hospital in a lather of excitement and a squeal of brakes. Orderlies, officers, partisans and visitors were just collecting their rations and sitting down to eat them in the mess when Dodd burst in, his face a-shine with a story to tell. At the sight of him, Frank Clynick choked on his M. &. V. The rest, turning at Dodd's apparition, burst into roars of laughter.

Dodd was covered from head to foot in flour.

He was indignant at the hilarity. "I tell you it was bloody bombs!"

That made them laugh the more. He had been bombed with flour bags.

"No, listen! One of 'em nearly took me head off!" Dodd insisted.

So it had. One of the flour bags had hit a mine. Dodd was even more indignant when he learned the truth.

"My Gawd—what sort of a bloody war *is* this, anyway?"

He was thunderstruck with the humiliation of it all and he subsided out of sight in a chair in the darkest corner.

Among the returning Allied bombers Scottie's group sighted a puff of oily smoke in the sky, and as he got on the radio to call up the flier, the smoke materialised into a Liberator bomber. It was blazing now almost from nose to tail. No answer came from the approaching plane and they watched it come, heading for the island, doomed. As it neared the north end of the plateau a shape streamed out and a parachute opened—and the only one to escape. The plane hit the water about a mile out to sea. Scottie and his driver clambered into a jeep and whizzed off for Vis harbour.

The parachutist came down on a hillside just behind the port and not far from the road which wound up to the plain. He landed safely, disentangled himself from his harness in a dazed way, stared round, and half-staggered, half-ran, towards an old peasant woman who stood halted there in astonishment, a figure graven in black with a shawl about her grey head, staring. The flier reached her with his arms outflung now and embraced her, crying: "Mother! My mother!"

He was only a boy, his eyes glazed with shock, and he was weeping. He kept hugging the old woman fiercely and

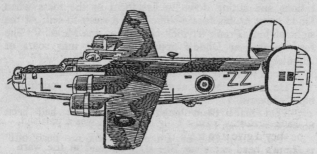

B-24 Liberator

repeating endearments. She stood bewildered, but held him too and patted him, and murmured softly in her Dalmatian dialect. She led him, hobbling now, to the edge of the road. He sat down on a stone and lit a cigarette, and he trembled.

Zena was among the first to reach him in a truck she hastily commandeered in Vis. The young airman turned a blank face to her as she came up, took his limp hand, and congratulated him on being alive.

Zena said: "I will show you where to go."

The boy turned a dazed inquiry to the old peasant soul, still holding her hand, and as Zena motioned him to climb into the truck, he clung desperately to the old woman, shaking his head wildly. His face contorted with weeping like a child's, and he cried with bitter despair: "Mother . . . !"

The old woman soothed him with a gentle enveloping embrace, stroking him, murmuring her alien endearments, and led him to Zena's truck.

Scottie and his party arrived.

"What's the old lady saying?" Scottie asked.

"She's saying: 'My son. My son!' " Zena said.

They brought the boy into Rickett, who gave him a sedative. At his thanks Rickett grinned. "We got it out of one of your own bombers," he said.

He examined the boy's ankle. It had swollen greatly and was hurting. He felt it but could not determine whether any bones were broken.

He had had scores of ankle cases from the rocky, trackless parts of the island and they were maddening. One could never tell the extent of the damage without an X-ray. That alone often meant posting injured Commandos all the way back to Italy for a check.

Rickett said to Zena: "If only I could *see* what was wrong with these cases. Now, if you could dig me up an X-ray—"

"Why don't you ask them in Italy?" Zena said. "You British have everything, haven't you?"

Rickett couldn't resist a dig back. "If I was a partisan, maybe they'd give it to me."

Zena's head came up. She stared round at the ward full of partisan wounded and sick. "But you *are* a partisan!" she stormed. And at Rickett's shrug: *"I* will find you an X-ray machine. You wait! *I* will find you one!"

She swept out very angrily. Of course Rickett could not take Zena's vow seriously. Her chances of finding him an X-ray machine in this hole were nil.

Her promise seemed even less likely to be fulfilled when an inkling came that Zena, too, might soon be transferred to Bosnia. Major Rogers, a New Zealand surgeon, had flown to work with the guerillas in the interior and he had stipulated that they give him Zena as his anaesthetist, nurse and interpreter.

But whether she stayed on Vis or not, Zena had decided it was time to complete her own personal preparations to meet the Germans. She persuaded the Commandos to give her a supply of grenades. Between spells of work with George and asking around the island for an X-ray machine, she spent some time in assiduous practice, throwing her grenades at imaginary Germans hiding behind the rocks on the hilly terraces which reared behind Vis harbour.

She returned from one of these practices livid with rage. "You fool!" she screeched at the Commando officer. "What sort of a joke is this to play?" And she held out a grenade.

"What's wrong?"

"You took the insides out of these grenades! That's what's *wrong!*"

The Commando officer managed a sheepish grin and hung his head, which taunted Zena to fresh anger.

"Did you think I wanted to *play* with these? What if I had thrown this at a German—and it hadn't worked? You want me to look *that* foolish?"

"I say!" the Commando protested. "Steady, Zena!" And then, rubbing his chin: "How did you find out?"

Zena's scorn reached thunderous heights. "You stupid man! I want to know how my bombs work! I opened them to see!"

In spite of the convenience of George's hospital to the quays where the schooners unshipped the wounded, Vis harbour was no place for a hospital.

The *Luftwaffe* was not long in demonstrating this. It tired of its practice runs and abruptly launched a heavy night raid on the little waterfront village which lay in a corner of the landlocked bay facing Hvar.

This time they all but flattened the place, hitting the bakery, a sardine cannery and a score of partisan billets.

Against all the stand-to Zena had undressed. She lay in a nightdress in her upstairs bed, unmoved by the example of the punishment meted out to a girl hospital helper who got into trouble simply for removing her shoes during the invasion alert.

Somewhat more prudently, George hopped downstairs to shelter under the staircase, for the bombs were raining around them; the screams of metal and the deafening blasts which shook the old house were terrifying. Cookie, who was already in the shelter when George got there, added to the din by setting up a screeching—but George, ever concerned about Zena, called up the stairs and implored her to come down.

"Why should I?" Zena sang back serenely. "I am sure the bombs will hit *you*, not me."

It was only when George threatened to come upstairs after her that Zena agreed to take shelter too, and came down shivering in a nightie which hung loosely on her thin body. George wrapped his overcoat round her and the three of them huddled together, awed by the sheer intensity of the noise, and the destruction falling all about them. In a lull they heard the shouting and the screaming from the houses nearby.

George hung his head. "I'm afraid there's going to be a lot of work for us," he said.

With a great whistle and an immediate explosion that filled their world with light and noise, a bomb burst on the quay outside, rocking the villa and shaking them in their shelter under the stairs with earthquake violence. Cookie huddled close to George and began to scream and wail again, to Zena's intense disgust.

"You are so stupid, Cookie. Is it better to die in bed of a terrible illness than a bomb? Or old age?"

"That's right!" Cookie wailed. "We must even quarrel when we are about to die! You have no nerves! You take my flowers off the table and you interfere in my kitchen and you don't care if we die! I will not work any more with you!" And she wept heartbrokenly.

She was still weeping when the other two realised that suddenly the bombing had all stopped. There was a banging at the door and George got up stiffly to admit a partisan orderly. One look at his face was enough to tell them that there was indeed work to do.

As they put on their coats and went, Cookie howled after them not to leave her alone. They could still hear her wailing as they picked their way along the rubble-strewn quayside.

The hospital itself had been hit. They were all night bringing in the wounded out of the debris of the houses. Bomb-blast cases with their lungs crushed and their eardrums shattered, traumatic amputations, repairs to faces and bodies rent with multiple bomb fragments, shattered limbs, head surgery, concussion . . .

Dr. Zon toured the village, rallying and directing the stretcher bearers. Some of the wounded he diverted up to Rickett's hospital, while in the theatre at Vis George Lloyd Roberts worked straight on through the night, all the following day and on into the next evening.

They found Old Joe, a frail old Americanised Jug who sometimes interpreted for George and followed him devotedly, under the rubble of the hospital, which a bomb had partially wrecked. Joe's chest was crushed and his lungs were full of blood. He awoke sufficiently to pass George the flicker of a smile.

Once George had asked Joe why he had come back to the Dalmatian islands after living so long in America, where he had worked all his grown life as a meat packer, a salesman, and in a dozen other jobs.

Joe had grinned and answered laconically, in the broad Yankee he had learned: "Well, it's okay for the dough, but it ain't no place to die."

They made him as comfortable as they could, but eighteen hours later Zena called George to him. He cradled the old man in his arms while Joe died.

There was no pause to eat, or even think of it. They only snatched enough time between operations to sip hot tea. After twenty-four hours Jim Rickett was through his major casualties and came down from Podhumlje to lend a hand. They were still operating and cleaning up nearly forty-eight hours afterwards. At any rate, it was getting dark on the second day when George finally submitted to the urgings of an English officer, Captain Barrett, to stop, and eat and rest. He allowed himself to be led away to the Allied Mission H.Q. in a bomb-scarred villa further along the harbour front. But Zena refused.

"I am so very tired," she said heavily.

George patted her. "Get some sleep, old thing," he said. "The others can manage for a while."

Zena was hardly asleep before a voice woke her. It was her husband. Dr. Zon said gently in the darkness: "The schooner is here, my dear. They are waiting for you."

Zena struggled up through a deep weariness to manage—"for me . . . ?"

"You are to go to Bosnia."

Zena moaned. She managed to summon words from her drowsy exhaustion. Slowly she said: "I cannot. Later. I will go by plane, tell them."

"You have to go. Don't make it any harder for me—please."

That edge to his voice made her wake up. A candle flickered on Dr. Zon's face. There were tears in his eyes, and she saw how tired and fragile he looked. His was the care of receiving and sorting all the sick and wounded along the whole coast. Delicate as he was, he had worked demoniacally through the raid and its aftermath. And now she, his wife, was under orders to join the partisans in Bosnia. Milo Zon loved her and was terrified for her on the awful trip by sea and by foot which lay ahead, and his anguish all but robbed him of words.

Zena got up, weeping strangely out of an infinite tiredness, and dressed.

At the quayside the schooner was a dark tangle of rigging under a luminous spread of cloud, and George was there, his handsome face a bewildered mask.

Very softly—for her—she said: "You are such a big man to cry."

All George said was: "I know. Why are they taking you away? Why?"

Zena said to her husband: "Take care of George. He is such a good boy." She might have been saying, *take care of our son*. She was frightened for his youth, his intense idealism, his vulnerability to hurt. It had made her fierce on his behalf.

The tall frame of Major Rickett loomed out of the darkness. He grinned down at her and said, in that strange way he had of being hearty, yet infinitely gentle: "God bless you, Zena. Be a good girl."

His appearance saved her from the desperately maudlin impasse which threatened, and she plucked up some spirit. "Ah! You are thinking you will not get the X-ray I promised, aren't you?" she rasped. "Well, you will have a surprise!"

"*I* believe you Zena," Rickett said with an air of mild injury.

"You will get a new assistant," she told George. "Milo will see to it. It is Lalla. She has been learning nursing and also English."

All this tidying up behind her seemed very much like making her will. Amid the shouting on the quay the sailors casting the schooner off were yelling for Comrade Zena to come aboard. She embraced Milo and George, and their tears made her cry too. George caught her arm. He could not believe she could be leaving him. "Why are they taking you?" he repeated.

She touched his young face. "Ah, you are so nice," she said, and turned and stepped into the boat.

At last the air raids on Vis forced George Lloyd Roberts to seek safer ground for his patients, and he moved up on to the plateau to a couple of cottages half a mile from Podhumlje. George and Jim Rickett christened

the new place the "Juggery". It enabled them to work
together even more closely now, and take in each other's
washing when the need arose.

George's new helper, the girl Lalla, was quiet, from a
cultured family, and dedicated. She had bright red hair
and enormous eyes. Lalla was shy of answering in English,
which she had been studying, out of a self-conscious
dislike for making mistakes. But she astonished Roberts
and Rickett when she did. For she spoke it exceptionally
well.

One of the fruits of a recent visit by a medical V.I.P.,
Colonel Penman, to investigate the situation on Vis, had
been, of all things, the surprise arrival of a whole crate of
warm sheepskin jackets. They were thankful for whatever
mercies the authorities back in Italy vouchsafed them,
and they donned these gladly. Those left over they divided
among their delighted Jug helpers, and in this way Lalla
acquired one; and though it was many sizes too large for
her, she was warm for the first time that winter.

About a week after this Rickett noticed that a loutish
commissar was wearing one of these prized sheepskin
jackets. He asked where the man had got it. Lalla
shrugged and said she had given it up.

It turned out that the commissar, coveting it, had
ordered her to hand it over. Which she had meekly
done.

There was Little Rickett or George could do, except
bide their time. But their turn did come. There came a day
when the commissar reported sick. Rickett was with
George. They held a grave consultation over him.

"I'm afraid this means hospital," George told him.

"You'll have to be shipped to Italy for your treatment," Rickett said.

They divested him of his jacket, which they returned
to Lalla, and put him into a set of rough hospital clothes.
A schooner was going to Italy and they put him aboard
this, neatly labelled and tabulated with his ailment.

"Let 'em work this one out in Bari," Rickett said, and
finished filling out their diagnosis. They clipped it to the
commissar's vest. It read: *Tabes Dorsalis.* *

Under her shy exterior, Lalla was avid for the drama

---

*Tertiary syphilis.

of major surgical work, and after venturing at first to be present at a few minor operations down at Vis, she had plucked up courage to ask permission to see the English doctors at work on an important case.

Accordingly, George had let her come in while he worked to save the life of a partisan who had been brought in with a bad abdominal wound. In a skirmish in the hinterland rising from Split he had been hit by a German bullet and they had brought him across to Vis.

The patient was very weak from four days' gruelling journey at night. Considering the risks the partisans took to bring their wounded out to comparative safety, the callousness with which they handled them was extraordinary. They carried them hammock-fashion in blankets, and dumped them with scant ceremony on the ground whenever a halt was made. It was rare to hear any of these dour, stubby guerillas complain. They knew the immense physical risks their comrades had taken to bring them through and they accepted suffering with remarkable stoicism. The Jugoslav doctors feared typhus among the fighting ranks—perhaps with reason—more than anything the Germans could do, and early in the garrisoning of Vis their orders went out that no casualties could be brought into their hospitals until they had been deloused. This was all very well, but when a casualty was in a bad way it was no picnic for him to be stripped and put under a cold shower with, say, a belly wound. George Lloyd Roberts was at pains to convey his views that this was taking public health a bit far.

With the same lack of ceremony two Jug orderlies brought in their belly-wound case. They hoisted him on the operating table with such scant disregard for his weakness, that the man's respiration almost ceased there and then.

Lalla slipped into their theatre, and her excitement and awe were evident as she stood pressed against the wall, watching, while Frank Clynick administered the anaesthetic. Jim Rickett had come to assist. As George incised and explored, Rickett clipped off the blood vessels and held the forceps while George tied off the bleeding points. In spite of Rickett's evident seniority and experience there was only a polite awareness that this was George's hospital and that it was he who was performing the operation. There was about them a punctilio and a calm interest as the exploration revealed the blood lying free in the peritoneal cavity and as portions of damaged gut were examined and repaired. Lalla watched them suture the perforations, murmuring among themselvs, returning the injured parts to their place with infinite care—and finally set about closing the abdomen.

In ninety minutes it was over. George called for Lubo and Johnnie, signed for them to take the sick man back to the shed which served as a ward. He warned them with threats of murder to be gentle, and their eyes rolled happily as they bore the patient off on a stretcher. The doctors took off their masks and had tea. Rickett motioned Lalla to a seat and poured her a cup.

After a while Lalla took courage from the tea, prepared her English phrase carefully, and said: "Do you believe that he will live?"

Rickett looked at her and smiled. He shrugged faintly. He didn't want to say yes or no, but in his smile there was strength and wordless hope. She put down the tea and walked outside, but before she could get to her bed the tears came and she leaned weakly against the wall, sobbing with happiness.

She had seen a life saved. She had seen it!

There was great activity up on the plateau now. The urgent build-up of force and equipment on Vis was beginning to tell. One morning they awoke to find an Artillery Battery had moved in, and some anti-aircraft guns. Spitfires were beginning to use the red earth strip, where the vines had already been cleared, for refuelling and as a forward reconnaissance base. A U.S. construction unit, after stubborn opposition from the partisan leaders had at length been broken down, was now clearing further vines to make landing room for the crippled Liberators which hitherto had only found graves in the sea or against the mountain.

The runway was still perilously short when a twin-fuselaged Lightning appeared in the sky, returning from a reconnaissance flight over Austrian territory, and came on the radio with news of engine trouble. Scottie talked him down and he came in over the harbour, misfiring badly, skimming the hillocks at the northern end of the plateau.

P-38 Lightning

The pilot furrowed the earth with the fury of his braking, ending almost on his nose overlooking the vine rows at the extreme limits of the runway. The shower of earth which accompanied his landing had hardly subsided when he was out of the plane and urging the mechanics who swarmed round it: "Just get me into that sky again. I got some hot pix to take back home."

The pilot was Chinese—or at least, Chinese-American. Apart from the incongruity of his accent he looked as if he had strayed way off course from a mission over Hankow. The R.A.F. mechanics looked inside his Lightning and came over to him, shaking their heads dubiously. His engine would take a long while to fix.

"*How* long?" he said.

"Three or four hours, mate, maybe more—to do a proper job."

"Are you kidding, a proper job? Just do what it takes to get me up in the sky. There's a lot of guys back in Italy waiting for me to show."

They went to work. At the same time a squad of partisans set to, furiously ripping up their precious vines and stamping the ground to give him a few extra yards of runway.

Under the pilot's impatient goading, the flight mechanics had his port engine running in two hours, though raggedly. They pleaded with him for an extra hour's work on it. But the reconnaissance pilot shouldered his way past them, pitched away his cigarette, and began climbing in.

"Nothing doing! There's a big raid going out tonight. They want to see what I've got before they take off. Thanks anyhow." He saluted and his almond eyes quite disappeared in an engaging farewell grin.

A big crowd of partisans had assembled at the end of the runway—with their usual disregard for safety. Their airstrip was still only day old, and this Lightning was the first twin-fuselage plane many of them had seen.

The Lightning roared and was in the air quite soon, climbing—but too steeply, it seemed, and suddenly its engine spluttered, cut. It turned on one wing and nose-dived, falling among the partisans. It exploded in a great blossoming of yellow flame as soon as it hit the earth.

Somehow the pilot was half-dragged, half-stumbled clear of the wreckage, alight all over, terribly burned. A fresh explosion spat gouts of burning petrol everywhere and set fire to the ground itself. Fifteen partisan dead and dying lay around, and more were crawling away, their heads and hands livid with burns, beating out their smoking clothes, rolling on the ground to put out the flames.

The hospital had been quiet and then suddenly it was full of burns cases coming in on stretchers and blankets. The Chinese pilot was brought in. He had scarcely any face left and his hands were red stumps.

They carried him in to Rickett, unseeing but conscious. From the tortured slash that was his mouth, his voice came faintly with his breath. "Can't see a thing. Can't see . . ."

Jim Rickett put a hand each side of his chest and said, low but cheerful: "Don't you worry old chap. We'll have you seeing in no time at all."

"You a doc?" It was hard to believe the voice, faint though it was, came from this man.

"We're just taking you in to tidy up your face."

The head nodded wearily. "Say, doc, you got a camera?"

"Why?"

"I'd like you—to take a photograph of me—you know—before you operate—" The words were coming raggedly now.

Rickett and the others stared. Then Rickett said conversationally, as though this were most natural: "Hard luck. Afraid we've no cameras here." He nodded to Dawson, and they took him up the stone steps and into the operating theatre.

As soon as the pentothal took effect they had plasma going and Rickett went to work gently cleansing the face with sterile saline. But oedema—the swelling from reaction—had begun already and was obstructing his breathing. He was soon fighting to fill his lungs. His tongue was also swelling and his skin was turning a dark blue colour of cyanosis from lack of oxygen. There was no oxygen to administer. Like penicillin it was not, presumably, an expendable store.

Rickett paused in the cleansing and immediately he did so, Dawson had the scalpel slap in his hand. He incised the trachea just below the Adam's apple. They had no proper tracheotomy set, but there was some rubber tubing used for plasma drip and Rickett cut a piece of this and inserted it through the incision in the throat so that he would have an air entry. He passed another length of tubing through his mouth into his stomach, for they would have to feed him.

Then they had to pause to give the pilot artificial respiration. That got him breathing properly so that Clynick could go on administering more anaesthetic.

Rickett cut away the dead skin, the charred remnants of his flying helmet and clothes, cleaning the great raw burned surfaces with saline, dusting it all with sulpha powder. He dressed it with a lot of padding to absorb the exudate. The best way to keep this protected and in place was with plaster of paris. The man could not speak, see or swallow. Communication with him was going to be limited. When the plaster was on, Rickett cut away an area of plaster over the ear so that the orderlies nursing him could warn him when they proposed to pour nourishment down the stomach tube.

He only hoped nobody would be clumsy enough to pour it into the breathing tube by mistake. The tubes were the same size, cut from the same length.

The next morning the pilot was conscious but entirely isolated and inscrutable in the diver's helmet of plaster. Rickett watched while an orderly spoke loudly through the orifice over his ear, saying: "Watch it, mate. Drop of soup coming up." The head seemed to move faintly. The orderly poured gently into the tube with a funnel.

After two or three days the drill became automatic. A light tap on the plaster; an announcement, loud but firmly cheerful of a liquid meal on the way. A hand, some kind of company and reassurance, briefly on his chest. The man could not even nod, but once he gladdened them with a weak raising of a hand.

There was much other cleaning up to do among the other burns cases.

The young girls, Anka and Filica, were blossoming into nurses in spite of their timidity. They used to stop in their bustling about the house at the door of the pilot's ward, which he shared with several partisan burns cases and two wounded sailors from an M.G.B. which had been shot up. The girls would pause there, struck by the pathos and solitude of the silent figure encased in plaster. They surprised the orderlies by taking over their jobs from them, and took turns in feeding him.

The difference in the partisan troops swarming on the island was growing clearer every day. With equipment now flowing to them more easily, most of them were wearing smart British or American uniforms and boots. They drilled briskly and with gusto. But nothing could lessen their instinctive greed for supplies, born perhaps of a long starvation. The habit of hunger and the desperate acquisitive provision for the morrow which it imposes are hard to lose. It meant that Rickett had to fight and scheme almost as much as ever for medical supplies from the partisan command. They went on shamelessly pillaging the crates which the *Prodigal* and other small craft dumped at night on the quay at Komisa.

The motley fleet now plying between Vis and the Italian mainland presented the Allies with a problem to which there was no really tactful solution.

The more partisan schooners they filled with arms and special supplies, the more ambitious grew the Jugoslav demands. From being pathetically short of everything, fighting a well-equipped and ruthless foe almost barehanded, the Jugs, like children under a sudden willing deluge of good things, grew insatiably demanding. Each new delivery of equipment now pouring into Vis they greeted, not simply with scant gratitude and a total unawareness of the

difficulties of supply, but, in return, with new and staggering demands.

The aplomb with which they did this began to annoy
their Allied contacts.

Moreover, this fleet of schooners and fishing vessels
gun-running from Italy brought every kind of threat to
Allied security. Manned by crews of Balkan seafarers of
every racial shading and political hue, and rarely carrying
credentials, their boats nevertheless expected simply to
berth at any Adriatic seaport below the German line and
to have the holds immediately filled with machine guns,
ammunition, petrol, clothing and food. The Allies had to
check every boat for enemy agents shipping on espionage
trips or even taking supplies for delivery to the Germans
themselves.

The culminating irritation to ordinary fighting men
was that, knowing the story of sweat, sacrifice, shortages,
sinkings and strained communications that lay behind the
delivery of much of this material, and expecting partisans
of all people to retain a healthy sense of the value of these
things, it was galling to be taunted by many a cheerful
villain flourishing a British weapon, pointing to the hammer and sickle emblem which already blotted out its real
origin, and lecturing them crudely by means of dumb
crambo and pidgin: "Hey, *tovarich*—Stalin *dobro*, eh?
Zivio Stalin!" And as often as not, gleefully firing a British
round into the air to emphasise his point.

At this time, to add further point to the irritation, the
Russians were supplying nothing but a stream of political
orders, not all of them calculated to ease the Anglo-
American burden. Many a hot retort to these ingenuous
Jug provocations fizzled out helplessly, for want of a
common language, in a waving of arms and a resort to
disgusted abuse: "Agh, go and get fog-bound, you ignorant
pack of ——s!"

But if disaffection sometimes rippled below the sur-
face on Vis, much came from the high tension of finding
themselves suddenly face to face with possible annihilation, shoulder to shoulder with strangers from a totally
different kind of war. Here they were all cooped up on a
rock from which there was to be no escape; bare, stony,
victualled almost entirely by sea—even to their water—

and with plenty of scope for getting on each other's nerves. The only natural abundance was of wine. Excusably, and for relief, they drank a lot of it.

Many reservations melted in the fierceness of ensuing battles together against a common enemy. The pettier differences vanished. They were to discover, grudgingly but without mistake, the qualities of each other, the spirit, the sudden endearing gaiety and individualism of the private soldier—Tommy or Jug. But it had to be owned that there would always be material for friction in so alien a pairing of forces, disciplined by such strangely different ideologies and only banded together, uneasily, by a caprice of politics.

Things were different at the hospital, where Jugs and Commandos lay in neighbouring beds. Among the helpless there grew a *camaraderie* far more intimate, even, than they could find in battle. From bed to bed they helped each other, fetching one another's rations, spoon-feeding the very sick, getting the convalescents to their feet and walking them about, bringing bedpans and urinals at need. The mess and its piano was barred to no-one. After dinner, if there were no operations, Rickett and George would find themselves hosting an incredible mixture of guests— American fliers and liaison personnel; Commando and occasional Navy visitors seeking some light relief from the incessant bombing of their billets down in the harbours; Dawson, Heron and his men, Lalla and the girl helpers who were enrolled as dance partners—Jugoslav style—to teach them the *kolo* and other national dances.

The floor shook under their feet as they joined hands and clumped about, grinning and yelling, in the naïve folkloristic patterns of the dance. Even the dark, grave commissars who looked in on the hospital on the pretext of a welfare tour, allowed themselves to be drawn into the gaiety, drifting closer to the piano, tippling solemnly with hilarious convalescents, orderlies, officers—and even unbending sufficiently to warble a partisan song or two.

One evening, having dealt with all the day's surgical cases, Rickett was organising the whoopee and leading their strange nightly motley in a rowdy jig when he caught the quizzical eye of Admiral Sir Walter Cowan on him. Rickett opted out of the dance and came to welcome him with a mug of wine. The old admiral accepted it with a nod, and surveyed the scene with a slow astonished wagging of his head. His stare pierced Rickett.

"You are a hoodlum, Rickett."

"Indeed I am, sir."

"How do you get 'em all eating out of your hand? You speak the language?"

"Well, sir," said Rickett, who had amassed about five words of Jug, "I am a hoodlum, as you say—"

He surveyed the orgy with quiet pride. "And I think I speak the language . . ."

On the fifth day after the Lightning crash little Anka came skipping into the ward, having plundered a bowl of thin soup from the orderly to take to the Chinese pilot. She marched up to him, leaned over, tapped lightly on his plaster skull and carolled one of the few English words she had learned.

"Soup?"

There was no answering sign. Anka tapped again and put her full lips close to the opening over the ear. "Soup?" she inquired again.

Then she noticed the stillness and knew. There was no flutter-and-hiss from the lower tube. The breathing had stopped.

He was dead.

Unseeing and almost unhearing, inscrutable and wordless inside the thick plaster dome, he had died the loneliest death of all.

TEN

The armed trawler *Prodigal* always brought a very mixed cargo to Vis. It brought something unthought-of—mail.

Rickett's first letter from his wife was a shock. Wives have their own intelligence service, and in spite of the heavy secrecy which cloaked every movement to Vis, Dorothy wrote: "Darling, I do hope you are having a lovely time on the island of Lissa . . ."*

The guilty thought occurred to him that if Dorothy knew that, she probably also knew he had donated all his winter underwear to Lovro and his squad of Jugs.

She and the children had moved back from the Island of Mull to their cottage at Stoughton, just out of Portsmouth. The bombing at home was plainly much in the past.

The *Prodigal* also landed a deputation from among its own crew. They came up the hill in a truck and paid a formal call on Major Rickett. He received them with the customary hospitality. He also noticed they had the goat with them. It had grown considerably and, having thus far managed to avoid being turned into stew, looked very pleased with life.

The deputation from *Prodigal* brought fresh news of strife down at the port. Two sailors there had nearly been lynched by infuriated partisans for teaming up with a couple of partisan girls. Indeed, they had only escaped thanks to the intervention of the Senior Naval Officer, Lieutenant-Commander Morgan Giles, with an assurance to the partisans that he would see to it that the men were

---

*English alternative map-name for Vis.

punished. Reluctantly they yielded them up. It was fortunate they had no inkling that British naval discipline took a somewhat more indulgent view of a sailor's love-life. The sailors were banished to Italy under heavy guard—ostensibly to be shot.

Rickett bethought himself of the romantic and sociable Private Dodd and wondered how, with his charming glibness, he would talk himself out of such a situation.

As the *Prodigal* party was leaving, its leader hesitated. Obviously he had something on his chest. He hemmed and hawed and eventually came to the point.

"It's this goat, sir . . ."

"If he gets any fatter," Rickett said, "there'll be enough on him to feed a battleship."

"Well, sir, fact is—we've made rather a pet of him. Nobody's got the, ah, well, heart, to knock him on the head and skin him . . ."

Rickett stifled a wild impulse to mirth and congratulated them gravely on their humanity.

"Well, sir, we were wondering—if you'd mind taking him back? I mean, well, it's not much of a life for a goat, is it—staggering round on a trawler?"

"It'll be a damned sight worse for him if Dawson ever gets hold of him," Rickett said. "However, if you're worried about the R.S.P.C.A. . . ."

And he took it back. No sooner was the naval jeep chuffing out of sight than he reeled inside, guffawing, and collapsed in a chair. Frank Clynick found him there a little while later, still grinning and wiping his eyes.

"I don't know what the Navy's coming to. Really I don't," Rickett said.

"What's up, Jimmy?"

"Don't tell me," said Rickett, "that sailors don't care."

The Americans were represented on Vis by a token force of Rangers, who took part in some of the combined Commando-partisan strikes at the Germans—now thoroughly roused to the defensive and still grouping amid inexplicable delay to put an end to the nuisance on Vis.

The American liaison officer was an amiable veteran of World War I, Major Reeves, who was mayor of a town called Pepak and who believed that the social aspect of liaison was as important as the military one. Accordingly he consumed a lot of wine at the hospital in the line of duty. Rickett had occasion to ring him up once on the field telephone after one of Reeves's nocturnal visits—and the phone was answered by a tired voice which said: "The late Major Reeves speaking . . ."

They saw little of the other Americans, who kept largely to themselves. While Rickett and the others were pounding biscuits and putting condensed milk on them in a forlorn attempt to simulate breakfast porridge, the Americans, small as their unit was, were enveloped in every kind of comfort including fresh bread, ice-cream, even a cinema.

But Rickett had occasion to make the acquaintance of one of their leaders, Captain Rogers of the U.S. Operations Group. He was a Texan who toted a revolver with which he could make a lightning "draw." This, he said, was taught to him by a grandfather who had fought the Indians. Rogers drew up outside the hospital in a U.S. Army truck, came in to Rickett and said, jerking a thumb outside at the truck: "Say, doc, come and have a look at this, will you?"

Rickett dropped what he was doing and allowed himself to be led out to the back of the truck. He looked in . . . A man lay in the back. Rickett examined him briefly.

"This man's dead," he said.

"I know. He got loaded last night on this Jug hog-wash."

"What do you want me to do about it?"

"Well, it's this way—maybe he died from this hooch, or maybe he died in the line of duty, from something else. It makes a few thousand dollars' worth of difference to his widow's pension. We've got to find out."

"I can't help you," said Rickett, and pulled a blanket over the dead man.

"We figured if you did a autopsy on him, maybe you could tell us what he died of."

"Not with *my* instruments. I haven't got that many that I can use them on a corpse. Sorry, Captain."

The American Captain departed, grumbling over Rickett's advice to ship the body back to the American

base hospital at Bari in Italy. Rogers toured the whole
island trying to find a passage for it. Finally he located a
partisan schooner which admitted it was leaving for Italy,
and he bribed them to take the body with them.

But the cold north wind called the Bora rose that day.
Soon Vis was being lashed by its blast which swept directly
down from the peaks of the Dinaric Alps. Great waves
boomed against the rocks and invaded the inlets, where the
little schooners hurriedly made fast—the schooner acting
as hearse included—until the Bora blew itself out. It was
this regular scourging of the Adriatic by the Bora which
immobilised shipping and made contact between the island
and Italy imponderable, often for days on end.

On this occasion the Bora blew for four days, and
while it raged no boat ventured out from Vis. Long before
it ended, however, the seamen on the schooner rebelled at
keeping a corpse on board. Komisa harbour authorities
persuaded the Royal Navy to transfer the body aboard the
long-suffering *Prodigal*.

By this time the body had not only become a play-
thing of the authorities, but it had also begun to smell
rather badly. It was with some disgust, then, in addition to
deep misgiving, that the naval crew received it aboard the
trawler. Burial at sea is the naval custom, rooted as much
in an instinct for tidiness as anything else, and it had given
rise to a profound superstition against carrying dead bodies.

The *Prodigal* left, shrouded in deepest gloom, as soon
as the Bora permitted.

It arrived safely enough at Bari next day, but in their
hurry to get the corpse ashore the sailors fumbled it and
dropped it into the harbour. They launched a small boat
and fished around in the oil-slicked, refuse-strewn waters
for it with boathooks for hours before locating it and
getting it back on board. In this state they finally delivered
it to the dead man's compatriots in Bari.

When word of all this reached Rickett, he paused in
his work, passed a hand over his forehead and wondered
aloud what comments the American pathologist had on
receiving a corpse, obviously dead from drink, somewhat
the worse for a dive into the slime at the bottom of Bari
harbour—and roughly five days old.

But they did hold their own post mortem on it in Rickett's hospital after all—verbally, over the usual drink before what passed for dinner.

"I reckon he was entitled to be written off as dying in the line of duty," Dawson said, "after all that lot."

He had a better right to it than some men had to the Purple Heart, according to Rickett. He said: "When I was in Algiers the Americans sent us a *pro forma* asking about all those who had been wounded, because they were going to be awarded the Purple Heart, irrespective of what service they were in."

For a moment Rickett's wickedness shone through, and he masked it by raising his wine mug.

"Well, we prepared it very conscientiously and eventually any fellow who sprained his ankle coming off a boat or contracted V.D. down in one of the native brothels was entered down as eligible.

"I took a picture of Eisenhower arriving at the *Lycée* there to award the Purple Heart to all these brave fellows, pinning it on their breasts and shaking them by the hand, with all the British craning out of the windows and cheering like mad.

"It was a beautiful medal, too. They were flogging them at seven-and-sixpence a head an hour after Ike had gone."

ELEVEN

One morning Captain Rickett woke in his little bivouac tent to a lovely dawn, stirred and peeped out for his usual view of the rosy Alps over on the mainland. A dark shape swooped through his tent and went winging over the rocks. At that the swallows rose all around him and took the air, streaking northward again like arrows.

There was a dew. It lay on the leaves of the blue gentians that now carpeted the slopes, and it winked in the rising sun under the nodding heads of cyclamen. The rock roses were showing buds and the colour spread visibly every day. The swallows were coming up from the Aegean, following the line of the coast and resting on the islands before flying on into the heart of Europe—perhaps on to England, for all he knew.

And with it all, the coming of spring, the war was changing. A new mood was spreading—at least across this island.

They were beginning to feel safer, perhaps. No lines had shifted. The Germans were still across that contented strait of pale turquoise which deepened lyrically to green as the light grew. Smoke rose here and there over on Hvar—fires. Breakfast, no doubt. Acorn coffee, black bread, tinned pork, jam for the German officers?

It was impossible not to be lulled, to feel safer, as long as they withheld their blow. And yet surely it must come? Could they allow the British this impertinence, roosting right under their noses, using the place to plunder their ships, kidnap their crews, as they were now doing almost every night?

In addition to the pugnacious Commando strikes with their varying tolls of wounded trickling back into the hospital, the accent of naval action around Vis had changed—from escort duty and anti-invasion patrolling back to one of purest piracy. Morgan Giles, Senior Naval Officer on Vis, tall, blond, as splendidly handsome as any fictional image of a naval hero, was the chief instigator of this nightly plunder. And his most redoubtable henchman was a bearded Canadian, Lieutenant-Commander Tom Fuller, who, at the head of the young men issuing forth in their M.T.B.'s and M.G.B.'s at night, had pioneered a audacious new technique of accosting enemy shipping. In the first week of April they had already captured eight German ships and sunk three more.

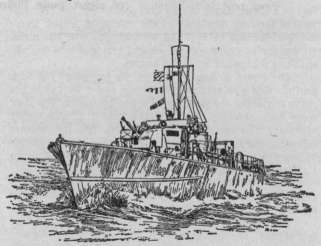

M.G.B.

Fuller's method was bold and fantastically effective. Lying in wait in a motor torpedo boat in the shadow of an island, and with a motor gun-boat for company, Fuller and his men would wait in absolute silence until they heard the approach of an enemy convoy. As soon as they could perceive it the motor gun-boat would roar out of hiding, put the helm hard over, and proceed down the line of enemy ships, spraying one after another with the fire of all its guns—while Fuller, issuing out in the M.T.B., raced to the nearest enemy vessel and crashed his craft alongside.

Yelling and flourishing Sten guns, he and his party would leap across and board her. In this way they captured, first a schooner carrying grain—after a brief passage at arms with a dazed crew. They put her in tow and brought her back in triumph to Vis.

The next night they bagged two more schooners in the same way and brought them in under tow, with the Messerschmitts out furiously beating the place for them at first light—fruitlessly. Other boats of Morgan Giles's flotilla took a leaf out of Fuller's book and were soon busily hauling in German convoy craft loaded with foodstuffs and adding them to the sizable prize fleet in Vis.

Fired now with ambition for bigger game Fuller tackled a big 400-tonner, the schooner *Libecchio,* off an island fifty-two miles away from the shelter of their hideout in Vis. It was an arduous haul from so far away, but he brought her in proudly, intact.

A brisk rivalry developed among these buccaneers in their small warships. It was fitting that the cheery Fuller held the record. His crew boasted that their time—twelve minutes—taken to board, subdue and put an enemy vessel in tow and under way, was the fastest achieved by any of them.

Many of these boarding parties were made up of Commandos, and Fuller and his colleagues made free and profitable use of loud-hailers through which they roared gruesome warnings in German and Italian to soften up the enemy before they came aboard.

The partisan seamen had also been performing with a dash and a courage which, with their creaking fleet, bordered on the foolhardy. They armoured their schooners in their small shipyard down in Komisa by fitting double gunwales and filling them in between with concrete. Others were sandbagged. All were armed to the teeth with captured Axis guns. They were slow but none the less dreaded in the ambushes they set, and when the Royal Navy arrived they found that these fierce bravoes who came swooping aboard the enemy boats out of darkness with a roar of artillery and small arms already enjoyed a reputation as fearsome as any desperado in the days of their forefathers, who terrorised the proud fleets of merchant Venice.

There were signs that their depredations, combined with the meal the Royal Navy was making of their vessels, now had the Germans thoroughly rattled.

It had not been achieved entirely without cost. On sea, the war was equally desperate and quite lacking in ceremony. If any boat failed to answer the recognition signal double-quick, they were shelled. In this way the M.G.B.'s had some brisk altercations with some of their own destroyers, in the dark. They kissed and made up afterwards, of course.

But reconciliation for these trigger-fingered clashes was not so easy when they brought their guns to bear on partisans in the darkness—and understandably. Pissy Parsons and some of his tearaways had been out on these M.G.B. patrols, and the trouble was, as he explained, that the Jugoslav boats usually had one hurricane lamp somewhere down in the hold which constituted their entire lighting and signalling equipment. When challenged, they would hold a noisy conference, and finally decide that somebody ought to climb down and fetch up the lamp to show a light—by which time British shells would be dropping around them.

In this way the Royal Navy had sunk several partisan ketches and schooners, and this had done nothing at all to improve Anglo-partisan relations. Parsons was heard to thank God for the Air Force. Unlike the Commandos or the Navy, it had no opposite number to tangle with. There simply was no Jug Air Force, unless one counted the vintage Jugoslav biplane that did occasional service as an artillery spotter on raids.

When Rickett was dispatched to Vis no provision existed to evacuate wounded. He and the meagre materials allowed to him were the only succour to the men of Vis, even for the most desperate cases. The idea was, presumably, that either they died there, and were buried, or they survived, and returned to their unit. Rickett did investigate another course—the partisan schooners in which they evacuated their refugees: but to commit the desperately wounded to the kind of berth that these provided was barely thinkable.

There was really no accommodation on these schooners for the wounded at all. Rickett first looked into their possibilities when he treated a handsome young Jugoslav girl fighter, a *partisanka,* who had taken not weeks, but eighteen months to reach them from a sabotage job in the Bosnian mountains. She had laid explosives to wreck a stretch of the Split-Zagreb railway line and a faulty fuse blew up the charges before she could get clear. She had crawled away badly wounded, and with a smashed leg. Her comrades lifted her into one of their blanket-stretchers and carried her between them back into hiding.

Wounds like she had were almost as bad as a death sentence. There were no doctors, no fighters to be spared to carry her on the long pilgrimage to safety. If she stayed where she was she would almost certainly die. Her partisan group was constantly on the move, and she could either travel with them, or lie there and await the hated Germans.

After hiding in a peasant hut for weeks she chose to find her own way out, and began one of those treks which, in the telling afterwards, was clouded with the vagueness of a procession of half-remembered nightmares. Her story had not even the distinction of being extraordinary. Hers was one of thousands of such journeys to this ultimate refuge—or to a bitter end, anonymously, at the hands of a German patrol.

Her name was Melitsa. She was twenty-five. She had come crawling down the ravines and through the woods, scavenging for food, hiding by day in hovels or caves peopled by scared but friendly peasants; begging a dish of polenta here, contacting, with luck, a partisan or resistance group there; sinking into the bliss of rest a while, then awakening roughly and scrambling for hiding before another sudden German alarm.

Often she had to crawl back the way she had come. At other times she would lie ill for weeks, starved, a scarecrow heap in the strawed corner of a barn, fevered and muttering wild nonsense, fed by a peasant wife who wanted to help but prayed for the time when she would move on and take with her the terror of vengeance from the *Chetniks,* the *Ustachi* or the Germans themselves.

It took her eighteen months of this to reach Vis. Her suffering had lent her a callous, gipsy defiance of the world, and her beauty, gaunt now and savage, had the character of an El Greco martyr.

Her leg, compound-fractured, had set partially at a

crazy angle, leaving a deep unhealed wound through which the bone still showed. The wound swarmed with maggots and the bone was infected with osteomyelitis. There was less pain after all this time, but there was only one thing to do, and that was to amputate the leg.

Under the primitive conditions of Rickett's hospital this would have been wrong, when there was a chance of getting her to a well-equipped hospital. What he had to do Rickett decided, was to open up the chronic wound and let out the pus, so that the sepsis amount should be reduced, give her a transfusion and ship her to the mainland.

But the anguish which burned deep in her eyes was not for her leg or for the other wounds, now healed. It was for something else—the thing which had urged her on all these eighteen months; the most powerful instinct of all. Melitsa wanted survival, not for herself, but for the fruit of her body. She wanted a child. It was the one dream that kept her going. She was terrified she would not be able to have one. Like many other partisan girls, she had amenorrhea, and she thought that the well of creation within her was dry. She ignored his talk of amputation for her leg and asked him many questions. Would she ever have children? Was the doctor *sure?*

Of course she would, Rickett said. He grinned at her. A round dozen, if she wanted to. Wait till there was peace again.

But Melitsa could not believe him. She could not believe that amenorrhea was psychological and part of the life they now led, that throughout the whole evolution of the human species it had happened to women in times of primitive danger, like now. Nature had thought of a law for their protection long before the partisans had.

Brief though it was, the crossing to Italy in a fishing boat would be almost as bad as any other part of her journey. The wounded either lay stretched out on the decks or were lowered through a hatch into the forward bilges where, in a space about twelve feet long where the ship's ribs tapered to the bow, the sick, the women, children and the partisan wounded lay jammed together, with a latrine bucket in the centre. An occasional match flicker revealed its infernal squalor. It stank—the kind of smell one remembered a lifetime. One dared not think what the passage would be like for these wretches if the Bora caught them.

As it was, the island's communications which depended on craft like these were constantly cut for days by the weather.

Since midwifery facilities on the island were nonexistent all civilian women, pregnant or otherwise, were likewise shipped on to Italy. All the same, Rickett had one or two birth calls from mothers too ill to be moved. One of them, lying in a cottage in complete darkness—the shutters had to be closed against the cold—gave birth to a baby shortly before she died of tuberculosis. There was much of it among the refugees. Out of the stream of these refugees another woman paused and collected the baby to take with her, on to wherever they would be going. She had lost her own child when their village was razed and in spite of their trials she was hungry to be hugging another. He remembered watching her going with the baby clasped fiercely to her in a greasy swaddle of linen. She would grow to believe it was her own; and it would most likely die, ultimately, of tubercular meningitis.

In spite of the steady refusal of base to supply them with anything they asked for, the official interest in Vis marked itself by a growing procession of brass. There was one curly youngster still resplendent in service dress and Sam Browne who had been flown out direct from War Office to have a look at the place. He stooged round whacking a swagger stick against his leg and being frightfully amiable in a drawly, tired way.

Rickett's cronies in the engineers had performed another of their innumerable services—they had blown a great pit in the back yard and installed a twin-seater latrine decorously girt with Hessian walls. The morning after he arrived the War Office wallah picked his way delicately out to this office and immured himself behind its screen. He was seated thus, enjoying the thin sunshine, when a strapping young girl *partisanka* came striding in, unbuckled and unbuttoned her clothing and baring herself to the fresh spring air, sat down beside him with a matey nod.

The young War Office envoy came tottering back a minute or so later and sank into his seat at breakfast, answering Rickett's inquiry about his health in a dazed way. Finally he mumbled something about supposing it would, ah, take one some time to get used to their unique toilet arrangements, which had so surprised him that he had all but fallen in.

"What do you mean?" Rickett asked, mashing up his biscuit porridge.

"Well, is it supposed to be for *everybody*, Major?"

"You mean," queried Rickett, innocently stupid, "we ought to have one for Officers Only?"

Another emissary came from the Foreign Office, for Force 133 and the mission established with the Titoists came under its control. As was usual, the military situation permitting, they gave him a party, which meant a binge at that now-famed social centre the hospital mess.

This young man's party was a particularly successful one and was going like a bomb by the time Rickett retired to his little bivouac tent on the hillside under the stars. The next morning it was still going in a desultory way, with several veteran partygoers still strewn about the place. That afternoon they shipped off the Foreign Office youth, incoherent with gratitude and still reeling from their hospitality, to continue his tour in Italy—where he arrived, it was reported back to them, with no recollection whatever of having ever been to Vis.

Another young Commando medical officer called Buswell turned up with a fierce moustache, baby pink cheeks and an unbounding energy. He had done rather well at the Garigliano crossing and the Churchills thought well of him, but since he had no surgery and was therefore of little use around the hospital, Rickett so contrived it that he was appointed to medical administration duties. To be rid of him one of the first jobs Rickett begged of him was to go back to Italy and hunt them out an X-ray machine. Rickett was a firm believer in the right man for the right job and he believed Buswell was born to race around and kick up a lot of dust.

In spite of Buswell's aggressive zeal he was met even in Italy with a blank refusal, but it kept him out of Rickett's hair for a while.

When Buswell turned up again on Vis he was sat

upon during a party and one side of his monstrous moustache was removed, revealing the features of a child underneath. He never got over his fury at being unmasked, and at future parties always drank prudently, with a brooding eye on those who were getting the worse for wear. When they were finally overcome with good cheer, Buswell would leap upon them and shear off a great swathe of their hair. Before long it began to look as if a strange epidemic had smitten Podhumlje. One could tell a regular partygoer by the amount of hair he had missing.

But a *camaraderie* had blossomed among them, born of a strange realisation: they were, in a sense, outlaws, cut almost entirely adrift from normal service administration —disowned. Their back door was almost shut except for food to stay alive and guns to fight with. The Commandos were inured to this cold concept of their role, but at least they had the tools for *their* trade. Rickett hadn't. They saw his need of them, and their need of each other, standing alone in this place. They were banded in an unspoken conspiracy to defeat all that withheld the things they needed—and in this the ordinary partisans, fellow-outlaws, joined Rickett's alliance.

At Podhumlje they lived on their wits. Indeed, it became almost a matter of pride to scorn any formal channel. If Rickett wanted an electrician any time of the day or night, the engineers and the little R.A.F. unit would send men running. The old base slogan, *It's not my pigeon, old man,* became the funniest slogan on the island. It was the engineers who installed hot water, bricked in stairs to give direct stretcher access to the operating theatre, coaxed life out of the generator, which in turn Rickett had coaxed out of Chicago Mary, via Zena. R.A.F. electricians had wired his theatre from material stripped from a Liberator. It was give-and-take, all of it. Anybody could help himself to the hospital's wine, or to its battered piano. Morgan Giles's eyes shone, for instance, when he saw Rickett had bagged an Aldis lamp—from where, he would not say—and had strung this up to augment his theatre lighting.

"My goodness," Giles said fervently, "I could do with that!"

Rickett unhooked it and passed the lamp over. "Help yourself." As was its custom the Navy had dug itself in very comfortably down at Komisa in the port's only modern block, which also boasted the only bath in the place. It was at the instance of Morgan Giles's assistant, "Spider" Webb, that Rickett came down to perform a minor operation on his chief. He decided to lay on a good show, turned up in a smart white smock, with sterile towels, and with Dawson almost presenting arms with the scalpel before he passed it to him, excised a small clot that had been troubling the commander.

Thereafter they had tinned ham and several other Naval N.A.A.F.I. delicacies including the right to stoke themselves a hot bath whenever the impulse drove them into their truck and down to Komisa for a clean-up.

It was during a break in hostilities that Navy House phoned warning Rickett to expect five casualties from a very badly shot-up M.T.B. The ambulance brought up a badly wounded officer, Lieutenant-Commander Smyth, and four ratings. Two of the ratings had to have their legs amputated from shell wounds which had done so much damage as to leave no other course. A third had several fingers amputated from messy gunshot wounds in both hands. The fourth was lucky with a clean gunshot wound in the buttock, but the Lieutenant-Commander had a bad thoraco-abdominal wound. An urgent operation saved him but he was thereafter immovable.

After ten days, with a load of Commando wounded in from a raid, Rickett prowled about during a pause in operating, checking the intravenous drips on the worst casualties and sorting out his next candidates for the operating theatre. He looked into the tent full of wounded where Smyth lay, and saw that he was a very sick man. It was hot now and the flies swarmed on him. The advent of warmth and flies was going to give the doctors another problem, for there were now more than 5,000 partisans on the island where in peacetime a handful of peasants and fisherfolk lived. The partisans had a most insanitary habit of defecating where they stood.

The sick naval officer was surrounded by moaning wounded, all in urgent need of attention, and there was nobody available to nurse him adequately.

That day one of the first Dakotas had touched down on their enlarged airstrip. Scottie had bagged the pilot and brought him up to his shack for a drink. While the U.S.

pilot was still collecting himself from a swallow of *rakia,* Scottie, with all his outlaw's radar working, asked if there was any room on the Dakota going back. The pilot replied that, why, sure, there was room for four or five.

"Excuse me just a m-moment," said Scottie, and got straight on the blower to Rickett, to whom he stuttered the news that they had room for five men on a plane leaving for Italy that day.

"Any g-good to you, Jimmy?"

Rickett thought of the chest-and-stomach case. Even after ten days, it was a horrible decision to have to take to move him, but he decided that here was a chance that could not be missed. Evacuating him by sea was unthinkable. He rang Morgan Giles who sent the officer's own crew up to carry his stretcher down on a three-ton truck to the airstrip. They bumped off down the track with the sick officer's knees bent to cushion the jarring, and got him aboard the plane together with four more of Rickett's worst casualties for Bari, where there was a clean, splendidly equipped military hospital, thoroughly organised and staffed for everything.

The grimness of their evacuation problem so stirred the Dakota crew that in a few days they were back on the strip at Vis, this time with an American nurse and an invitation to load the plane up with wounded—which they did joyfully, despatching amputations and those casualties who would be a long time, if ever, returning to their units.

This was too good to be anything but a shortlived joy. The Americans clamped down on these illicit mercy trips, with perfect logic. Let the British look after their own casualties, they said.

Jim Rickett later had a chance to visit his thoraco-abdominal casualty in Bari. He found him with a pelvic abscess and other complications to demonstrate the gravity of the decision to move him. But it was obvious that he was going to recover, which was more than could have been said of his chances in this sweltering, fly-blown tent on Vis.

They owed their next victory to—the partisans.

Dr. Zon was their emissary. He appeared at the door of the hospital, smiling and exuding a gentle satisfaction.

"We have something for you," he said.

Outside, several partisans were unloading paper parcels and bringing these in.

"What is it?"

"Unwrap it and you will see."

It was only after a lot of unwrapping, and puzzling over the shiny pieces of metal which came to light that it dawned on them what it really was.

It was an X-ray machine.

Modern, gleaming—and all in little bits.

Dawson was on the blower to his mates in the engineers like a shot, babbling for them to come on up and lend a hand.

Rickett stared at Dr. Milo Zon. When he found words he said: "Where on earth did you get it?"

Dr. Zon smiled happily. "We—kidnapped it," he said.

Before she left Zena had scoured the island for anybody who knew the whereabouts of an X-ray machine. On the night she left for Bosnia, weary as she was after hours of operating, she had left the task to Zon and the others as a solemn trust, and warned them within an inch of their lives if they failed her.

The partisans had watched the daily wonders a competent surgeon like Rickett could perform on their wounded, and they hatched a plan. Over on the German-held mainland, a port as big as Split would surely have an X-ray machine to spare. They asked around until they happened on a chemist who remembered a clinic in Split which owned one. He gave them directions, and a landing party took off at night in a schooner for the mainland.

Stealing into Split was truly walking into the lion's den, for it was the big military nerve centre and it swarmed with Germans. But Zon's party walked in with arms under their ragged coats, strode into the clinic and held it up, delicately unbolted a gleaming German-made X-ray machine, asked for a supply of brown paper and wrapped it up piece by piece, walked out again through the thronged streets to their rendezvous downcoast with their schooner.

And they had done this for Rickett. Or more truthfully, for Zena and for Rickett.

He was all but overcome. He could only grin, and

walk around the jigsaw of pieces, and grin again. Zena was now in Bosnia, but her indomitable power remained with them. She had raged at him: "But you *are* a partisan, Jim!" It was the best she could say of any man.

They had not risked their lives to bring it back for one of their own doctors, but for him.

The engineer lads arrived, and their R.A.F. electrician. They had hardly ever seen X-ray apparatus, except to get their insides photographed. Much less had they ever attempted to put one together. And in pieces, it was strange how little it looked like *anything*. They started work by picking up one gleaming piece of metal, arbitrarily, and then looking for the next piece which it seemed likely to fit. It was maddening, and absorbing, and thrilling, and slow.

But gradually it came to life, rather like a miracle.

An engineer said: "The thing about these German things is that it's all nice and logical. The square bits go in the square holes, and the round bits go in the round holes."

He stood back and surveyed the assembly. An electrician brought up some gun-turret wiring and tapped the lighting circuit and soldered leads to the machine. They started the old generator going, and now the doubts assailed them all.

With their combined ignorance, it didn't seem remotely possible that it would work.

"It'll kill us all," Dawson said.

Rickett flicked the switch, but instead of a blue flash, there was a purring, a hum.

"Well, who's going to be first?"

"You, sir." The verdict was alarmingly unanimous.

He shut the shutters and in the gloom stepped behind the screen, and grinned down at them hopefully, not without misgiving. They weren't looking at him, but goggling at the screen, and he could tell by their fascination that it was doing something interesting, anyway.

"Blimey, do we all look as scraggy as that?"

"Look at all those holes in his liver. That's what you get from this vino!"

Frank Clynick's smooth face was shining in the strange green light. "I can see his heart beating," he said. "You're alive all right, Jimmy."

Later that afternoon Rickett took a nap in the mess after a spell of operating. It had been a long day.

He awoke to the sensation of something warm and liquid on his chest. When he opened his eyes he thought he was in a tent. Then he saw that the goat, Herbert, was straddling him—and urinating over him.

Rickett scrambled to his feet and bellowed for Dawson, who came rushing. His O.C. pointed a quivering finger at the goat and barked: "All right, J.J., he's all yours!"

Dawson allowed no gleam of satisfaction to cross his long face. He said simply: "Right, sir." He pounced on the goat, and bore him out.

There were several alarmed objections when they learned of the fate in store for Herbert, but Rickett was adamant.

That night, to celebrate the installation of their X-ray machine, they had roast kid, and they tapped a new barrel of wine. By this time details of Herbert's crime had leaked out. Professor Heron raised a glass to toast his memory and looked at Rickett with an awful leer.

"Don't say goats can't talk, Jimmy," he said.

TWELVE

In the quietness ensuing since the last big Commando sortie they had got their self-made hospital functioning sturdily. They would almost have resented help if it had materialised from Italy at this stage, so proud were they of all their rattletrap apparatus, the kidnapped X-ray machine, their store of pillaged medicaments.

But whether responsibility for their welfare was being shuttlecocked back and forth between authorities back in Italy or not, there was one thing that Rickett could never quite forgive them for, and that was their denying his Commandos actual medicines to save life—in particular, penicillin.

In 1942 Professor Florey had come out to 95 General Hospital in Algiers, where Rickett was working, to try out penicillin on the first war casualties. It was a fine hospital with several top consultants from London, now in uniform, on its staff. A complete ward was turned over to Florey so that he could experiment with the penicillin. He appeared in civilian clothes. Rickett heard one ranker say: "Gorblimey—a real doctor!"

Before Rickett had left for Vis, penicillin was in general use in hospitals throughout Italy and North Africa where results in reduced postoperative infection and wound sepsis had been dramatic. The doctors were treating the thousands of refugees with it. But the Commando fighters on Vis were not allowed any, and that, he raged, was criminal.

Partisan fatigues had been busy widening the high stone-walled lane, 100 yards long, which ran off from the main trans-island track down to the hospital cottage. Getting ambulances down here had been deadly slow, with two inches to spare on each side. They could get a three-tonner down here now and turn it around, which meant that the way was clear for every vehicle on the island to be pressed into service, delivering casualties right to their front door, if the rush started.

They were naïvely pleased with all this. Their en-forced independence had become precious to them. Life here had narrowed down to a humble, peasant focus, in which the things they built out of nothing gave them a primal thrill of achievement. Apart from the hospital equipment, all that surrounded them here—the animals, the wine, the vineyards, the view—was steeped in change-less time.

It would have been interesting to refer the next problem that confronted them to one of those elegant emissaries of the Foreign Office.

The problem arrived in the shape of Private Dodd, in a fearful cloud of dust. He was white, but not this time from German flour-missiles. He hung around in Rickett's sight for hours, an anxious figure dancing in the back-ground trying to catch the O.C.'s eye, until finally Rickett had finished sick parades, ward touring, conferring with the cook, and going through a minor list of operations with Clynick, Dawson and Lalla in attendance.

Dodd finally got alongside Rickett as he was taking a cigarette before the evening meal. He looked hunted. Finally, bucking up with an inane smile, he confessed.

"Well, I've torn it, sir. You'll never guess what I've done."

"You're quite right. And I'd rather not try, Dodd."

"Well, sir, there's a lady I happen to know who's up the—well, she's—" he paused, then almost yelled it. "Christ, sir, I've got a *partisanka* in the family way, and she's—!"

Rickett slowly cupped his face in his hands.

"—and you know what those Jugs'll do to her when they find out! They don't mess about, sir. Ask those boys from 2 Commando, or those sailors off that M.T.B.—!"

"I know," Rickett said. But he was wildly tempted to laugh. It was so absurd. There was always something fun-ny about it—though, God knows, enough tragedy, too, even in the ordinary course. But here among these crazy partisans—!

And of course, it *had* to be Dodd.

He wiped the grin off his face and tried conscientiously hard to consider it seriously. It was a fix, all right.

Dodd's own contribution was especially inadequate. He said solemnly: "We've both agreed, sir, it mustn't be allowed to happen again."

Rickett surveyed him blankly. Private Dodd was at all times quite unbelievable. The boy essayed his wide, gay smile but it only worked in a ghastly kind of way.

"She's as scared as hell, sir."

Rickett got up. "I'll see what ought to be done," he said heavily.

"If you're going to the Juggery, sir—I've already discussed the matter with Captain Lloyd Roberts," Dodd said lamely.

"Oh you *have!* Are you canvassing the island? Have you tried Dr. Petak?"

"Oh no, sir, not *him!*"

Jim Rickett came to confer with George Lloyd Roberts. Neither was kidding himself any longer about what might lie in store for the girl when her pregnancy became apparent. She couldn't be rescued and shipped out to Italy, and after discussing it from all angles they knew that the only solution lay in terminating it.

But neither was prepared to do this, each maintaining it was the other's job.

"After all," George Lloyd Roberts argued, "Dodd is a commando, and the Commandos are officially your job."

To which Rickett retorted that it wasn't Dodd who was pregnant, but a partisan girl, and that was officially George's job.

"I tell you what," he said. "Let's toss for it."

They did. Delicacy prevents its being recorded here who won the toss, but it may be said that a couple of days later a very comely young *drugarica* was carried in on a stretcher professing all the symptoms of appendicitis.

For this she was duly operated on. And while he was about it the officiating surgeon, to use his own picturesque phraseology, made a slight detour and "gave her uterus a very friendly squeeze."

Private Dodd was extravagant in his gratitude, to the

point of making fantastic promises. His potency had quite overawed him.

"I'll never touch a woman again, sir," he said.

The girl Lalla was proving to be a jewel—dedicated to her work, very intelligent, willing and devoted to both George and Rickett. Now that the Juggery was only a short walk away, friendship had merged their functions even more closely and Lalla often came over to assist Rickett or to interpret for him.

Like Dawson she had a knack of anticipating their needs—even to the extent of always having a pin at the ready to test for nerve damage in wounded limbs. The procedure was to prick the flesh lightly, instructing the patient to tell them if he felt it. It provided an interesting study in human reaction. The patient would answer "yes . . . yes . . . yes . . ." and if there came a prick which they did not feel, there would be silence—naturally. Yet there would always come a time when, having felt nothing, they would offer—"no." It was the same with the Jug patients. Rickett would listen with amusement to their "da . . . da . . . da . . ."—and then, as positively, "nishda!" They called the pin, which she always produced while they were groping for one, "Lalla's dada-nishda."

Having Lalla translate for him was particularly valuable in diagnosis. One of his partisan patients in the morning sick line-up came complaining of internal pains. Lalla translated the symptoms and Rickett said: "Ask him if he's had his bowels open."

Lalla turned to the partisan and addressed him a long speech. This was answered by a torrent of words. Lalla heard him out gravely before resuming the interview with another flow of verbiage which Rickett began to fear would never come to an end. It did, though, and the partisan's reply to this encompassed most of the Balkan theatre and took only a little less than the length of a one-act play. This question and answer went on for a further full five minutes. Finally Rickett said, with what mildness he could muster: "What does he say, Lalla?"

That cut them off in full spate. Lalla lifted her large eyes to him and shrugged laconically.

"He says No," she said.

Now that the X-ray machine was functioning well it soon occurred to Rickett that if he went on screening patients for too long there was a danger of burning them and producing cancer. He knew nothing about X-rays and so went in mortal fear of doing some damage with it.

He muttered some of his fears to Professor Heron.

"We've got to get some film somehow. Then we'll be able to switch it on, take a picture, and switch it off again."

"Wonderful," Heron said. "All we have to do is send the partisans back to Split for some Jerry developer, and while they're about it, kidnap somebody who knows how to process the film."

But by strange luck a Commando sergeant was lunching at the table, and he pricked up his ears. He cleared his mouth and said, "I could get you some film, developer, fixing, cassettes, the lot, sir—if I can get to Italy and back."

"Italy!" somebody scoffed. "That's one way of wangling a leave pass."

"I have a brother," observed the Sergeant, wiping his mouth, "who is a sergeant in the base medical stores at Bari."

He could not have produced a better effect if he had said his uncle was the Pope. Rickett stared, started gobbling his food, and when he had finished, hopped into the fifteen-hundredweight and tore off up to Borovic, where he found Brigadier Churchill at home, poring over maps and reports with his staff and some hefty partisan officers.

Rickett produced quite a creditable salute and, somewhat out of breath, said: "No questions, please, sir—request four days' leave to Italy for Sergeant Pursell of No. 2 Commando."

Brigadier Tom Churchill looked up. He smiled faintly and said: "Given."

They tore down to Komisa to see Morgan Giles and flourishing the leave pass, wangled Pursell aboard an L.C.I.

In a few days the Sergeant was back, tottering under an enormous packet. He ripped it open in front of Rickett and everything fell out—films, cassettes, fixer, darkroom bulbs, everything they could dream of wanting.

Sergeant Pursell was rather patronising about his feat.

"The trouble is, sir, you don't go to the right people," he said.

It was true they only had wood with which to make developer trays, and these leaked; but they kept topping them up and they produced some splendid pictures of the islanders' insides.

The X-ray apparatus proved its worth in unthought-of ways. The sense of a big battle impending attracted a padre to the hospital cottage. He was genial and highly conscientious and he arrived with his retinue while tension was at its height. Everybody was at action stations and Rickett's team was bustling around scrubbing, disinfecting, planning ward space, getting everything ready for casualties. Rickett turned and with misgiving watched the padre set up shop, announcing that his place was with the wounded.

There was a bit of moaning that a priest would turn the place into a cloister.

"We are all sleeping out, of course," Rickett said, in a lame attempt to discourage him. The padre smiled and replied briskly: "That's all right, old man, I've got my tent"—and pitched it right beside the steps into the operating theatre.

Everybody pulled the padre's leg mercilessly. An officer from Brigade H.Q. told him gravely that for camouflage purposes his tent would have to be flattened every day; and so with great diligence the padre would strike his tent at daybreak and pitch it again at night. He was a sport. He took all the ribbing in good part. And nothing would budge him.

Rickett gave the problem some thought. One evening when Father Grote's presence in the mess had stricken the hell-raisers round the piano with near-paralysis and reduced them to decorous wailings of *Roll Out The Barrel* and *Run Rabbit Run*, Rickett seemed unusually preoccupied.

Finally he came out with it in a confidential murmur, aside. He sipped his wine and said: "You know, padre, I'm getting a bit worried—well, not *worried*, because you're a priest and therefore celibate . . ."

He paused, contemplating the whole matter judiciously. "But the fact is—there's no lead lining inside that wall where you've put your tent . . . and with this X-ray machine working at all hours, of course, it *does* have an effect on fertility. Mind you, I know it doesn't matter to *you*. People do like to know these things, though . . ."

The next day the padre's tent was struck and they found it about three miles down the road.

Later their paths crossed in the wards and Father Grote halted him, hem-hemming in a confiding way. He said: "Of course as you say it doesn't mean a thing to me, this business of the X-ray. But I've got my batman to think of, and he's a married man."

THIRTEEN

The true quality of the partisans was epitomised in the arrival on Vis, early in April, of one of Tito's crack officers, Colonel Zuljevic. He was a swarthy, handsomely chiselled giant who had risen, like most of the partisan chiefs, on sheer courage and military skill. He came from Bosnia, straight from Tito's headquarters, with orders to lead a series of offensive operations against the Germans on the Dalmatian islands, and his appearance was clearly to demonstrate to the Allies, themselves flushed with the success of their recent sorties, what the partisan armies were capable of achieving. For Zuljevic brought with him a reputation as the most aggressive leader of all.

He lost no time in fulfilling this reputation. As soon as he landed on Vis Colonel Zuljevic called on Brigadier Churchill in his little H.Q. cottage up in Borovic and plunged into a conference on the general tactical situation. Then he outlined a plan. It was for a mass attack by partisans on the islands of Korcula and Mljet, their neighbours on the eastern quarter which they could see from their H.Q. in all their steep serrations as they discussed the battle plan.

There were now enough partisans on Vis, and with enough arms for a large operation. They had their own artillery now: a British officer, Major Kupp, had trained the partisans to use a number of captured Italian 75 mm. guns which had been made over to them. In addition they had quantities of mortars and machine guns. Zuljevic asked for naval and air support. With enthusiastic backing from Churchill, he got it promptly.

For the Navy Lieutenant-Commander Morgan Giles

contributed landing craft and M.T.B. escorts, and the R.A.F.'s Forward Fighter Group came in with air support.

Colonel Zuljevic's little fleet sailed out of Vis on the 19th March to gather first, overnight, on the almost-deserted island of Lagosta, à ruin of wrecked Allied installations to the south of the German shipping lanes, and from there to leapfrog to the attack, first across to the more distant island of Mljet.

The partisans lunged across at Mljet on the following night with sudden ferocity and in two days of bitter fighting they destroyed the entire German garrison on the island, leaving the dead piled around their fortifications and withdrawing with forty-six prisoners.

Italian 75mm Gun

Two days later the great stony peaks of Korcula were resounding to the noise of battle and the roar of covering aircraft as a fresh partisan force swarmed ashore from the boats and charged into action on the western end which confronted Vis. They overran it to the east through village after village. The fighting reached its fiercest in the fortified town of Blato, where a German battalion held out with bitter determination, most of them preferring to die fighting rather than be taken prisoner by the partisans. It took two days of the bloodiest fighting to clear Blato and with it the strongest defence concentration in the western sector of the island.

Everywhere with the partisan forces there were Commando signallers who wirelessed back news of the fighting to Vis. There was also a Commando doctor, Captain Leitch, charged with the job of setting up a Regimental Aid Post to handle the partisan wounded. Rickett and his comrades had watched Leitch's departure on this mission with some relief. He was an unruly character who had been instantly attracted by the hospitality of their mess. It offered a cheerful refuge from his feuds with his C.O. and Leitch sought its solace and its wine frequently. His troubles seemed to be so great that often he started the process of drowning them around breakfast time, so that any of his Commandos wanting medical attention had to get up pretty early in the morning to derive any coherent benefit from it. By mid-afternoon his advice for a boil on the arm would be to "chop the——thing off." By evening on such days his sociability had so declined that to enter the mess with Leitch around was to take one's life in one's hands. He had an unpleasant habit, in the discussions that arose around their log fire, of fetching out his Colt .45 and waving this under people's noses to emphasise the points he chose to make.

Leitch landed unopposed in the darkness on Korcula with several boatloads of partisans, who in their eagerness to get to grips with the enemy began storming up the steep, rocky mountainside at such speed that, encumbered as he was with all his medical gear, he could not keep up with them, and soon he was left on his own.

Captain Leitch came staggering up to a derelict house, kicked open the door, found it empty, and decided to take shelter here till morning. Curiously, its cellar was full of wine barrels. He sampled one and decided this place would make a very good Regimental Aid Post.

Leitch settled down to refresh himself and await what the war brought him.

By 2 a.m. he had drunk himself into a state of rosy content with the world when gunfire burst out all around him, and with it the popping of mortars. A party of partisans burst into the house, reloading Sten magazines and holding a noisy conference. They ignored the solitary figure of Leitch seated with his feet up on a rough table, and, their hasty debate over, gathered themselves and rushed outside again. When they had gone Leitch, grumbling, got to his feet, bolted the door, and returned to his wine.

About an hour afterwards another battle arose in the darkness and the house shook to the thump of explosions and the chipping and whining of bullets which spattered the stone walls. Leitch raised his eyes as someone tried the door. It shook to a furious hammering. Leitch ignored the knocking and a chorus of guttural yells from outside, until the door heaved under an assult and it burst open.

A knot of German soldiers came tumbling in. At the sight of Leitch they halted. An officer among them motioned the others back and they lowered their weapons as he advanced on Leitch.

"British officer?"

Leitch grunted sourly in answer.

"We wish to surrender to you."

"Why?" growled Leitch.

A hesitation. "We—do not wish to surrender to the partisans . . ." the officer ventured.

Leitch turned his bleary gaze on the German and surveyed the anxious crowd of soldiers behind him with distaste. He motioned to the door. Obediently they began to back out through it as he advanced on them.

"Out!" Leitch growled. "——off! I'm busy!"

And he shut the door on the goggling enemy and returned to his drinking.

They didn't bother him again.

On the third day, with half the island in their hands, the partisans withdrew from Korcula with their booty, leaving 300 Germans dead. On this occasion they took prisoners—nearly 500—with them, as well as a valuable haul of equipment: four 75 mm. guns, 20 mortars, 38 machine guns, piles of small arms and ammunition, radios and a fleet of German trucks. Before they left they distributed the captured food back to the civilian population. They would need all the comforts one could give them. The German reprisals among them would be savage.

Zuljevic's men had put out of action nearly 1,000 Germans in two operations which were remarkable for their skill and ferocious heroism. Their style of fighting was entirely different from that of the Commandos, but on this showing quite as brilliantly effective. It had not even been all that extravagant of life, either. The partisan casualties were only a third as high as the enemy's.

Still, there were 300 partisan wounded returning to Vis in the boats under cover of dusk. It was an enormous total for two surgeons to face, equipped as George and Jim Rickett were.

Navy House phoned as soon as they had news. Dawson went into action like a demon, getting the sterilisers going, marshalling Anka and Filica and the orderlies from Heron's ambulance gang. Private Dodd looked in and was immediately collared to get the generator going beneath the stretcher stairway.

The first batch of wounded came grinding up from Komisa in a mongrel fleet of trucks. They were the priority cases, roughly sorted on arrival, and there were about eighty. The partisan bearers who off-loaded them in the darkness were directed where to lay them down with shouts and gesticulations, and when the reception tent was full, they laid them all around it outside under the stars. Rickett came round peering at them in the white glare of a hissing Tilley lamp, directing plasma resuscitation, tabbing the urgent ones. He motioned Dawson and Clynick into the operating theatre.

They started operating at 8:30 p.m. The longest part about it, with all this urgency and the horde of wounded waiting downstairs, was the preliminaries—the injecting of the pentothal, setting up the saline and plasma drips, waiting for the orderlies to clear the instruments for re-sterilisation.

But they kept quiet and worked steadily, grimly, through the messy and familiar drudgery of excision, débridement, the patient cleaning and removal of dirt, dead tissue, mortar fragments or a cruel shard of H.E. shell, picking out strands of clothing fabric, clipping the blood vessels which spurted under the knife, tying, powdering with sulpha, straightening their aching backs for the brief moment between the removal of one patient and his replacement by another in an endless, bloodied procession.

Dawson's precision was a joy; the long, horsey face

opposite Rickett, intent and absorbed, never allowed itself the luxury of any expression beyond watching. His hands hovered and selected, slapped a Spencer-Wells clip into Rickett's palm as it rose whenever blood gushed, proffered a ligature and unclipped as Rickett tied. Occasionally Dawson's eyes flickered round to check on the orderlies at their work. Once, when Rickett dropped an instrument, Dawson reached and knocked it spinning from the hand of the orderly who retrieved and wanted to return it, then poked out a foot and kicked it into a corner.

There were many girls among the casualties. One of the first was a stomach wound and she had lost a lot of blood. She came in escorted by an orderly holding the plasma bottle; she was conscious and angry in a fevered way that somebody had deprived her of her rifle. The operation was a long one but Rickett had already hit on a standard way of keeping them under; Clynick, now very adept at the whole busienss, would inject a vein, strap the hypodermic on the arm with Elastoplast, and connect it up with a saline drip containing a measured quantity of pentothal. They rarely used ether and there was no bottled gas anaesthetic. They could gauge the girl's sensitivity to the pentothal by inviting her to count as she slipped into unconsciousness. Slowly, they would add the same amount again of pentothal and begin operating. Twice in the ensuing long stretch of exploring and suturing intestine she stirred faintly and began to tense. At that, Clynick undid the clip pinching the rubber tube and ran in more anaesthetic with the saline drip.

It was almost as if the battles had been fought in the stony field outside the cottage, for these wild fighters were borne in still clutching their Sten guns and abusing the orderlies who tried to disarm them. It scandalised the others in the theatre but Rickett was tempted to humour them.

"If it makes 'em happy," he said, and shrugged, and bent to work. In their attachment to their guns he found something inexplicably moving. It was childlike of them, theatrical, yet passionately real. He interrupted an altercation between a fiercely whiskered old warrior and Heron's men for possession of a Sten, and restored it gently to the owner who tucked it beside him on his stretcher.

For a moment his eyes met Rickett's, and a kind of

recognition lit between them, compounded of humour and wry villainy. Under his walrus froth of black moustache the old soldier's grin dawned and he showed his thick broken teeth; he wagged his head, threw a derisive stare at the orderly, then grinned again at Rickett with fiercest affection. In less than a minute he was on the table and snoring happily under the pentothal.

Two patients later they loaded a fat, brunette *partisanka* on to the table who bristled with military impedimenta. In the act of removing her belt, the orderly fumbled with a grenade which was hanging by its pin. It dropped to the floor, where it rolled under the table and Rickett's eyes bulged—he saw the pin was nearly out. As the orderly dived after it the grenade knocked the leg of the table and was still. The orderly came up with it in his hand and a wild, scared question in his stare. He stuttered: "Will it—?" and Rickett shoved him, urgently, rasping: "I don't know—just get rid of it!" By the time the words were out the lad was halfway down the stairs and racing outside. Having waited and heard no explosion, Clynick and Rickett exchanged glances, and it was Dawson who put it into words.

He said: "I imagine the pin has to be right out."

But from then on, they frisked the partisan wounded as part of their routine procedure before operations, unclipping the grenades which swung from their blouses by the pin and turning more out of their pockets.

It was about midnight when the lights overhead began to glow suddenly with a hectic brilliance and they halted. The generator was roaring. Then the lights blew, and Rickett was straightening in the pitch black with the memory of them dancing in his eyes like a cluster of coals. He heard a rush on the stairs and Private Dodd's voice, dismayed. "It's that throttle, sir! It's gone haywire again!"

Clynick kept the patient under while they found three bulbs, all that were left; two of these they soldered to the bare wire hanging over their heads. Dodd was ordered back to crouch in the hole under the stretcher stairway and hold the governor on the generator. He had to judge the right speed by the glow it produced in the third light bulb, which they fixed on the generator itself.

Thereafter they operated in the wavering glow as the current alternately surged and flagged. The operations

went on—laparotomies and the equally dreaded thoracic
wounds, several amputations, a trepanning, the slow cleaning and exploration of what was left of a man's face, on
and on, intent on the case in hand and only rarely aware
of the great rabble of wounded choking the stairs outside
and the reception yards below, all waiting somewhere
beyond the weak pool of light in which they worked. They
only grew conscious of the host of them when the theatre
door opened and the babble, pointed with wailing here and
there, invaded the room.

Somewhere towards five o'clcok in the morning they
were coming to the last of their critically urgent cases, and
by now the lighting from the generator was fluctuating
wildly, sometimes fading almost to extinction and then
returning with alarming brilliance. Rickett sent an orderly
down to check on Private Dodd, who had been crouched
under the stairs for hours now, holding the throttle on that
infernal generator.

The orderly came upon Dodd in a blissful daze,
clinging to the remnants of consciousness, his filmy look
fixed on the control-lamp as in a dream. The two girls,
Anka and Filica, had taken pity on Dodd. He had the kind
of guileless charm which invited it. At intervals during his
cramped vigil, as the lights wavered and reflected the
cramp and weariness of the solitary man seated under the
stairs, they visited him with wine. Dodd simply opened a
grateful mouth and let them pour it in. By five o'clock he
was wrapped in a beatific half-dream while the lighting
system of the hospital glared and paled like a neon
hoarding.

But by dawn they had cleared the worst of this first
batch of casualties. Morgan Giles had sent up a donation
of Navy rum and they had a stiff tot of this all round.
Dawson, the poker-faced sultan of their establishment,
ushered Anka and Filica in to clear the mess from the
operating theatre and to scrub it out while he superintended a thorough resterilising of all the instruments and
the mackintoshes and towels. The others turned in for a
brief doze with a warning from the Navy ringing in their
ears that more casualties would be arriving in port any
minute.

Three hours later the phone was ringing to say that
another 150 wounded were on the way. Marie was up and

cooking a hot meal and by the time the first trucks came rolling down the lane and turning round to unload they were all fed and ready to go again. Rickett recommenced operating. They lost count of time until he called a halt for more sterilising, scrubbing, and a meal. Then he looked at a clock. One-thirty. By three they were starting all over again and only halted well after darkness had closed in and they had called in reinforcements to manage the obstreperous generator, one man clamped to the governor for every half-hour that passed. They dared not risk blowing the last of their precious lighting.

At eight o'clock on the second night they were wolfing down another meal and by this time the routine for coping with the tides of wounded was defining itself. It worked best, Rickett calculated, to pause about every five hours for a good meal. While they ate it Dawson put the girls in to scrub out the theatre and saw that all the instruments went through re-sterilising. Rickett made his helpers rest alternately for two hours each on their beds. In that way he counted on getting the best out of them. He helped himself to benzedrine tablets—scrounged, he remembered wryly, from the kits of crashed aircraft. For he could not rest himself. He had to look into the after-care of the wounded, check the drips, the condition of the cases he had already operated on. They had no qualified nursing. He had to sort fresh batches of wounded amid the confusion, the yelling, the groans, the engaging blandishments with which some of the casualties sought to catch his eye, into a degree of order for operation.

When he returned to the theatre it would be damp and steamy, but clean, and Dawson was always waiting with fresh towels and their humble array of instruments at the ready. They carried on, nobody sparing a superfluous word, simply slogging through the appalling pile-up of shattered limbs and ripped organs that passed through the tiny ill-lit room.

The next stop they made was about three in the morning. His orderlies were not bothering now to go off to their own beds for rest; they simply lay down between the sterilising tables and slept there till Rickett roused them again. He himself dozed during a theatre-scrubbing session somewhere towards morning, but there were always more post-operative patients now to care for and he had to instruct some primitive kind of nursing for these.

In the middle of these sessions Colonel Orchard, a hygiene expert visiting the island to check on the medical situation—for Rickett had been bombarding Italy with complaints—presented himself at the theatre to help. Orchard took off his coat and buckled to; he washed and prepared the wounded men and girls, shaved limbs, held patients while Rickett excised their wounds, and plastered.

This flood of casualties soon demonstrated that the raffish Dr. Petak was not alone in his strange ideas about wound treatment. The partisan doctors now working in the field used the same primitive techniques. Among the waiting patients were numbers whose wounds had been excised at an aid post on Lagosta island, then immediately stitched up tight before wound sepsis declared itself, and encased in skin-tight plaster without a vestige of padding. By the time they arrived at Vis many cases were so heavily infected—some already even to the point of gangrene—that Rickett was resorting to amputation to save lives.

Typical of these was a leg-wounded old Jug who managed to catch Rickett's eye as he came round with his lamp looking for the worst among them. He gestured to his plastered leg.

"Kako si, drug?"

"Boli, boli." The man moaned and beckoned Rickett. The pain dewed his brown face and he kept muttering *"boli,"* while with an eloquent chopping motion of his hand he was begging Rickett to cut off his leg. When he opened the casing Rickett found a severed artery in a filthy wound. To stop his bleeding to death the partisan doctor had rightly tied it off. But in consequence, for that alone, gross swelling was inevitable below his shattered knee as the smaller veins and capillaries dilated to by-pass the severed artery by assuming its load.

In imploring Rickett to cut off his leg, the wounded man's diagnosis of his own plight was only too accurate. Rickett took the limb off above the knee. It went much against the grain. Even in this predicament, overwhelmed by casualties, one's instinct was still to preserve, to save.

Side by side with these botched plaster cases came the

oddest contradictions—the ruthless amputations. Rickett
supposed the field doctors thought to relieve those back at
Vis of the work on compound fractures and unsaveable
limbs. At any rate, they had guillotined without mercy. It
would not have pleased them to know that in this they
were simply following a German doctrine: to save work,
amputate. Yet guillotining of limbs without leaving a flap
to cover the stump often involved re-amputation later,
anyway.

The Germans, however, went one stage further in
their own ruthless surgical philosophy. Under any kind of
pressure they ignored the bad stomach-wound cases. They
simply left these to die—whereas the Jugs always really
tried to save their own as best they knew how. In a part of
the world where life was held cheap they took unprecedented risks to save it, as long as it belonged to a comrade.
Their loyalty was something to marvel at.

In this way, sorting between shifts, checking the
already operated and committing those strong enough to
evacuate to truck trips down to Vis harbour, swallowing a
regular hot meal and dosing himself with benzedrine,
Rickett managed to stay at the operating table well into
the third day, still without a sleep. He often felt his eyes
closing now, and on an impulse of fear for the patient, he
paused, blinked, shook his head like a wet dog, took a long
breath or two, and bent to work again.

It was while he was sorting cases that he realized he
was no longer any use. He found himself staring at a
wounded partisan who smiled back at him and indicated
his wound with a shrug and chattered something at him in
Serbo-Croat. Lalla was interpreting question and answer
for him, but now she was mute and her huge eyes were on
him, waiting.

He had asked all his questions, and received all his
answers, and now he sat down and blinked.

None of it made any sense, neither question nor
answer. He tried, but he could not fit them together,
simple though he knew them to be.

A reflex instinct had kept him at work in the swift
mechanics of wound surgery. It was his mind which had
let him down first. He could no longer diagnose.

Not until he slept.

Five hours later Frank Clynick woke him and he

fought up through depths of unconsciousness to meet him, to rise till he was standing, and then to walk around the field and the tents full of stretchers. He was awake and alive again and now, in the sea of casualties, he could see it all clearly.

In one more stretch of operating, he would be through. Somehow he and the others had waded almost clear through the sea of wounded—and now, incredibly, it was nearly over. He walked through the stretcher rows checking the drips and grinning at the upturned faces.

"Kako si, drug? Boli?"

"Nishda boli . . . Dobro! Dobro!"

And they would cackle at him, if they could, these gay unshaven villains, and for their mischief and their gaiety and guts he loved them deeply. Lalla smiled with them at him, and averted her head decorously at the riper sallies from the beds. When he returned to the operating theatre, ready to tackle the last big batch, he walked into something of a crisis. Lalla had preceded him and waited with her eyes blazing. They had a wounded German prisoner sitting on a form outside the theatre. A Commando soldier guarded him from a curious crowd of hospital helpers. Lalla turned as Rickett came up, her mild face contorted with hatred, and spat on the German, mouthing her elementary German. *Deutscher schwein. Dreck. Du kommst für hilfe, schwein?* The Commando moved her aside, gently. Rickett took a look at the haggard German. He had a bullet through the elbow, but the ulnar nerve appeared intact and the arm could probably be saved.

The German was a little quivery at all this partisan interest in him, but determined to appear unconcerned. His pale eyes sought Rickett's and he said, with an eloquent motion, apropos of his arm, almost hopefully: *"Abschneiden? Cut off, ja?"*

At that moment the Intelligence Officer appeared and drew Rickett aside.

"Jugs took this one. Though not without a struggle."

"So I see."

"Quite. Well, they lent him to us for interrogation and all that. He's yours now."

"What do you mean?"

"Well, to patch him up, what? We've had a little

man-to-man talk about German dispositions and at the end
of it I promised him I'd do what I could. So you'd be
doing me a favour if you'd—"

Rickett massaged the stubble on his chin and his
speculative stare cut the I.O. short. He said coolly: "I have
no time to be messing around with Jerries, not while
there's a partisan or a Commando case left to be treated."

"I see." The I.O. stiffened a little. "I don't think that's
frightfully—"

"—you might try George." Rickett jerked a thumb
towards the Juggery. "He may be through his list. I'm still
busy. Besides—" Rickett found himself making a rare,
cynical resort to the rules—"technically he's a partisan
prisoner."

He watched the I.O. stalk off in a cloud of disdain to
the Juggery to tackle George. While they waited, Lalla
came close and spat again on the German and screeched
abuse. Rickett slapped her on the bottom, hard.

"That's enough nonsense, Lalla. Wait for me in the
theatre."

Lalla straightened, gaping with shock—and obeyed.

The I.O. came back and in silence removed his
prisoner to the Juggery. Rickett scrubbed up again and
came into the theatre. After a further five-hour stretch he
was finished with his last case. In the end all the Commando medical orderlies had come up from their stations to
volunteer help. They only knew about first aid in the field,
but they tackled the after-care of the wounded under his
directions. And with theatre work under Dawson they had
taken a lot of the weight of the lighter casualties by
cleaning and dressing wounds, and bandaging.

In all this time, in spite of their crude machinery, they
had not once run out of sterile towels, or jaconet, or
dressing. That was Dawson's diligence. Anka and Filica,
though really still in their adolescence, had not faltered in
the gruesome drudgery of cleaning out the theatre and
scrubbing it down every several hours, while between
times they flew among the beds with water and comforts
for the wounded and brought Rickett and the other workers their meals.

In eighty hours they had sorted, dealt with, dressed
and evacuated down to the waiting harbour schooners
more than 350 casualties—all heavy ones, since the minor

puncture flesh wounds had either been sent back to their
units to await their turn or—as was more frequently the
case with the partisans—had simply not bothered to report. The Jugs considered it unmanly to report with a light
wounding. They would rather wait till it started to fester
and give trouble, and then, as likely as not, they would
simply prise out the mortar fragment or H.E. splinter with
a knife, and carry on.

Rickett had done nearly fifty major surgical operations on top of 200 or so lesser ones. They had retained
about fifty serious cases, unfit to travel.

Apart from Dawson, the imperturbable Frank Clynick, the orderlies who came rushing up to Podhumlje to
help, Dodd, Marie, bustling in with great hot platters from
the wood oven, and a veritable beehive of partisan stretcher workers, there were those quietly devoted ones like
Lalla murmuring question and answer—and then breaking
clean out of character into rage at the sight of a wounded
German prisoner.

He touched Lalla on the arm. "Why did you spit on
that Hun? It's not like you."

Her enormous eyes turned on him, but they remained
remote and she lifted her shoulders disinterestedly.

"I saw them shoot my husband," she said. "I had to
watch him die."

Rickett went back to his little Italian bivouac tent on
the hillside. It was dusking. The wind whined among the
rocks and drummed on the tent canvas and he fell asleep
vaguely dreading that it might herald the Bora. That
would put a stop to evacuating the wounded to Italy for
three or four days.

He did not wake as usual at dawn. The sun was high
when he uncramped himself and got up. It was hot and
still and peaceful. The sea was green and placid as bottle-
glass. Deep down in it, dappled sunlight washed over the
rock ledges and flashed in the eddies. There was no
Bora.

Nor were there any more truckloads of wounded,
when he came down the hill to Podhumlje. The reception
yard was empty.

FOURTEEN

There was always a terrific reaction after such a big burst of surgery, and the standard therapy for this was a party. They had one, a whopper, in the house farther down the lane where they had their mess. They threw open the doors and windows and let the sound of it drift on the soft night air, now rich with the promise of summer. The noise of it attracted a mixed flock: a shy commissar, quite young and very military; several of the partisan helpers from over at George Lloyd Roberts's Juggery; drifters from the neighbouring British ancillary units, and the R.A.F. camp.

Of course, the redoubtable Captain Leitch turned up—though sheepishly, for he was in disgrace. Leitch was under sentence of banishment from Vis. His C.O. could stand no more. He poked his head in the door and said humbly: "May I bring my cloud?" the cloud being, presumably, the one under which he was leaving. He had left his gun behind, which everybody noted with frank relief.

Having taken on the lowest tasks about the hospital during this prolonged emergency, Colonel Orchard was now an open convert to Podhumlje's cheerful anarchy, where personality came first and rank came almost nowhere. Though he had already demonstrated a good head for liquor, the colonel passed out in the arms of a hilarious band of partisan convalescents after falling for their invitation to drink brotherhood with them, Jug-style, one after another, in great swallows of *rakia* which drained his glass for every new brother he acquired. Frank Clynick whisked him away on a stretcher as though the mess was a battlefront. That was the gentle Clynick's mission. At these parties he could be relied on to hover, collar the casualties, see the lost to bed. He was the alcoholics' Florence Nightingale.

Lalla was invited. She slipped into a corner and sipped shyly at the gin which Rickett dispensed from a hoard inside an ancient cupboard. George Lloyd Roberts joined them from the Juggery. He was proud of his Hun prisoner's progress, and of the fact that so far he had prevented his Jugoslav patients from tearing the man to bits.

"Bit haughty, though, this Jerry. They really ask for it, y'know."

He had installed the German in an adjoining shed among half a dozen Jugoslav wounded and threatened them all within an inch of their life if they laid a hand on him. It was not George's threats which held them at bay; but what they felt for him, their doctor, and his care for them, was greater than all their hatred for the enemy who lay in a stretcher in their midst.

In spite of the German's pleas to amputate his arm, the danger of gangrene was receding and under conservative treatment the arm was regaining some of its movement. Rickett knew why the German wanted it amputated.

He said: "If he's disabled he thinks it'll give him a sporting chance of surviving as a prisoner."

"Why should it?" Lalla flashed suddenly. "If they can kill babies and old women?" She lowered her lids over the blazing in her eyes and shrank back again. In the ensuing silence George downed his drink and said briskly: "He's going to survive in *my* Juggery, anyway." And he lounged over to join the group around Scottie at the piano.

Rickett changed the subject. He raised his glass to Lalla. He said: "It's only three weeks since you took over from Zena. You had about two words of English then. Now you speak like a Cambridge don. You're a ruddy marvel." At his smile Lalla hung her head.

"I am a very bad translator," she said.

"What absolute rot."

"It's true. Otherwise—I could translate, for example, what our partisans say—about you—in the wards. They say things for which I cannot find the right words."

This was the girl, Rickett remembered, he found crying outside the theatre after they'd finished operating on a bad abdominal case. She had said it was because she was happy. It was this girl, so passionately tender, whom Zena had instructed to look after George. Who was to look after Lalla? Yet perhaps in giving Lalla a means of forgetting herself, Zena had had the right idea.

Zena was very wise, and echoes of her would long pursue them all.

Before she left—discreetly early in the party—Lalla showed Jim Rickett a photograph of her husband. He was a rotund little solicitor with a wide grin. One morning the Germans had scooped him off the street with a score of others as hostaages. He had only as long left to live as it would take the Germans to announce their next reprisal against the partisans, and when this arbitrary moment came, they herded him and the others they had snatched into the town market place, backed them against the church wall, and mowed them down with a Spandau.

Spandau (MG 42)

Friends among the townspeople held on to Lalla while they all watched.

But what was the use of Rickett's knowing this? It added nothing new, now, to his awareness of their suffering. It was another tiny detail minutely filled in on an enormous canvas. You took a step forward for a close glimpse, and this is what you always saw, and you had just another moment of being transfixed with pain.

Now that there was no operating list awaiting him, Rickett felt he could safely enjoy the party, and for once he didn't put down his drink early and retreat to his bivouac on the hill.

The next morning Colonel Orchard arose and surveyed the chaos around him. He said: "Where's the hangover? As far as I'm concerned the party's still on."

Rakia left one like that. It was perhaps for this that a Jugoslav party customarily lasted three days. But Rickett had had his holiday and he was off to the Juggery to see if George needed a hand. When he arrived George was in a state, shouting and fuming.

"Where are those bloody scissors of mine? I suppose somebody's taken them to cut their toenails with!" Nobody could find them and so, muttering, George started on a round of his wards.

When they came to the shed next door, the German's bed was empty. He had vanished during the night.

In vain George grilled the partisans who lay stacked like sardines on all sides of the empty bed. They merely stared back blankly and shook their heads and shrugged. They had not seen him go, they said.

"Perhaps he got up to urinate, and fell in," one of them suggested.

"We can only pray that may be so," another said.

Lalla, scarlet, translated amid the laughter. George was furious. He turned on his heel and stormed off to report it to the commissar who currently shadowed all their work at the Juggery. He warned him that unless they found his patient for him there would be the devil to pay.

"Perhaps he has escaped?" suggested the commissar, and drew on a cardboard-tipped cigarette.

"Then find him!" George roared. In this mood his way of giving orders brooked no denial. The commissar got on the telephone and began mobilising search parties. They brought in dogs and combed the hills—a delicate hoppity-hop business since the Jugs did not know where they had laid their own mines.

It was not till towards evening that they stumbled over the escaped German, miles from Podhumlje, on a slope overlooking the sea where some low bushes struggled for life among the stones. He was lying beneath them, semi-conscious now, and in a bad way. He still had George's missing surgical scissors in his hands. With these he had stabbed himself three times near the heart, but in his weakness each blow had missed, and one had only succeeded in piercing his lung.

It looked as though he would die anyway, but that it would simply take longer than he had intended.

He fought for breath with his remaining lung and struggled to talk at the same time. On each breath he muttered through ashen lips, "... *konnte nicht mehr* ... *konnte nicht weiter ...*"

They brought him back on a stretcher.

Surprisingly, the German rallied well. Under conservative treatment, again, his chest healed, his colour returned, and he began to show promise of a good recovery.

Dr. Zon entered to check on George's accommodation. There were more wounded than there were beds. Inevitably the fate of the German came up.

George shot a glance at Jim Rickett and dug his heels in.

"I don't want him moved yet," he said.

Dr. Zon straightened from examining the prisoner and, gently inexorable, led with his next question. For the sake of a bed space, and considering the condition of those awaiting treatment, could the German not go now to a camp and convalesce there?

George Lloyd Roberts hesitated. It was plain from the imploring glance he shot at Jim that he hated handing the German over to the dubious fate of a partisan prison camp. But sooner or later he would have to let him go. Also, he was under Zon's orders.

He said heavily: "Very well."

"He could report back here every few days, perhaps?" Rickett suggested. George seized on that. "He must!" he said.

"Of course."

And the convalescent German was removed under guard to make way for more pressing cases.

A week went by, and the German patient was not brought back for a check, as promised. It was not like Dr. Zon to let them down. George and Rickett tackled him

with it when next he called. By that time, ten days had
elapsed since they had handed the German over.

Thus confronted, Dr. Zon halted, colouring. His helplessness and embarrassment were plain. He wagged his
head slowly, sighing.

"A terrible thing—terrible!" said Dr. Zon. "It was
necessary   for ... another   operation ... And—"   he
shrugged, spreading his hands, appealing for their understanding—"he die ..."

By May, Vis had become a fortress. As each day went
by its accent changed a little more, from that of a
beleaguered outpost facing annihilation to a garrison
which, by holding the enemy poised in check with its sheer
pugnacity, had won itself the time to organise, arm heavily, reinforce, and enlarge into a bastion.

Everywhere in the islands around them the enemy
now crouched in heavily defended attitudes, emerging only
in massive patrols. It was becoming increasingly difficult to
ambush them or attack their concrete fortresses without
heavy loss. The threat of invading Vis had receded from a
seeming certainty, with the day-to-day drama of stand-to
and swift counter-action, to a mere possibility.

Waiting for it had become almost boring. Yet if the
Germans were aroused to a proper decisiveness Vis could
still fall, and bloodily, to a well-co-ordinated onslaught
from the three enemy divisions it held down immediately
around them.

But waiting for that, growing slowly becalmed in
more orthodox warfare, was becoming boring. The island
now possessed a regiment of field artillery encamped on
the heights and two anti-aircraft regiments to deter the
Luftwaffe's playfulness. Nobody bombed Private Dodd
with any more flour. There was a field company of
engineers, a bomb disposal squad, a beach group.

And then, one day, the island lost its code name *Ham
Hill* and became, instead, *Number One Forward Base*.

They all knew they had become part of a base,
however far forward, by the appearance of a newspaper on
the island. Its title was devastatingly apropos—*Vis-à-
Vis.*

And for Rickett, signs that the rear was catching up

with the front came wafting across from Italy. The Army, now belatedly alive to the medical situation on Vis, was at last proposing to ship across a fully-equipped field hospital. Even if it was coming far too late, now that the really desperate days were gone, it would still be very welcome. Rickett was overjoyed by the prospect of relief, and while Heron muttered that this was all so like the Army, he could only think of the freedom it offered from the overwhelming weight of surgery and all the cares that went with coping alone.

Their Jugoslav comrades greeted the advent of May with revelry, for in Tito's calendar May Day was a quasi-religious festival, and they had the recent victories of the redoubtable Zuljevic to celebrate. Accordingly they decided to give the rank-and-file a treat. As a contrast to the private executions that went on over on Bisevo, they made plans for the public hanging of a German prisoner.

For this they saved a prisoner specially.

It was perhaps unfortunate that the detachment guarding their May Day sacrifice started their celebrating early, on the afternoon of April 30th. By evening they were well in their stride and at midnight a kind of Conga-line of partisans set off for the cells with the idea of looking their prisoner over and putting him in the right frame of mind for the morrow.

This part of their amusement proved a little boisterous, however, and during it they inadvertently kicked the German prisoner to death.

May Day on Vis proceeded a little lamely, without the *pièce de résistance*.

In the middle of the same night there was a slight commotion in George Lloyd Roberts's Juggery, an event recorded in his scrawl in the school exercise book which he used to enter up details of his surgical operations. A badly wounded partisan—one eye removed, jaw badly damaged, and on top of that, a gastrostomy operation—had been slowly mending since Korcula, and demonstrated his slow return to health by leaping out of bed in reply to the provocation of a nurse. He fought with her—and won. And having done so, he dropped down dead. Johnnie, in commenting on the affair, had but one observation. He swigged at his wine, the reward of further blood donations and remarked that this was one soldier who wouldn't have to face a tribunal for attempting illicit relations with a *partisanka*.

Now the airstrip down the road was operating at full blast, relays of Spitfires were landing to refuel before foraging farther across the water into the Balkans. It was large enough now to take Dakotas which braked precipitately in clouds of red dust and disgorged special stores. The partisans, echoing Tito's phrase, began to boast proudly of Vis as the "Malta of the Adriatic". Their numbers had swelled to the point where watering them had become the major supply problem. Geologists, engineers, and other experts from Italy had surveyed the island for untapped sources and now a special detachment of Royal Engineers arrived, drilled for water at the only likely spot near Vis harbour, and found it.

It was as brackish as the famous Tobruk water. The Navy had converted an infantry landing craft into a water carrier which brought water from Italy every forty-eight hours—the Bora permitting; they mixed this in the brackish well and pumped the resultant blend, which was tolerable, through an intestinal maze of pipes all over the island. But it remained strictly rationed.

Before long new officers were bustling about the island organising sporting events and educational lectures. A cinema set up business in Komisa for the British troops. They even had a visit from an E.N.S.A. concert party. The Director of Military Operations of Allied Force Headquarters visited the island and issued directives to make it impregnable to attack. With all these mounting evidences of garrison civilisation, their raffish little hospital up at Podhumlje seemed marked for an early doom.

Before the rule book entirely blanketed Vis in gloomy sanity Rickett found himself chuckling over another piquant unorthodoxy of this island war. It was provided by Churchill's Brigade Major, a slim, fair warrior called Alf Blake who had all this time, he now revealed to Rickett, maintained a direct phone line with the partisan postmaster of enemy-occupied Hvar.

"You *what!*"

"Quite true," Blake said. "Simple, really. You see, the Germans never woke up that there was a phone cable between Hvar and Vis. Every now and then we just get on the blower and ring him up. If the Jerries are about, he doesn't answer. If they aren't, he does—gives us the lie of the land, invites us over. We borrow a boat from Morgan Giles and go chuffing across at night, and there's the post master of Hvar waiting at the end of the jetty to receive us. Er, he's also the Mayor, you see. And while his boys keep tabs on where the Jerries are, the villagers kill a goat and we all have a beano."

"You're pulling my leg!" Rickett said.

"I am not. Then when we've all had a good feed they show us where we can help ourselves to furniture for our officer's mess—which is the real reason we went last time—and we load this aboard the boat. Then, a swim in Hvar Harbour, and back home twenty-four hours later. It's a real old gallivant."

That was just what Rickett was looking forward to, when the field hospital arrived—a real old gallivant. He might at last be free to go on a sortie—a "party", they called it—with his Commandos across to those shapes, blueing and sharp-etched in the evening light, that were Brac, Hvar, Korcula, Solta. He would no longer be the only qualified surgeon on Vis to tend the wounded. There would be no authority, nor any inner voice to order him to stay behind, and wait.

Meanwhile the aggressive Colonel Zuljevic was girding himself and his partisan force to cap their triumphs on Mljet and Korcula with a fresh demonstration of their military prowess.

This time they picked on Solta, which Colonel Jack Churchill had attacked with such brilliant success two months before. Again the Navy, the Air Force and the Commandos rallied to help with boats, fighter-bombers, and wireless signallers to keep contact with Vis.

The technique was to be the same—a "big bash" with an assembly of guns, mortars and automatic arms and a superior force to overwhelm the defenders.

But this time the Germans were ready and dug in, concentrated in a single fortress system of concrete emplacements behind a formidable mass of wire and minefields. Not only that, but as soon as the partisans swarmed ashore and swung into the attack, roaring their heady battle songs and surging forward through the minefields and the withering defensive fire with incredible courage, heavy guns from the mainland opened up and soon a great barrage of high explosive, on a range already accurately registered, was exploding and creating a terrible carnage among them.

In spite of all these things the partisans penetrated all the Germans' outer defences and, indeed, seemed on the point of overcoming all resistance—when the Germans rallied desperately. With a fanatic bravery they mounted a counter-attack with close artillery support which forced Zuljevic's invaders back.

Thereafter it was attack and counter-attack, with the R.A.F. repeatedly bombing the German positions and with the partisan mortars and artillery pounding them continuously for two days. But hammer as they did, they could not reduce the final desperately tough German core, now centred around two pillboxes and five fortified houses and holding on with all the heroism of men who believed that to surrender meant death, anyway—and a death far more ingnominious.

Nevertheless, Zuljevic had marked another signal beating-up of an enemy island. His men returned with their wounded and 100 prisoners captured early in the battle. These were shipped to Bisevo, to the mythical "prison camp" there. And with this operation, the Allies now had a clear demonstration of the new task which lay before them.

One of these days they were going to be ordered, not just to beat-up or ambush the Germans across the water, but to *take* the islands, and hold them.

On this showing it was not going to be easy.

Having coped alongside George with another sudden flood of wounded, Rickett fell to gloating over what it would be like to stand back and watch others tackle it, see some decent hospital equipment in operation, watch the wounded getting dealt with straight off the boats.

"They're probably going to get a proper evacuation of the wounded going at last, too," he said.

Heron snorted. "Within a week, we'll be up to our arses in general hospital bull. Wait and see."

Rickett had to smile at Heron's sudden pessimism. He took a leaf out of his book and quoted it back to him. "The trouble with you, Professor, is—you worry too—— much."

One evening a new captain walked into their mess and sat down as though he owned the place. He grinned in a friendly way at them all and said: "Hullo, chaps. I'm Wright. Where's the grub?"

They stared. Marie was used to this. She just loaded another plate with stew and handed it over, via Anka. Wright hopped in. It turned out he was a dentist, and he had come to Vis because, he explained, his part of Italy was buzzing with stories about the place. He had also heard about Rickett's hospital. It was news.

And so he had come over to, um, review the dental situation. By the way—how were Rickett's teeth?

Straight after dinner Wright was leading the singing and the revelry. Next day he got up and started his dental review, which consisted of a boating trip across to Bisevo, in company with George Lloyd Roberts, to explore the blue grottoes there. They came back raving about these. "Much better than Capri," said Wright, the connoisseur. Next day was gloriously hot and he went swimming, and that evening all the new chums he had made on Vis came along to the mess for a party.

This went on for fifteen halcyon days. Then Wright came into Rickett, still jaunty and philosophical, and exhibited a very rude signal he had received from his masters recalling him to Italy.

Rickett had to grin. "Never mind," he said, "I'll write you a reference." He sat down and wrote an elaborate and glowing report which detailed the pioneering dental work Wright had done under conditions of considerable difficulty on Vis. He watched Wright journey disconsolately down to Komisa and the boat. He was probably the last adventurer to visit the place. Soon there would be no adventure left . . .

It was hot now. Flies were a problem. They swarmed on the food so thickly that you could hardly see the bully beef for them. They tormented the wounded who trickled in from reconnaissance sorties and lay sweating in the tents. Rickett and George began instructing the partisans earnestly in public health, and under the threat of dysentery they began revising their more primitive habits.

Now there was bathing in a sea like green silk, and walking about stripped to the waist to soak their limbs in a baking sun. The war here lay momentarily quiescent behind concrete and wire. It was slipping into orthodoxy, identifying itself with the war elsewhere—except that elsewhere the war was moving now.

The stalemate in Italy was breaking. The Allies took Monte Cassino and advance units were moving to join up with those breaking out from Anzio.

The Field Hospital arrived in Vis. As soon as the news came over the phone Rickett and the others were vaulting into his skeletal jeep—a vehicle made entirely of stolen stores and presented to him by the engineers. They buzzed and bumped their way down to Komisa. When they came round Komisa's stony point, past the white cube of Navy House and on to the quayside, the boats were already in and unloading stores on to the mole. Rickett, Clynick and Dawson could only stand and stare. An L.C.I. was disgorging hospital beds by the hundred. Dawson's eyes gleamed at the sight of some of the gear and he lifted an edge of tarpaulin to peer underneath and identify the stuff in the crates.

"Hands off, mate," a staff sergeant said. He turned and bellowed: "Right, this lot first! Where are the ruddy trucks?"

Clynick introduced himself to one of the young R.A.M.C. officers coming ashore and said: "We're the surgical team here. Anything we can do?"

The Lieutenant turned and inspected him. "I don't think so," he said. "Thanks all the same."

Rickett was soon shaking hands with the C.O. Major Charlton, dark, thin, quietly pleasant, about his own age.

"Your show's up on the hill? Right, perhaps you'll show the way?" He turned, "Quartermaster . . . !"

They had to mobilise the island's entire transport pool for twenty-four hours to shuttle the stores and tents up to Podhumlje, and it was several days before they were sorted out. There were 100 personnel including half a dozen officers, a stiffening of regular N.C.O.'s, a very regimental quartermaster; tentage for their two hundred hospital beds.

Two hundred!

By the time all the tents were pitched their little stone hospital structure had all but disappeared in the sea of canvas. Charlton, the C.O., was an agreeable fellow, and content to let the hospital run in well-grooved tracks. Which meant it was run by the regular staff sergeants, and the Q.

The first result of this was apparent at dinner. Dawson came whistling in to the meal and stopped short. He was about to sit down when he suddenly realised, colouring, that there was no Marie, their fat old Jug cook; *no* Anka or Filica handing out dishes. No other ranks. Only officers seated around the table, and mess orderlies. They were looking at him a little askance. He backed out and the scandalised stare he turned on Rickett burned deep into him. Rickett felt a hideous blush of embarrassment scalding his face.

Likewise, after coming to sample Rickett's drinks in the mess, down the lane, the officers moved in *en masse* as by natural right. The place was suddenly an officers' mess, as rigidly exclusive as "Shepheard's" in Cairo or Bari's "Imperial." Rank had returned.

Nor had they simply settled down in the same area. They had moved in and taken over the existing establishment. The houses had become the central focus of the new order. Their own cosy, crazy little cottage set-up was being devoured in a lava of organisation and bull.

And paper work. The amount of it struck Clynick almost speechless. The Jugoslav hospital helpers had melted away, clearly unwanted, and suddenly the new organisers were making it plain that they had little use for the scruffy and unregimental handful they had stumbled upon—and which, in their view, had gone native.

The first thing the Quartermaster wanted to do, having surveyed their hoard of medical loot, was to put it on a list.

"Don't talk nonsense," Rickett said mildly. "Most of it's American, anyway." By now they had hoarded enough gauze from their raids on American shipments to the partisans to wrap up the whole island in it.

Nevertheless, down it went on a list.

And when Dawson went to collect some from this, his own proud hoard, he was told to sign for it. At that he lost his temper, offered to knock a staff sergeant's teeth out, and was told he would be put on a charge.

Frank Clynick, the gentlest and most untempera-
mental of men, was explaining their cafeteria plan for
sterilising the few instruments. One of the new M.O.'s
listened with indulgent patronage. He let Frank finish,
allowed a well-measured silence, then murmured dryly:
"Very interesting." Rickett got a similar rebuff when he
started talking about sorting a large mob of wounded for
operation. Their advice was not only unwanted, but unwel-
come.

The culminating injury came when the Field Hospital
appropriated their X-ray machine.

Rickett's temper broke for the first time since he'd
been on Vis. He bellowed suddenly at a quartermaster-
sergeant: "You damn fool! This is partisan property,
personally on loan to *me!*"

At which a very suave M.O. interjected a smooth
word. "Nevertheless, you will agree it's a very handsome
piece of property. It has a most useful place here. Unless
you wish to take it home with you—?"

Rickett came into the C.O., Charlton. "Look here—
I'm going!"

"Do you think that's wise, Rickett?"

"To hell with that! Anyway, between Force 133 and
the Army, nobody will know the difference if the three of
us vanish into thin air. All they'd miss of us would be the
way they've passed the buck between each other for
months for our supplies."

"Oh, surely now—"

"I tell you, we could lose ourselves for the rest of the
war! So I'm going to help the Jugs."

Charlton was really rather nice about it. He smiled a
little wearily and said: "Well, I quite understand. I shan't
raise any objections."

"Thank you!"

And Rickett moved with Frank Clynick across to the
Juggery to work for the partisans. They might not be able
to take the X-ray machine away except at the point of a
gun, but they made sure of the piano, and before a lot of
raised eyebrows among the junior officers, superintended
its removal by a joyous crowd of Jugs.

Frank and Jim Rickett had work enough with George
and the partisans, but not Dawson. He had seen his

preciously hoarded stores gobbled up by a crowd of spit-and-polishers from base, his whole motley little organisation which he had ruled, perhaps ruthlessly, but so well, trampled on with patronage and derision. He'd had enough. He would never go back to a general unit. He knew all the originals on the island, and he did his last piece of string-pulling. He wangled it with his pals in the Commandos. He was off, first to be parachute-trained, then to join Churchill's men.

As he said goodbye to Rickett, Dawson looked darkly over towards the welter of canvas encrusting Podhumlje. He said: "I don't care how many they've got over there. Just wait till they get their first shipload of wounded. They're going to find out!"

And Dawson went off to join the Commandos.

Rickett and Clynick now stayed away from Podhumlje's mess and lived entirely at the Juggery. A couple of the M.O.'s tried to be a little sociable, but it took a great effort to comprehend the wildly impartial friendliness of Rickett and George and their crew, or to be hailed by the villainous Johnnie with a whack on the back and a yell of: "Up your pipe, sair! *Dobro!*" The scenes in the Juggery wards were a little strange to them too: men, women, young boys all mixed with a complete disregard for sex amid a most un-British clamour, with doctors examining them, often in the most intimate particulars, with signs only of the most detached interest from any of the surrounding beds.

The most unsettling sight of all was provided by the black-whiskered Lubo, pipe in mouth, seated astride a naked woman on the floor in the centre of the ward, shaving her in preparation for an appendectomy and following each contour with scholarly concentration, surrounded by a judicious audience who only now and then ventured a word of advice.

Not that advice was necessary. Lubo was so skilled and meticulous at these rites that Rickett, receiving the patient on the operating theatre and waiting for the pentothal to take effect, had occasion to send back his compliments with the remark that the *partisanka* was well barbered enough for a gynaecological operation.

The whole shambles at the Juggery with its brutal

stoicisms, its squalor, however unavoidable, its don't-give-a-damn-for-any-body, lay in a realm beyond the understanding of No. 2 Field Hospital. In Rickett's and Clynick's preference for a set-up like that, the newly-arrived unit could only see a prime case of demoralisation.

The two of them had simply gone to the dogs.

FIFTEEN

In the last week of May the Germans suddenly launched a large-scale offensive against Tito's forces in central Bosnia. They had opened this by dropping parachutists right on Tito's headquarters on Drvar, and at the same time they drove in on Drvar from five different directions with powerful armed columns and infantry.

They were obviously intent on cutting off all escape from Tito's main stronghold and destroying the heart of the partisan movement. For Tito was its heart. It was his image which inspired the partisan chiefs on Vis, his voice alone which commanded. Even the big raids they launched from Vis were selected and ordered from his headquarters in Bosnia.

Tito and his staff escaped capture in the first German lunge by a hair's breadth, but German tanks were in Drvar only twenty-four hours later; these linked with the parachutists, and the German ring began to close in remorselessly on Tito.

Though the partisans counter-attacked fanatically they could only manage to hold open a narrow escape route through which to evade the German thrusts, and as the situation grew hourly more desperate, Tito radioed both Allied Force Headquarters and his commanders on Vis with a call for a large-scale diversion along the Dalmatian coast. It was to be immediate, and violent enough to make the Germans turn their attention from their onslaught on Bosnia to the threat materialising suddenly out of the fortress of Vis.

In week of hurried air-landings of emissaries on Vis, the combined force of Commandos and partisans thrashed out planning difficulties and devised the main details of a

Hurricane

big combined operation—against the enemy forces holding Brac, the biggest and toughest of all the islands.

The attack would have to be a big enough diversion to forbid any enemy troops being moved up inland to reinforce Tito's besieger's in Bosnia—at a time when the Germans thought they at last had the Jugoslav leader cornered.

Brac now presented a very different problem to any attack, however powerful. Its main positions were a series of strong points surmounting the hilltops in the centre of the island, each supporting the other, heavily manned with artillery and a regiment of the crack 118th Jaeger Division.

So well-sited were these defences that they could be counted on to hold out against vastly superior attacking forces. They would undoubtedly inflict tremendous damage. The Germans had shaved the steep hillside approaches which they commanded clean of scrub, trees and

bushes, giving them an uninterrupted field of fire and rob-
bing the attackers of any cover whatever. Every piece of
open ground was mined and heavily wired.

Brigadier Churchill had been called to England to
report on the activities of the Special Services in the
Mediterranean, and his brother "Mad Jack" again assumed
command of the British forces on the island. These were
now further swelled by the arrival of No. 40 Royal Marine
Commando from Italy, giving the British forces now on
Vis a total of 2,000 men. There were more than three
times that number of partisans.

Here at last was Rickett's chance to go on what he
called a party. Or so he had hoped.

Except that No. 2 Field Hospital, for all its gleaming
equipment, its modern generators, its tentage and its beds,
had only one surgeon.

And he had gone down with a gastric haemorrhage,
and had been shipped back to Italy.

From Charlton came a call to Rickett which he
received with disgust and profound misgiving. The C.O.
was taking a team with the attacking force, armed with
plaster for splinting those wounded who needed it for the
trip back to Vis.

He left Rickett as C.O. of No. 2 Field Hospital, and
its only surgeon. The partisans wanted George Lloyd
Roberts to go with their attacking force, and George went
gaily, though in truth he would have been better employed
in his theatre at the Juggery when the wounded started
streaming back. George took Lalla with him. She was
terrified. But when George asked her, she was more
terrified of showing her fear, and she nodded. Johnnie and
Lubo went with them, too.

Plans were only finally revised at a co-ordinating
conference on the morning of 1st June, just before the
operation sailed for Brac. At dusk their invasion fleet
assembled—eight L.C.I.'s, several minelayers, sundry
smaller craft, an escort of Morgan Giles's M.T.B.'s, stiffened by two destroyers from Italy, and the Jugoslav fleet
of twenty schooners and caiques crammed with the 26th
Division of the Jugoslav Army of National Liberation—
possibly the biggest and noisiest choir ever to take the
water.

Caique

Awaiting them all on Brac was a garrison of 1,200 Germans supported by three batteries of guns, disposed in four heavily defended and separate positions on the island. The island lay athwart the harbour of Split, the largest German-held port along the whole mainland. A heavily-

defended artillery observation post on the highest point of
Brac overlooked the beaches on which any invasion force
from Vis would inevitably have to land. The first boats
sighted would undoubtedly call down a holocaust of shells
on a range already precisely registered by the main position's artillery.

By midnight the convoy was skirting the western end
of Hvar island and splitting up to steam straight for their
beaches on the south side of Brac. Ahead of them, an
advance party already lay in hiding on Brac, ready to
tackle the observation hill commanding the beaches. The
partisans were there to guide the boats in, as they always
were.

The main force of partisans and Commandos came
quietly inshore and in the dark landed without a whisper
of opposition. By two o'clock in the morning most of them
were climbing steadily inland and the artillery was unloading on to the beaches ready to range on to the enemy
points at dawn. Another force, mechanised with jeeps, gun
trailers and ammunition carriers, landed in the fishing
harbour of Bol to tackle the Germans entrenched away on
the eastern end of the island. The Navy performed the
unloading and turn-round with a slick, silent perfection
which the soldiers had now come to regard as their
standard job.

By the time dawn broke, there was not a sign anywhere along this coast of the small ships which had landed
4,500 troops, 16 guns, 20 vehicles, and large quantities of
stores and ammunition on Brac.

Well before day broke, however, the advance party of
Highland Light Infantry attacked the Germans' observation post, creeping silently to the wired-in-minefield which
surrounded it and starting to breach the wire. But the
Germans, alert and trigger-fingered, soon spotted them
and put down a hail of bullets, mortar shells and grenades
which, with the mines exploding all round, turned the
slope into a sudden hell. The Highlanders replied with
Stens and mortars, but against the heavy concrete emplacements they found they were no more use than stones.
Clinging desperately to a steep, bare rock face, firing and
trying to wriggle through a complicated minefield, they
were finally battered back by the storm of fire to what
cover they could find.

Sten Gun

Immediately they had reformed they put in another assault to rescue their company commander and another officer who lay wounded in the middle of the enemy minefield, and while they managed to get in and pull them out of the open, it cost them dearly in casualties.

Some 2,000 feet below and behind them they could plainly see the invasion ships unloading in the moonlight—with not an enemy gun in action against them. The German observation hill had been too busy with their attack to start directing fire on to the beaches, and the assaulting party now concentrated for the rest of the night on worrying it continuously with their fire to keep the defenders at work, or under cover. So they neutralised any enemy attempt at artillery observation. At the same time they radioed for heavier support for a renewed attack after dawn.

The main battle opened at first light with rocket-firing Hurricanes roaring in on the enemy's main positions and all but silencing the artillery which started to range on Bol harbour. Elsewhere the R.A.F. attacked the northern port of Supetar to support a Commando drive on the town and to seal it off from rushing help to the main German bastion-system high in the middle of the island. While the Commandos locked with the town's defenders—and had a grandstand view of the U.S. Air Force bombing mainland positions in Split—the men of No. 43 Royal Marine Commando were still desperately clambering up the sides of one main enemy strong point in order to launch their attack on the heels of the Hurricanes. But they were well over an hour in reaching the wired minefield and after a further half an hour of trying to penetrate it, they had to abandon their assault in the face of the firepower which greeted them.

Meanwhile the partisans to the south of them were also thrown back in the attack on a neighbouring point in this system of near-impregnable hilltops. The Allied troops were feeling the inadequacy of their artillery support, which was being widely dispersed in answer to the calls on it.

It was only after strafing, rocketing and bombing the German observation hill, and a gallant renewed attack by a company of partisans called in to reinforce the assault that this post finally fell—yielding a mere twenty Germans. It was a grim tribute to the efficiency of the wire, mines, the strength of their concrete, and above all, to the mood in which they were determined to defend Brac.

The attackers on this small post had lost twice the total number of defenders in casualties. For anybody minded to take this as a sample poll, it boded ill for the rest of the operation.

All that day the partisans and Commandos took turns in attacking the main steep, bare strongholds commanding Brac, with more concerted artillery and fighter support now. Each time their assaults were shattered under murderous fire, which strewed the slopes with wounded and dying. For all these efforts the partisans had wrested possession only of a couple of outposts, for which they had paid dearly. Matters were not helped during the day by an inter-Allied dispute on the co-ordination of one of the attacks, for the partisans did not like complex plans or timings. Spitfires hawking around above the village of Nerejisce near the main German positions twice strafed their own troops—once as they filtered around to attack the German heights from a new direction, once as they came stumbling back after a mauling from the German guns.

While Jack Churchill's headquarters radioed Vis urgently for reinforcements for a large-scale attack on the morrow, the partisans carried on their attacks in darkness: but now control and co-ordination of these was additionally hazardous, not only because of the language problem, but because with the onset of darkness came atmospheric conditions which blanketed all radio communication.

Early next morning troops of No. 40 Royal Marine Commando and a further 300 partisan reserves from Vis were churning across the night sea in L.C.I.s towards Brac to stiffen the attack.

A dawn stocktaking shed one bright ray on an otherwise sinister picture. Away to the east the Allied force had captured five enemy strongpoints and occupied the town of Selca which these covered; their score was 100 prisoners and 130 enemy slain, and they were now closing in to besiege a large enemy force in the town of Sumartin.

Spurred by this, partisans and Commandos agreed on a heavily concerted attack on the enemy's still-intact main positions in the centre of the island that afternoon. Jack Churchill went on an exhaustive reconnaissance all around those forbidding hills, now sullen and almost quiet under a broiling sun. Further disputes with the partisan commander on tactical details delayed the Allies until evening, when No. 43 Royal Marine Commando went into the attack again under cover of an artillery barrage. After an hour's bitter persistence they forced a gap through enemy wire and minefields with bangalore torpedoes while German guns flashing from the neighbouring hilltops blasted them from three sides. The survivors reached and carried their hilltop, held it for half an hour, drove off a fierce German counter-charge which however split them in two, and with their losses mounting all the time tasted the bitterness of an order to withdraw from a position so hard-won, now untenable, for they had lost touch with their Brigade H.Q., and could not call for support to hold it and avoid being cut off.

A further irony was that half an hour later their comrades of No. 40 Royal Marine Commando attacked the same objective, rallied by Colonel Jack playing his celebrated bagpipes—at the same time as No. 43 Commando was withdrawing down another slope of the same position. No. 40 Commando in turn wrested the strongpoint for the second time that night from the enemy, fired success Very lights to announce it, and were immediately swamped by a German counter-attack of unprecedented ferocity, backed with machine-gun and mortar fire from all round them. In this attack their left-hand troop was wiped out, the Commando headquarters overrun, Colonel Manners killed, Colonel Jack Churchill knocked out by a mortar fragment and in the ensuing wild confusion the remnants of the Commando struggled back minus almost all their officers, dragging their wounded with them, their ammunition practically finished.

Major Maude, taking command, came down last, searching for wounded and stragglers in the dark, the surviving troops taking it in turns to cover each other's withdrawing with their casualties until they had all reached the bottom of the hill.

By this time George Lloyd Roberts and his helpers in the surgical station which they had set up in an old stone house with a winepress above the beaches were overwhelmed by the wounded pouring back from the battle around the central stronghold of Brac. George was operating on the most urgent Commando and partisan cases in the open air, on an old stone table—with several interruptions to shelter from bombing attacks by the *Luftwaffe*.

A gunner doctor, Captain Kieft, came up from the artillery battery positioned on the beaches to lend him a hand with anaesthetics. From where they were George could plainly see a company of partisan women who formed and put in a furious frontal attack on a neighbouring hill position, wildly singing. They went down like skittles as the German fire came down and scythed through their ranks.

In the evening George and the others had to move indoors to avoid showing lights. They carried on operating on a table, but the place was so derelict that as George was working on a bad abdominal case the rotten flooring gave way and he fell through up to his waist in a shower of dust and filth. He stood there grimy from head to foot, cursing in English and Jug. Lalla helped him out. They planked the hole with loose wood and carried on.

In these conditions any kind of antisepsis was just a theory. By the end of the second day he was reeling with tiredness. They had spent two days packing their stores for this, a sleepless night crossing in an L.C.I. and lugging their gear up the hills to their casualty station, and had started immediately dawn broke, operating on the first casualties to straggle in. Through the day the wounded grew into a flood. Soon it was no question of coping with all of them. George scribbled a signal and handed it on for despatch to Vis. It was: EXPECT HEAVY CASUALTIES. SUGGEST AIR EVACUATION ONLY HOPE.

Neither would Jim be able to handle this awful tally. George addressed it: S.M.O., Vis.

A signaller misread the addressee and flashed it to S.N.O., Vis—the Senior Naval Officer, Morgan Giles, who retransmitted it to Admiral Morgan in Taranto.

Late on the first day George made brief contact with a partisan doctor, Beliakov, dapper in a smart blue uniform, who was briskly content with his own role in dealing with casualties. He boasted to George that by mid-afternoon he had performed thirty-eight amputations. Chopping off arms and legs—particularly the way an ordinary Jugoslav doctor did it—was a drastically simple matter, but to achieve this physical total was ghoulishly impressive. And not least because it was unnecessary. Obviously Beliakov did not know any better than the others how to treat shattered limbs, and the mere sight of a compound fracture had him reaching for the saw.

By the end of the second day George was forced to stop and snatch a couple of hours' sleep. Guarded by R.A.F. fighters and M.T.B.'s, the second night's convoy of wounded was ploughing back to Vis.

There Jim Rickett had already been on his feet for over twenty-four hours, operating. He had not received George's signal but he did not need it now. One glance out in the yard or in their field full of tents, or along the road where the growl of engines in low gear announced more truckloads on the way was all he had to know.

He had decent lighting this time, but in spite of all the dazzling equipment which now surrounded him, there was not much else of any use.

What they really needed now was half-a-dozen more surgeons. The gas-and-oxygen cylinders were more nuisance than they were worth without a qualified anaesthetist to help.

Also, it was proving hopeless to try and organise the evacuation of these masses of wounded. Most of the boats were too busily in use between Brac and Vis, ferrying reinforcements and stores and bringing back wounded, to spare for the run across to Italy.

It was no satisfaction to see the grim predictions Dawson had made so amply fulfilled. *They're going to find out!* Now, all round him, the people of No. 2 Field Hospital were finding out. The shock of it had paralysed most of them into dazed inactivity. The most sickening thing was the triage—the sorting of the wounded. At least, Rickett had thought, he would be able to leave that safely to the flock of junior medical officers cluttering the place up. That is, until he had gone out touring through the tents just to see that everything was going all right, and had found the younger doctors blundering about amid unparalleled confusion.

Most of them were lost. He could find nobody proficient even in plasma resuscitation. They had no experience of sorting badly wounded men into priorities for operation and they were simply fumbling around with the slow bewilderment of blind men in an unfamiliar place, while

the unattended and the deathly sick piled up in mountains
from the trucks. They had not a clue how to look at a
bloodied wreck of a man and cleave straight through all
the inessentials of his condition to get to the real truth of
what needed to be done. It was not a matter so much of a
lot of questions so much as of assessing, from the whole
complex of experience that went to compound one's medical instinct, a man's true condition before placing him in
some order on the stretcher line for the operating table.
One did it from pulse, colour, respiration, palping. anxiety
state; on likely symptoms of, say, internal bleeding; and
thence to elementary precautions like refusing food or
water to the abdomen cases—God, how old these youngsters made one feel!

So, on top of operating, Rickett had to do the sorting
himself.

He had even to supervise the after-care. This hospital
had been sitting on its tail since Sicily doing cold garrison
surgery—pyelograms, hernias, appendicectomies; there
might not have been any sort of war on, so far out of their
depth were they among battle casualties. And the flashes
lighting the toothy peaks of Brac across that moonlit
stretch of water promised still more of these.

He had never thought to have this nightmare again,
but here it was. He had ten times the staff and about a
quarter of the efficiency of the little stone hospital that he
had built with Clynick and Dawson and the Jugs. Where
was there a Dawson?

Rickett straightened from examining one case and
was about to dismiss him as a superficial wounding who
could be returned for ordinary sick parade attendance
with his own unit when he noticed a small black spot on
the man's temple. He bent closer again, peering. There was
a droplet of fluid oozing from it. He brought his light
nearer. Greyish.

"Make him next," he rapped.

Through the tiny hole, cerebral fluid was oozing. That
was how careful and alert one had to be in sorting what
mattered from what didn't. If he had not perceived what
lay behind that small black spot, the man would have
died.

In another tent a badly wounded partisan girl lay
among the others, her whole front spattered with blood

from chin to thighs. She was an obvious candidate for early surgery but the first thing that Rickett did was to request the little Welsh orderly to remove her clothing so that he could see the damage more closely.

To his astonishment the orderly goggled and did nothing. It dawned on Rickett. He didn't want to undress a woman!

Curtly he made it an order. Only then, with averted head and eyes, the orderly gingerly exposed the girl's bleeding chest and abdomen. They were punctured with mortar fragments.

Rickett looked and tabbed her in the queue for his table.

On the third day the decision was taken to evacuate Brac.

The withdrawal began in broad daylight, in full view of heavily manned enemy positions on the mainland. Over there, German troops were massing and could be counted on to pour across to Brac at any moment now, probably as soon as night came. In their exhausted state, with more than enough blood already spilt, the Allied troops could not be expected to withstand a heavy German counter-blow. With the Navy showing its usual daring and with Spitfires from the new airstrip on Vis maintaining a constant watch, the bulk of the troops had been collected from all over Brac and embarked by mid-afternoon of the third day.

Spitfire

The last part was slow and difficult—carrying the rest of the wounded down the steep stony paths of Brac with a small rearguard of Commandos and local partisans to cover them. The coolness and loyalty of the partisans who stayed to carry on a life of hide-and-seek on Brac were remarkable. It was not until nearly midnight that the partisan outposts on Brac saw the last British troops safely reembarked. Then they grinned, made a few tersely obscene gestures in the direction of the unconquered German peaks, and melted away into the dark hill folds.

At the eastern end of Brac lay a segment of mainland and the enemy port, Makarska, which had an excellent view of the withdrawal throughout the day. Twelve enemy E-boats lurked there. A short distance away at Split there were more. Against a mass irruption of enemy craft bent on ripping their evacuation flotilla to bits the Navy could only muster three or four M.G.B.s in working order. Their boats lay naked, too, to the other imminent threat—of those lofty concrete redoubts where so many had fallen, and whose guns could be expected to reopen fire at any moment.

In spite of these overshadowing spectres the Navy showed no whit of impatience as they lay the long hours in wait for the remaining casualties to be brought down. With the courteous solicitude of a host-team at a sporting meet they welcomed the last exhausted fighters to stumble aboard with lemonade. They opened the galleys for them to hash up something hot and then, serenely nonchalant, began a search of every landing and cove along Brac's southern shoreline for stragglers. Not till they had completed this did they set course for Vis. And in all this time, the E-boat packs did not venture to try conclusions with their tiny escort.

It was true that the Allied force had never planned to stay on Brac; occupying it would have been suicidally premature. But ordinary soldiers are less concerned with broad strategical concepts than winning the immediate battle for a hill or a farm, and having invaded Brac, nothing short of sweeping it clear of Germans, however briefly, would have satisfied them. Their bloody losses would have been much easier to bear.

Brac was also a demonstration of a strange military truism: Commandos and partisans were better off fighting separately. Individually, they had each scored brilliant successes on operations of their own. They had profited, too, from using each other's specialists; the partisans borrowed Commando signallers, aircraft cover, escorts, and for their part the Commandos relied heavily on partisan espionage, the advice of local guerillas and particularly on guides. The Jug guides met them with unfailing loyalty at every rendezvous; their reliability and coolness became a byword among the British. They were fine men, rich in personality and courage, hard-bitten but gay, and loyal to an incredible degree. Even when a brush with the Germans turned a whole area around them into a hornet's nest, the guides not only covered their withdrawal; they beat the countryside, searching for stragglers and wounded, as though getting the Commandos away again, all properly accounted for, was a sacred charge on local hospitality.

Yet it had to be faced that they could not fight side by side as military formations. Liaison was poor—with the language problem, co-ordination was haphazard, tactical disputes frequent; their styles were diametrically opposed. A precisely-timed battle plan meant nothing to a partisan; they had few watches between them and little use for them. It was dangerous to urge a complex scheme upon them too insistently because they would then agree—but being reluctant and unconvinced, ignore it in practice. Their individualism as fighters was untameable. All they wanted to do was to tackle a hill or a strong point in their own way. It must be said they did this with magnificent dash, even with skill—but a skill that was uniquely their own.

Many could not have read a military manual anyway, and they suspected what they did not understand.

Still, the whole object of the operation had been to relieve the sudden overwhelming enemy pressure on Tito up in Bosnia.

And they had achieved this. Because of it the Germans were unable to summon troops from the coast to help tighten the ring around Tito's partisans; on the contrary, the ferocity and size of the Allied attack alarmed them into rushing reinforcements to the coast opposite Brac from inland, to await the opening blows of what might, for all they knew, develop into an invasion thrust at Europe itself.

This was the news which greeted them as they sailed

back to Vis. It was June 4th, 1944—the day the Allies driving up from Anzio were entering Rome.

Two days later the real assault on Europe began in France with D-Day.

The battle was not over for Major James Rickett. He no longer knew what day it was, nor what hour. When he felt hungry he stopped and ate. When the theatre became too much of a mess he waved the orderlies in to scrub out and took a tour of the teeming wards to see how the new staff was carrying out his schooling on after-care. He sorted his wounded, haggard, and bitterly derisive of the triage already attempted. He took a brief cigarette, tried to marshal his thoughts to see if there was anything he had forgotten in the fearful administrative picture confronting him whenever he emerged from the theatre.

In the middle of thinking of it he found his mind wandering and clapped another couple of benzedrine tablets into his mouth and pitched his cigarette away and returned to the theatre.

The next case on the operating table was a Commando soldier with a through-and-through wound of his groin and testicles. To Rickett's relief the testes themselves were intact and the scrotum could be cleaned and stitched. But when he probed among the shattered mess of the groin he made a dramatic discovery.

The main artery to the leg, the femoral artery, as thick as one's thumb, was sticking up in the middle of the wound—and was completely severed. Through it the man's lifeblood should have gushed out within minutes of his being hit on Brac. Instead, after a buffeting journey down the mountainsides, into boats, across the water to Vis and up more hills in an ambulance, almost twenty-four hours later, he was still alive. He had not even lost any more blood than a lot of lesser casualties, and his pulse was quite good.

But as soon as Rickett began gently to clean the wound a great fountain of blood gushed clear across the room, and the assisting doctor slapped a Spencer-Wells clips into Rickett's hand, then the ligature.

The miracle for this man was that this huge artery had gone into spasm immediately after he was hit, contracting the artery; a tiny clot had sealed it off, and this had held for all the intervening time, against all the shocks to which it had been subjected on the way back—until now.

And now Rickett was going to be able to save that leg. The other smaller vessels would take up the load. There would be an oedema resulting lower in the leg, which he would relieve with an incision down the calf. As the leg slowly mended, he would stitch if the calf swelling went down, or skin-graft if it did not. But that was a job more properly to be done in a decent general hospital in Italy, like so much else that lay around them here.

And that reminded him. Not a boat had arrived from Italy to evacuate the wounded. Yet they must have been aware of the magnitude of this battle, for it was co-ordinated and directed from Allied Force Headquarters. Perhaps they were quarrelling about whose pigeon it was.

Then the next patient was carried in and he had no more time to reflect on this.

There came a time, again, when he could no longer think. Once more, it was during the sorting. He found himself sitting and staring at a pallid youngster, a partisan, with his arm in a dirty sling. He looked at the elbow wound, made the boy flex his fingers.

"Boli, drug?"

The boy shook his head. Rickett tried and didn't know what else to ask him. He waited a while, with the boy's eyes on him mutely.

"Where's your family in all this? Family . . . where?"

The youngster's face lit up and he answered in a torrent of Serbo-Croat through which Rickett caught the words Italy. Well, he had diagnosed where the family was, but he couldn't frame a few simple questions nor make sense enough of the answers to assess the damage to an arm. All he could do was to swap chat and kid himself he could last a bit longer yet. The youngster was tapping at his breast pocket and fumbling and Rickett bent forward and helped him pull out a tattered photograph, over which he frowned, mustering a grave interest. A fat old lady in peasant black with two grimy toddlers clinging to her skirts, and the patient himself, strapping and chest-puffed, standing ridiculously to attention beside her with his rifle in an on-guard attitude.

The boy's eyes were hungry on his every expression, and he smiled affectionately over the picture and handed it back. There was another wait but he could not think of anything. He could not diagnose.

He said: "You sleep now. I'll see you in the morning." Miming, he got his meaning through. The lad grinned back contentedly, restored his picture to his pocket, patted it, winked.

Rickett winked back. He wandered out and blundered up the road to the Juggery. The sky was aswarm with stars, and still. There was no breeze to whip him back into wakefulness and in an empty room he fell on to a bed and slept.

An urgency woke him at dawn and he came back to take a kind of bird's-eye view of the chaos around Podhumlje and sort out what remained to be done.

An orderly said: "They've landed in France, sir."

"Really?" It was a rebuke, almost, for chattering of unimportant things.

In another day the surgery was practically all cleared up. But the following morning came an accident on the tail-end of all this involving cases as bad as anything that had passed through his hands, as far as he could remember, for the past four days.

Three sailors down at Komisa were cleaning down an M.G.B. that had been used for bringing back some of the casualties. They were getting the ship ready for action again out among the islands that night. It was hot. They had stripped down to shorts and were washing down the walls of a cabin with petrol when somebody started up the boat's generators.

A little electric fire bar which had been left switched on from the night before started glowing into life. Immediately it did there was a great flash as the fumes and the bucket of petrol itself exploded, and the cabin became an inferno.

By the time the fire appliances had put out the blaze and the three sailors were pulled clear they were burned completely from head to foot except for a ghostly whiteness around their loins where their shorts had protected them from the searing blast of the explosion. This small skin area offered the only place possible for the insertion of a canula bearing the saline drips they would need as soon as their terribly burned bodies started exuding. To do this Rickett had to find a vein, and the saphenous vein in the groin was the only choice. But being deep-set it involved cutting down.

The cleaning of charred and peeling tissue from that first roasted but still-living body took Rickett six hours. As he was finishing it a message came through from Navy House, one that stunned him as a miracle might.

Navy House repeated the message for him over the phone: "That's what they say—*Hospital ship on the way*."

A hospital ship!

A big white boat fitted out with everything imaginable including operating theatre, beds, a staff of doctors, *surgeons*, a score of Queen Alexandra nurses . . . !

All that on its way to Vis. At last they had pulled their finger out in Italy. He was giddy with happiness and relief. All that he could say was, repeatedly: "We're really getting some service now! Must have been that last rocket I sent. Yes, this is really service!"

The weariness, the reaction closed in. The best thing to do, then, would be simply to smother the two remaining burns cases in vaseline, wrap them carefully in gauze and lint, and with the case on which he had already operated, transport them carefully down to the outskirts of Komisa to await the hospital ship's berthing.

The rest of the wounded who could travel would be moved down in relays and held outside the town to avoid the air raids till they were embarked.

But—the burns cases first. He still could not believe his good fortune, this white vision dazzling him of the coming relief. He saw the three sailors off in an ambulance and went back to the Juggery and poured himself deliberately a large tumbler of wine, and sipped at it, marvelling over the whole thing.

The news spread all over the island.

That night, quite late, while Rickett was busy with further operations, one of the Commando doctors, McWilliams, came hurrying up in a jeep, and he was white to the lips.

The hospital ship was in.

It was a Jugoslav schooner.

It was scarcely fit to travel cattle. There was one doctor aboard—a general duty officer, not even a surgeon. This officer had accepted the burns cases but he had no instruments, and he had sent up a plea via McWilliams for

the loan of a cutting-down set so that he could get the
canulae into the veins of the remaining two victims and get
saline going.

The astonishing thing about this glossy field hospital
now surrounding Rickett, for all its gas and oxygen cylinders and proper tables, was its entire absence of the actual
instruments of surgery, so that he only had the small kit he
had always had.

He had only two scalpels, for instance. To struggle on
with one scalpel in this situation on Vis was impossible. He
had no specialised instruments anyhow. Some of his basic
instruments were not even duplicated. It was now quite
obviously lunatic to count on any kind of succour from
Italy.

Rickett got an orderly to make up a kit: scalpel,
dividing forceps, aneurism needle, canula rubber tubing,
ligatures, and saw to it that the lot was wrapped in sterile
towels. He handed the package to McWilliams and said:
"You know what these are worth to us. Tell him if I don't
get them back before he sails, I'll come after him. And I'll
have his guts for garters."

Early in the morning the schooner sailed, with the
doctor still cutting down to get drips going into the burned
men—and bearing Rickett's instruments away to Italy.

For him, it was about the last straw. It was a tiny
matter to set on top of a whole, savagely treasured collection of frustrations and mishaps and blunders and petty
follies one suffered successively from the administration of
war. He had known patients who had endured one setback
after another sunnily enough—until something ludicrous, a
small culminating irritation, a boil on the neck, a tooth-
ache, reduced them suddenly to a wild anger, or even to
tears.

So it was with him. He got on the phone to Morgan
Giles who, as an original settler on this island, understood
immediately that even though Rickett was only talking
about a small bundle of surgical cutlery, it was important.
Giles ordered an M.T.B. to sea and it ploughed off on a
hundred-mile race to Bari. It was waiting with bared teeth
for the schooner they called a hospital ship when it
berthed. They snatched the instruments back and returned
with them to Vis.

As it chanced, the instruments had not availed any.

The first çase had lived. The other two took several days to die.

There were several bold attempts to rescue Jack Churchill before the Germans whisked him off Brac into Germany. As the Commandos expected, the island was now stiff with reinforcements, ferried across from Split. These had landed on the north and east of the island as the Commandos pulled out on the other side.

One of the first acts of the Germans as they emerged from their entrenchments and combed the island was to set fire to the house which had served as a Commando dressing station on the way back to the beaches. They burned alive the old couple who had tended the wounded.

A partisan agent who had volunteered to go into the port of Supetar to find out Churchill's fate had vanished. Commando intelligence officers were dodging heavy patrols to try and glean some news of British prisoners. Three troops of Commandos landed again on Brac the next night with artillery to hold a beachhead through which their scouts and any rescued prisoners could escape. News leaked back to them through civilians that Allied prisoners including three high-ranking officers had been taken under guard from the centre of the island to Supetar.

At that news the doughty Morgan Giles produced his coolest proposal yet. He offered to send three M.G.B.'s through the mine-infected channel—a mere 500 yards wide—separating Brac from Solta, round the northern side of the island and into Supetar harbour. It was full moon. They would deliberately show themselves to stop any shipping leaving Supetar, except warships, oˤ course. Unfortunately they would also have to lie in full view of Split, the focus of all the German strength in Dalmatia. Their most piratic leader, the Canadian Tom Fuller, led the three ships in. They had loudhailers and German interpreters aboard, and with these they proposed to harangue any enemy craft they ran into and browbeat them into giving up their prisoners.

Even the hard-bitten crews under Fuller on the M.G.B.'s decks goggled when, having sailed clean through the mined strait, they manoeuvred till they lay athwart

Supetar harbour, every detail brightly visible in the brilliant moonlight, while behind them, almost as plain, the gun-infested position of Ciovo and the mainland stood out in sharp relief.

They began cruising gently in to Supetar on a sea as smooth and luminous as glass.

Not a shot nor a flare greeted them. The harbour was bare of shipping. In vain they waited there all night, motionless on the flat calm until, an hour before dawn, Fuller decided to go right in to prod the enemy into some show of spirit. He came right in. Then some 20 mm. guns suddenly opened up. He danced back, firing at the flashes, and pretended to take cover behind a spit of land. But now it was getting light, and they had at last to turn and streak back through the mine channel for home.

Next the R.A.F. had a try, and Allied scouts crouching in the hills round Supetar itself watched while the Spitfires, carefully briefed and knowing the local situation perfectly, came skimming in over the rooftops, circling, scanning the panic scene below. Everywhere the Germans were dropping their stores, abandoning vehicles, and scattering wildly for cover. But there was no sign of any prisoner-gangs reported to be loading the ships there. After circling low four or five times, each fighter pilot picked off a sea-front building and with great care came in and laid his bombs on it. One hit an ammunition store and soon the whole seafront was ablaze.

The Commando scouts and partisans came scrambling down the mountainside to the very edge of the town looking for prisoners taking advantage of the confusion to escape, but they could see none.

Finally, in spite of this tenacious loyalty to their friends and leaders, the rescue parties from Vis had to give up. They only withdrew when it was clear that the Germans had somehow managed to spirit their captives away from the undefeated fortress of Brac.

A week later Tito himself was on Vis. He had escaped the Germans in Bosnia and after a week of hazard and adventure boarded a British destroyer at night along the Jugoslav coast.

The Marshal's arrival on Vis was kept an elaborate secret from all troops on the island. Tito was housed in a

cave on Mount Hum not far from the cottages of the
Commando Brigade H.Q. An army of partisan sentries
guarded the narrow pathway up to the cave. A special
anti-aircraft squadron of the R.A.F. Regiment surrounded
his habitat with guns. A special security section arrived on
the island from Italy.

But after a fortnight or so of this the Marshal
shrugged off some of these security trappings and made his
appearance among the men. He celebrated his escape with
a lavish luncheon party to the island's commanders, re-
viewed the British troops amid considerable international
pomp, and made speeches of praise for their gallantry and
comradeship.

In that June of 1944, the most fateful month of the
war, the Germans across the Adriatic in Italy were re-
treating to the north, and the line there was at last drawing
confortably abreast of Vis. June saw the island's character
change from a precarious outpost facing an enemy host
alone into a busy and thriving base. It would require a
major reversal in the tide of war, a dramatic rebirth of
enemy aggressiveness for the Germans to mount an invasion against it now.

Everybody sensed it.

The buccaneers were leaving. Among the first to go
was Admiral Sir Walter Cowan, saddened by the loss of
Colonel Manners on Brac and of Jack Churchill, whose
sword and bagpipes were now on show in Vienna. The
island gave the venerable Admiral a royal send-off, with
every gun in harbour firing in salute and with guards of
honour, British and partisan, lining the way for him to his
boat.

Rickett was invited to a farewell drink. Sir Walter
eyed him over a gin and said abruptly: "No place for
roughnecks any more, Rickett. I stayed too long. Missed
the boat to France. Got to do some catching up now." He
stomped off to shake hands with the others.

If that old storm bird was going, it meant that Vis
was indeed getting too cosy.

Now the Commandos, once led by Manners and
Churchill, were also preparing to leave.

It was true the atmosphere at the Field Hospital,
where Rickett was still having to stand in and do odd bits
of surgery, had undergone a marked change of heart

towards him since the revelation of Brac. But it was no longer a time for the friendships they had forged in those early days—the days when he could wish aloud for something impossible, like an X-ray machine, and with Zena pointing an imperious finger and no further questions asked, the partisans had shoved off to go hunting among the Germans for one.

Here, nice as they were, they wouldn't tear up a single form to oblige you.

George Lloyd Roberts, too, was very tired after Brac. His handsome boyish face had thinned. He coughed and was querulous, and lost his temper now at the slightest interference from anybody, particularly from the commissars who plagued his hospital with their supervisions. Rickett sent George to Italy for a thorough checkup.

Not long after George got back again, Rickett was operating on a minor case when he nicked his finger with the scalpel. The next day it was swelling. A mild sepsis set in. One of the young doctors noticed him treating it.

"Something wrong?"

Rickett shrugged. "Finger's septic."

"Oh I say!" The M.O. sounded really concerned. "I'd look after that. It can be very nasty."

Rickett smiled. "I will," he said. Here was his chance. He made a large bandage of his hand. In the mess at lunch another M.O. came over. "I hear you've got a bad finger. I hope you've got a good doctor." He beamed.

Rickett got on the phone to the R.A.F. Forward Group superintending the now-busy little airstrip. He invoked the Old Pals Act.

"Scottie? Jim Rickett here. Look, I've got a walking wounded case, but it's quite urgent to get him to Italy. Can you get him out for me?"

Yes, Scottie could.

Rickett got the driver Strudwick to take him down in the terrible Lizzie the engineers had made for him out of spares. The R.A.F.'s jaw dropped inches when Rickett himself climbed out with a huge bandage and presented himself for evacuation by the old Hudson bomber that was warming up.

They flew low over the sea to avoid the Messerschmitts that still hung around in the sun for prey. Back in Bari he whipped the bandage off, entered No. 2 District

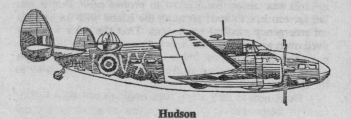

Hudson

H.Q., and finding nobody there, sorted through their Top Secret files in the office till he found an interesting one, and settled down to read it. It started with a mass of signals and bureaucratic shuttling which showed him all too plainly why nothing had ever started on its journey to him in Vis in those precious early days. It was amusing to see, though, how the apprehension of a medical crisis on Vis had begun dimly to percolate through the sheafs of messages between A.F.H.Q. and Force 133 and L.F.A. and other mystically symbolled authorities who had juggled with their fates.

The messages ended on a note of high alarm.

An M.O. entered. Rickett tucked the file away. They exchanged introductions.

"Rickett? Any relation to that fellow on Vis?"

"That's me."

This brought an electric change. He swooped on Rickett and whirled him down the corridor to Cameron's office, where the Brigadier pumped his arm till it was tired. They only got down to business after a royal fêting.

"Now then. Tell me—what do you want for Vis?"

Rickett pondered that one wryly. "Well, it's a bit late, sir, now."

"Really? Tell us the things you could have done with, then—"

"It's a long story—"

"Never mind! Tell us what gear, the sort of organisation it needs, what strength . . ."

"Well—" Rickett lit a cigarette, and launched into the long tale.

The Brigadier kept making notes, to his great uneasiness. At the end of it Cameron said breezily: "Right. Will do."

It was useless for Rickett to protest again that it was all far too late to start rescuing the island with an armada of emergency medical equipment. That the crisis was now well over, and the war was moving on.

But the supply machine it had taken so long to get into gear was now turning too ponderously for anybody to dare stop it.

And now that his job was over, there, the kind of convoy he had once had wild dreams of solemnly set sail for Vis.

Major Jim Rickett only returned to Vis for a party. He had arranged for his own successor and one for George, who was ailing and growing daily more allergic to commissars.

Rickett managed to get back on the island by dodging the wharf guards at Manfredonia and stowing away on an L.C.I.

It was the Jugs who threw the party for him and George.

They summoned all the old cronies who remained, the pioneers, from all over the island. Johnnie recruited a crowd of flare fishermen and their lights danced over the warm summer sea in search of delicacies for the feast. The fish factory brought up piles of anchovies and under Lubo's generalship several of the island's wiliest surviving goats were finally outwitted in their own guerilla fastnesses and turned up next day on the banqueting spits.

The girls from the Juggery, Anka and the shy Felica included, combed the hill slopes for flowers for the white tables, but not till the engineers had vetted the ground with their detectors for mines. The tables sagged under the accumulated weight of fish dishes and *grigorica* and roast kid and drink.

It started under the stars just after dusk, with the shape of Mount Hum deepening against a satin sky. The night was so still that the harbour sounds rose and floated up among the hills around them. It was a strange party to do honour to the two British doctors, and yet appropriate; it was a monster-sized shindig whose ancestry was directly traceable to their early revelries in the cottage mess at Podhumlje.

But this one had oddly official overtones. Rickett sat

between two large, important female commissars. Brigadier Tom Churchill was there, back from England. Colonel Meynell of the beach group arrived. There was Morgan Giles and Spider Webb from Navy House; several officers from the H.Q.; Rickett's engineer lads who had built his theatre almost barehanded; a cluster of bemedalled partisan veterans, Johnnie, Lubo, Lalla; everybody washed and combed a treat, about fifty of them sitting out at a banquet on top of a rock fortress under the stars.

It began with great official decorum and took several hours to loosen up. The sure signs that it was proceeding successfully and that nobody needed leave began appearing around midnight as the eating shambled to a close, and the impromptu *Zivio*'s, the glass-clinkings, began to multiply. They had finished the long ritualistic toasts of death to the Fascist beast, and the sonorous invocations of Stalin, Churchill, Roosevelt, Chiang Kai Shek were by now degenerating into a diligent but mis-directed search for some of the war's less distinguished generals. The venerable Dr. Zon made a wildly extravagant speech in halting English about Rickett and George which ploughed on through a rising ferment of jollity—and was abruptly terminated by a hefty fighter springing to his feet and roaring *Domovino! Domovino!*

The chant was taken up and the singing started. Then the dancing, the *kolo* and the other folk-steps, with Rickett first up to dance, ruddy of face, kicking his long legs out in front of him, ring-a-rosying with a brawny, heavy-breathing lady commissar. There were personal toasts to drink with everyone, and drinks of farewell and everlasting brotherhood, especially with Johnnie and Lubo, who lured Rickett aside into suicidal salutes in *rakia*.

He remembered vaguely a young M.O. coming up to him, raising his glass, saying solemnly: "I don't know what we're going to do without you, sir."

He had leered at that, and remembered the Professor. He said, somewhat thickly: "The trouble with you fellows is, you worry too bloody much."

There was Lalla in tears at their going.

The party faltered around dawn. Frank Clynick came into his own, bearing the casualties off to their rest. The hard livers rallied limply until mid-morning, but the remnants of the merrymaking collapsed as the hot summer sun rose high.

Rickett and George were hoisted bodily aboard the *Prodigal* in their home-made jeep and decanted gently on to the trawler's deck. George was asleep with a sad smile on his face. His shirt fell open. There was something printed on his brown chest in lurid red characters.

Lipstick!

No girl had ever dared own to stuff like *that* on Vis.

The words said, *Gotevo, 08.00*.

Only a lady commissar would use such chronological precision.

"Had it—08.00 hours."

They were clear of Komisa harbour and Rickett looked back at the island.

"George," he said. "Were you leading a secret life on Vis?"

Join the Allies on the Road to Victory
BANTAM WAR BOOKS

These action-packed books recount the most important events of World War II. Specially commissioned maps, diagrams and illustrations allow you to follow these true stories of brave men and gallantry in action.

☐	12657	**AS EAGLES SCREAMED** Burgett		$2.25
☐	13643	**BATTLE FOR GUADALCANAL** Griffith		$2.50
☐	*12658	**BIG SHOW** Clostermann		$2.25
☐	13014	**BRAZEN CHARIOTS** Crisp		$2.25
☐	12666	**COAST WATCHERS** Feldt		$2.25
☐	12916	**COMPANY COMMANDER** MacDonald		$2.25
☐	*12927	**THE FIRST AND THE LAST** Galland		$2.25
☐	13572	**GUERRILLA SUBMARINES** Dissette & Adamson		$2.25
☐	12665	**HELMET FOR MY PILLOW** Leckie		$2.25
☐	12663	**HORRIDO!** Toliver & Constable		$2.25

*Cannot be sold to Canadian Residents.

Buy them at your local bookstore or use this handy coupon:

Bantam Books, Inc., Dept. WW2, 414 East Golf Road, Des Plaines, Ill. 60016

Please send me the books I have checked above. I am enclosing $_____
(please add $1.00 to cover postage and handling). Send check or money order
—no cash or C.O.D.'s please.

Mr/Mrs/Ms _____

Address _____

City _____ State/Zip _____

WW2—1/81

Please allow four to six weeks for delivery. This offer expires 7/81.